The Night
Detectives

Books by Jon Talton

The David Mapstone Mysteries
Concrete Desert
Cactus Heart
Camelback Falls
Dry Heat
Arizona Dreams
South Phoenix Rules
The Night Detectives

The Cincinnati Casebooks
The Pain Nurse
Powers of Arrest

Other Novels
Deadline Man

The Night Detectives

A David Mapstone Mystery

Jon Talton

Poisoned Pen Press

Copyright © 2013 by Jon Talton

First Edition 2013

10 9 8 7 6 5 4 3 2 1

Library of Congress Catalog Card Number: 2012952567

ISBN: 9781464201325   Hardcover
      9781464201349   Trade Paperback

Poisoned Pen Press
6962 E. First Ave., Ste. 103
Scottsdale, AZ 85251
www.poisonedpenpress.com
info@poisonedpenpress.com

Printed in the United States of America

For Susan

And for David Strang, 1938–2012

Chapter One

The dead talk to me in my dreams. When I wake up, I can't remember what they said.

Chapter Two

It felt wrong from the start.

The man who sat across from us wore a sleek charcoal suit and a starched white shirt with French cuffs. I made the suit for a Dsquared2 right out of the *New York Times* Men's Fashion supplement, retail price $1,475. Its perfectly draped cuffs broke over tasseled black loafers that might have cost more than the suit itself. You didn't see that kind of suit in our part of town, much less when it was 108 degrees outside and this was only the first week of May. Yet he didn't sweat.

Still, somehow, $1,475 didn't buy elegance for the wearer, or peace of mind for me.

The suit lacked a tie, which irritated me. I like suits. I am a clotheshorse and they are also handy for concealing my firearm. Today, the rebels wear suits, which are the zenith of great clothing design. Show me a man with stubble and dressed like an adolescent and I'll show you today's version of 1950s conformity. Unfortunately, Phoenix weather only allows me to wear suits six months of the year. I looked at his open collar and thought: here was a suit quietly longing for a smart tie to complete it. The man appeared the same way: incomplete.

He introduced himself as Felix Smith, sat before Peralta's desk, and said he needed our help. We already knew that part. Smith had called the day before, dropped the name of a criminal lawyer who was a friend of Peralta's, and set up this afternoon's meeting. I pulled over the second client's chair and faced him.

"I want you to investigate a suspicious death."

"Let's start with the name of the deceased." Peralta had produced a yellow legal pad and pen.

My partner, who was also not sweating, was in one of his many tan summer suits with a conservative tie. I wore khakis with a long-sleeve linen shirt—this was, after all, Skin Cancer City—but even in the air conditioning, a layer of sweat formed beneath the fabric. In a city where so many people either came to die or, as in the case of illegal immigrants hiking across the desert, died trying to come, I was a native. I was one of the few my age who had stayed or returned. But my body held the DNA of the British Isles and when the temp crept over one hundred five I couldn't stop sweating.

The only cool thing against my body was the Latin cross by the Navajo silversmith Harrison Bitsue that had belonged to Robin, Lindsey's half-sister. Robin and I had walked over to the Heard Museum and she had fallen in love with it. So I bought it for her. I didn't know if Robin was a believer. She would have scoffed at organized religion as she did so many things in the world. But it was all that had come back to me from the medical examiner. I had restrung it on a longer beaded chain and now wore it all the time.

Felix said, "The girl's name was Grace. Grace Hunter."

Peralta asked more questions in his familiar deep voice. Each time, Felix gave a short, precise answer. He held a smart black portfolio but it remained unopened. Grace Hunter was twenty-three. He gave her date of birth and Social Security number, both of which we would need for records searches. She had died on April twenty-second, a little more than two weeks previously. The police had ruled it a suicide.

Peralta took notes. I studied Felix Smith and couldn't shake a feeling of discomfort.

He looked around thirty and his hair was dark and cut short, pushing down on a low forehead. Sitting straight with his hands palms-down on his thighs, his body conveyed strength and self-possession. But he had a nose that looked as if it had been mashed in multiple fights, pocked skin that had ingested too much sun which gave the impression of a flash burn, and the remains of bruises around unsettling, old yellow eyes. Even with his head immobile, those eyes restlessly swept the room.

Joseph Stalin had yellow eyes.

I guessed that his driver's license identified them as hazel.

He wasn't as big as Peralta, but he was plenty big. His head was large, about the same width as the muscled-up neck that held it. His hands were large and hard, with big knuckles, and underneath the suit his plank-like shoulders looked capable of violence. The brawler's face and body didn't go with the tailored suit and the high-shine, pricey shoes. Unless he was somebody's muscle.

But maybe I was being jumpy, paranoid. Peralta kept telling me that.

My agitation kicked up a notch when he said where the girl had died: San Diego. I wanted to start nervously shaking my right leg, playing drums with my hands, or leave the room. After the first jump, I made my leg stay still.

"They say she jumped off a balcony. It was from the nine-teenth floor of a condo." His voice was steady, one note above a monotone. Peralta waited several seconds before going on.

"And you don't believe that…"

"No."

Peralta wrote down the address where it happened. It was downtown, near the beautiful Santa Fe railroad station.

"Who is she to you?" It was the first time I had spoken besides the introductions after he walked in the door.

The cat's eyes focused on me. After a pause: "my sister."

"Why not Grace Smith?" I asked.

His eyes narrowed and he assessed me, finding me wanting. "She had a different last name."

I suppose it made sense. Lindsey and Robin had different last names, different fathers. Maybe Felix and Grace's mother remarried. Maybe Grace had been married. I persuaded myself I was being overly suspicious.

I said, "I'm sorry for your loss."

His gaze would have cut me down if it had been a gun.

He produced a photo from his portfolio and slid it across Peralta's immaculate desktop. It was five-by-seven and glossy. The young woman had butterscotch hair with blond streaks, stylishly cut to hang slightly above her shoulders, large brown eyes, very pretty. She didn't look anything like him. Great smile and something more, something magnetic. The camera liked her. She liked the camera.

When the suit sleeve and French cuff rode up with his reach, I saw a multi-colored tattoo on his lower arm and almost unstrapped the gun on my belt. I had recently made enemies in the drug cartels and didn't know if our business was settled.

"This condo." I studied his face. "Was it hers?"

The skin around his eyes tensed. "No."

I waited and after a full two minutes he talked again.

"It belongs to a man named Larry Zisman."

It sounded vaguely familiar but I couldn't place it. Smith sensed it, and continued.

"He was an All-American quarterback for the Sun Devils back in the seventies, then he played pro for ten years before his knees were wrecked."

"Now I remember," I said. "I never read about this in the newspaper."

"Funny about that," Felix replied. "Larry Zisman is a celebrity with a lot of powerful friends."

"Is he married?" I asked.

"Very." Felix adjusted one leg and very slightly winced. It was the first time his face had given away an expression beyond tough.

The next question was logical enough, but Peralta didn't ask it.

"Note?" Peralta could be more taciturn and economical in his language than anyone I had ever met.

"No. She didn't leave a note. Nothing. That's one of the things I don't like."

"What else makes you doubt the police?"

"She was naked and her hands were bound."

Now he had my attention for reasons beyond his appearance. Peralta grunted and I heard his pen scratch along the paper.

"It's a good department," Peralta said. "San Diego. You need to understand that these things are usually what they seem, however much the loved ones want it to be otherwise."

I wasn't sure about that. I had seen botched death investigations, even by good departments.

"I have confidence in you, Sheriff. That's why I'm here."

"I'm the former sheriff." Peralta said it without any emotion, then pulled out the sheet with our fee schedule and handed it across to Felix with his meaty hand.

That was another thing that didn't feel right: "former sheriff."

Until four months ago, Peralta had been the sheriff of Maricopa County for what seemed like forever. Everybody I knew thought he would be sheriff as long as he wanted it, unless he decided to run for governor. I was one of his deputies and the Sheriff's Office historian. It was good work for somebody with a Ph.D. in history in this or any job market.

But those assumptions had been based on another Arizona, before millions of retirees and Midwesterners had collided with the huge wave of illegal immigration before the big housing crash. It was a bad time to be a Hispanic running for office and Peralta lost, even though he was a life-long Republican. There would be no Governor Peralta in today's Arizona. He took the defeat stoically. Instead of moving on to any of the lucrative consulting offers that had come his way, or encouraging the feeler to become San Antonio police chief, he set up shop as a private investigator. And here I was, too, as his partner. He was my oldest friend.

Our office was shabby compared with the places Felix Smith must have been accustomed to, based on his suit. We were on Grand Avenue, the bleakest thoroughfare in a city with abundant competition for the title, in what had once been a little motel, an "auto court." Most of the motel had been bulldozed long ago—Phoenix loved clearing land and leaving it that way. The new mayor was trying to encourage art projects and gardens on vacant lots, but I wondered if the effort would do much good.

Robin had found a 1948 post card of the motel: a charming affair with half a dozen buildings, each with two rooms, a swimming pool, lawns, and palm trees. All that was left was the former front office—a small, square adobe with enough room for our two desks, some file cabinets, and places for clients to sit. Except for our comfortable chairs, the décor was spare. Recently, Peralta had added a black leather sofa.

We were barely moved in. Peralta had sprung for a bookcase for me, but I hadn't put a single volume in it. Boxes of correspondence, all for Peralta, sat behind my desk. Speaking requests for him came almost every day. We really needed a secretary. Behind the office were a bathroom and a storeroom, the latter having been remodeled and fortified by Peralta for gun storage. Robin had named it the Danger Room. We each had a key to it, but it was mostly Peralta's playroom. A super-sized Trane air conditioning system had been installed.

Outside, sixty-year-old asphalt was the best you got for parking. It was as much potholes and the crumbled remains of petroleum products melted and reformed, summer after summer, as it was a parking lot. A carport next to the office was for our vehicles. Mine barely fit thanks to the size of Peralta's extended-cab pickup truck. The only other improvements had been a heavy-grade fence with a section that rolled across the driveway to seal things up tight when we were gone and restoring the old motel sign of a cowboy throwing a lariat. The neon was new and blinked happily into the night. And some well-concealed security cameras. We both had made enemies over the years.

Across the wide, divided avenue stretched railroad tracks and an industrial district. It was two miles and a new lifetime away from our old world: Peralta's palatial suite of offices, and my beloved aerie on the fourth floor of the art deco 1929 county courthouse. No more badge. No more cold cases to solve. After I had left academia—or was I thrown out?—I had taken Peralta's offer of a job in the Sheriff's Office reluctantly. I hadn't even intended to stay in Phoenix. I would be back long enough to sell the house. But I stayed.

It came to seem natural. Deputy David Mapstone.

Then it went away with great suddenness. Much else did, too.

"The point is," Felix said, "I want another opinion. A deeper investigation. I couldn't think of a better person than the former sheriff of Maricopa County. I want the best. Your reputation is very good, too, Doctor Mapstone."

Doctor Mapstone. That had been my grandfather, a dentist. I was merely a guy with too many history degrees. Once I had been mildly proud of the honorific. Now, for reasons I didn't fully understand, it irritated me. Like when somebody other than Lindsey called me "Dave."

He would be getting the best with Peralta, no doubt about that. Perhaps he was pleased that neither of us was awed by Zisman. I recalled now that Zisman's nickname had been "Larry Zip" and he had led many thrilling comebacks when he was at Arizona State. But I wasn't a rabid sports fan or sports historian, and Peralta's passions were golf and baseball. So we wouldn't approach this case as hero worshippers. Still, flattery seemed very out of place coming from this rough-looking, expensively dressed man.

"Was she suicidal?" Peralta asked.

"No."

"Bi-polar? Any mental illness? On any anti-depressants?" Spoken like the former husband of a psychologist. "Did she have a history of emotional problems?"

Felix shook the big head sparingly several times. "She was a sweet girl."

"Did she have enemies?" I asked.

"Of course not." It was the first time his voice had showed anything other than a careful detachment.

I asked other questions. When was the last time he had spoken to her? Two days before her death. How was she? Everything seemed fine. No change in her voice? Nothing new going on in her life? *No. No.* His voice grew more taut.

Expanding on my winning interpersonal skills, I continued. "What was she doing in Zisman's condominium?"

"What the hell business is…?" He stopped himself.

"We're going to need to know." This from Peralta's deep, authoritative voice, before which the toughest cops had quailed.

Felix allowed the slightest sigh. "I don't know. I know what you're thinking. I didn't even think she knew the man. She had a boyfriend in San Diego. I can give you his name."

Peralta leaned back and said nothing. Felix rolled his head and knocked out a kink with such force that his neck emitted a sharp pop and I wondered for a second if he might have injured himself.

He was fine. "Money won't be a problem." He floated the fee schedule back across Peralta's desk.

Peralta tapped his pen against the pad. He didn't need a case. Sharon, his ex, had made sure he was set up with money for life and his only vices were guns and beer. I did. I was already digging into savings that had never been plentiful. Lindsey had a good job and her paycheck dropped into our joint checking account every two weeks. But I was reluctant to use her money. I had never thought of her money and my money during our marriage, but that was before the *annus horribilis* we had gone through. Money would be nice right now, but I wasn't sure I wanted it from this particular case.

"Let me take down a little more information and we'll make a preliminary investigation," Peralta said. "After that, I'll decide if we're going to continue."

"Fair enough," Felix said.

The "little more information" took another forty-five minutes.

Afterward, Felix pushed across a thick envelope. "I hope ten thousand is enough for a retainer."

My greedy heart leapt. My nervous leg didn't celebrate by calming down.

Peralta studied the contents. I could see hundred-dollar bills.

"I didn't want to wait for a check to clear," Felix said. "I'd appreciate it if you can start now."

Maybe Peralta nodded, but the man stood. He handed each of us a card with his name and number. No address.

"What's your line of work, Mister Smith?"

"Between jobs."

Peralta didn't push the question so I let it be.

Felix shook our hands. He gave me a long, vise-like shake. I gave it back as hard as I could and met his stare full on. If he was packing, my peripheral vision wasn't good enough to pick it up.

"I hope you don't mind if I also check you out." Peralta's voice snapped the moment.

"Not a bit."

Felix pivoted and pulled out a platinum money clip. From this, he handed the big man a driver's license. When Peralta had written down what he wanted, he gave it back and thanked him.

Felix let the money clip fall into his pocket. "You can't be too careful."

He turned and walked to the door. As he opened it, a hot gust from the outside caught his left cuff, raising it briefly. Above the pricey loafer on his foot, I saw something that looked like it was out of a *Terminator* movie. A lower-limb prosthetic, very high-tech, titanium and graphite. He definitely hadn't received it through the average health-care plan. I had read about ones embedded with a microprocessor that were worn by wounded soldiers.

When I looked up again, I saw him watching me watching him. The yellow eyes hated me.

Chapter Three

"Feeling guilty?"

I did a little. I walked to the front window and raised the blind. Felix the Cat was sitting in a Mercedes Benz CL, silver, new, insolently bouncing back the sun's glare. The driver's window was down. Who needs air conditioning when it's only 108? He had a cell phone against his head and he was talking animatedly, very different from the stone-like expression he had mostly shown us. He didn't look happy.

"A rig like he had on his leg would only be issued to a disabled veteran." Peralta made more notes as he spoke, his large head and shoulders hunched over the desk.

I let the blind fall and turned back toward him. "The cartel could afford it." I told him about the car, which was not issued by the V.A.

He looked up. "Mapstone, you see Zetas and Sinaloa in your sleep." His tone softened subtly. "Which is understandable, after what you went through."

Yes, I was jumpy. But I saw other things in my sleep.

"I can guarantee you that Chapo Guzman doesn't even know who you are," Peralta went on. Chapo was the boss of the Sinaloa federation. And maybe he didn't. But his lieutenants did.

"Did you catch the tat?" I asked.

He nodded and went back to writing. "Everybody has tattoos now."

"Do you?"

"Maybe." No smile. This passed for raucous Mike Peralta humor. I didn't laugh.

"We shouldn't take this case."

"Why not?"

"Oh, I don't know." I prowled around the small room, absently slid out a file drawer, closed it. "He paid in cash."

Peralta opened the envelope and counted. He peeled off five grand and held it out to me. The bills looked as if they had come out of the U.S. Bureau of Engraving that morning. I made no move to retrieve them. Someday soon I would need to set up an accounting and tax system in the computer if we were actually going to have a PI business.

Peralta gently tapped the Ben Franklins. "Paying clients are nice."

"Cash," I persisted. "Who pays in cash? A criminal."

"That's why you're going to run a background check."

This was a man who until recently had bossed around hundreds of deputies and civilian employees. Now only I was available. I made no move to pick up the phone. "He says his last name is Smith. *Smith?* Right."

"Some people are actually named Smith." He left my share of the retainer on his desk and slid the envelope containing the remainder into his suit-coat pocket.

"And his sister has a different last name?"

"Families are complicated nowadays. Lindsey and Robin had different last names."

Bile started up my windpipe. *Lindsey and Robin.* I wanted to curse him. I bit my tongue, literally. It worked. I gained deeper knowledge about the provenance of a clichéd expression. And I said nothing.

Peralta, typically, bulled ahead. "How is Lindsey?"

"Fine." How the hell should I know? She's only my wife, a continent away physically and even further in the geography of the heart.

"When did you talk to her last?"

I told him I called her on Sunday. I called her every Sunday, timing it so I would catch her around noon in D.C.

"She'll get tired of Washington and Homeland Security," he said. "It's a temporary gig, right?"

"I guess."

It was a temporary position that seemed to have no end.

"When she's ready to come home, we could use her here."

I said nothing. Yes, she was the best at cyber crimes. That was the job she did for Peralta when he was sheriff. But the last place my wife wanted to be was back in Phoenix.

I started coughing again. Three wildfires were burning in the forests north and northeast of the city. The previous year had been the worst wildfire season on record and we were off to an ambitious start now. It was the new normal. Yesterday the smoke had combined with the usual smog to obscure the mountains. Somebody flying into Sky Harbor would never know why this was called the Valley of the Sun. The gunk was sending people with asthma to emergency rooms and making me cough. Quite an irony for a place that once claimed clean, dry air that had made it a haven for people with lung ailments.

But that was the least of the reasons why Lindsey didn't want to be here.

Sitting back down, I said again, "We shouldn't take this case."

Peralta's obsidian eyes darkened further. "Why?"

"Felix the Cat in his fifteen-hundred-dollar suit, paying you in hundred-dollar bills. He's hiding something. Maybe Zisman had a mistress or not. Maybe Felix is using us for some vendetta against Zisman. The guy's pretty clean from what I remember. He actually came back home to Arizona after making it big and has tried to help out poor kids. Now here's some dude in an expensive suit who wants us to play morals police."

"He only asked us to investigate a suspicious death," he said. "Remember, Felix bridled when you implied Grace was involved with this Zisman."

That was true. Why was I fighting against taking this case?

Peralta swept his arm wide. "Half the bigs in Phoenix stash their mistresses in San Diego condos. Big deal. But we have our first paying client. Have a sense of celebration, Mapstone. This might not lead anywhere. It probably won't. If not, we'll refund most of his money. Bringing the family comfort and closure is a big thing. We can get out of town for a few days, go to a nice, cool place."

I was still about to gasp from Mike Peralta using the word *closure*. I managed, "You go. I'll hold down the fort. Who knows, we might get another client."

"You're coming with me. You know San Diego."

"It's changed a lot since I lived there."

"Well, you *used* to live there."

I tried not saying anything.

"You won't see Patty."

I could feel my cheeks warming. "This has nothing to do with Patty."

"I know you," he said.

Yes, he did. He had known me as a young deputy he trained. And then all the years I was away teaching, finally ending up in San Diego. And he had known me when I was married to Patty in San Diego. One marriage dead. Another on life support.

"It's been a long time, Mapstone. She probably doesn't even live there any more."

I stared at the wall. Patty would never part with that house in La Jolla.

The room was still. Only the sound of intermittent traffic on Grand Avenue penetrated the walls. Then a short train rumbled past and the sun started coming through the blinds. Peralta pretended to ignore me.

"Fine. I'll go. Fuck you."

The gunfire put me on the floor.

It was a loud and mechanical sound. One long burst, chucka-chucka-chucka-chucka-chucka. Then two short bursts. I pulled out my heavy Colt Python .357 magnum with a four-inch barrel, rolled away from the door, assumed a firing position, and waited for the shooter to break in. He would be looking at his eye level. I would be below him and put three rounds into his torso before he could take his next breath.

An engine revved and tires screamed against pavement. Then all I heard was silence. The eighty-year-old glass of the windows was untouched. The front door was secure. I wasn't sweating anymore. The ancient linoleum floor was cool. It smelled of old wax and fresh dust.

When I glanced back, Peralta was emerging from the Danger Room. In his hands was the intimidating black form of a Remington 870 Wingmaster shotgun, extended tube magazine, ghost sights.

He racked in a round of double-ought buckshot, producing the international sound of Kiss Your Ass Goodbye.

"That was an AK-47," he said.

"How do you know?"

"Because I was shot at enough by AKs in Vietnam that I'd never forget the sound."

I stood and moved along the wall toward the door.

"Mapstone."

I turned.

"Let's go out the back door."

Chapter Four

We stood away from the jamb as Peralta opened the back door. Nobody poured AK rounds through. He tossed a black duffel bag out to draw fire. Nothing. He nodded and I knew what to do.

I stepped outside into the oven and ran along the southeast wall while Peralta went around the other side. It was like the academy so many years ago. The carport was on my side and gave me cover to slide between the cars unseen from Grand Avenue. Felix's Benz was stopped in the closest traffic lane. Nobody else was around. Across the median, a small car zipped by going toward downtown without changing its speed. No traffic was headed in the other direction.

Both hands on the Python, I swept the parking lot and made a slow trot toward the Benz. The sun was in my eyes and the scrunchy pavement was loud under my shoes. Peralta was coming from the other edge of the building in an infantryman's crouch, moving quickly and with a grace that belied his big frame. We reached the car at the same time.

Felix the Cat was very dead.

His face was gone. The nice suit was plastered in blood and bone fragments. More blood, brains, and miscellaneous gore were sprayed across the seat and interior of the car. One bubble of tissue had fallen halfway out of his skull and it took me a few seconds to realize that beneath the blood was an eyeball. His left hand still clutched the cell phone I had seen him holding while he talked in our parking lot. In the passenger seat lay the silver bulk of a Desert Eagle, a nasty semiautomatic pistol. It had done Felix no good. His right hand was in his lap. He had never even been able to reach for the gun. Maybe he had it on the seat when he was still in our parking lot. Or maybe he pulled it out when the other car came beside him.

There was something else: the shooter had been so close and so skilled that no shell casings scattered on the pavement. Not one. I had counted at least nine shots.

I did one more look-around and holstered the .357. Whoever had done the shooting was good. Felix had pulled out onto Grand Avenue when they caught him. His driver-side window was still down; no glass shards were to be found. And only one round had penetrated the fine paint job of the car door. The others went right to target.

I turned to Peralta and asked if he had any evidence gloves.

"I want to see that cell phone and the last number he called."

He shook his head. "Give me your gun."

"What?"

He held out his hand.

I hesitated, and then I slipped off my holster and handed it to him. One, two, three cars sped by.

"I'm going back inside," he said. "You're going to call 911 and sit on the curb. We're not the law any more."

I dialed as he trotted back to our office. The excitement over, my body resumed sweating.

In the distance, I heard sirens.

Chapter Five

It was ten p.m. when the Phoenix cops finally cut us loose. Out on Grand, it had been a full response: half a dozen marked cruisers, chopper, news helicopters, Phoenix Fire paramedics, crime scene, and the avenue blocked for hours. Back in the air conditioning of the office, two young detectives had interviewed us. Peralta was cagey. No, he outright lied. Nobody could tell when Peralta was lying, certainly not this pair. He had come back outside and taken control of the narrative and of me.

Here's the way he told it: we were waiting in the office for a potential client when we heard the shots and went out to find the Benz and the dead body. That was when we called the police. Had this potential client given a name? No, Peralta said. It was a man and he didn't give his name. Peralta didn't think to ask for it. We were here and he told him to come on by. Were the detectives thinking this was the man?

They didn't say. They did ask if we knew a subject named Derek Zimmerman.

"Is that the D.B.?" Peralta gave them his best command stare and they responded.

"Maybe, Sheriff."

"Never heard of him. Have you, Mapstone?"

No. I hated him. Why was he lying? I felt all this, forgetting that I had wanted to muck with the investigation by reading the recent calls on our late client's cell phone.

"How about Felix Smith? James Henry Patterson?"

"Who are they?" Peralta asked.

"We're only starting our investigation," one detective offered. "But you might be glad you didn't get this case. The guy was carrying multiple driver's licenses."

I thought about the Desert Eagle on his passenger seat.

They left their cards. If we remembered anything else, please call us at this number…I had done the routine a hundred times myself, when I was on the other side of the badge. Then they left.

"Why did you do that?" I whispered it, as if the detectives were listening at the door.

"I want a trip to San Diego."

"Our client is dead."

"Exactly."

Afterward, I drove east a few blocks on Encanto Boulevard and was enveloped in the trees and grass of the park and the historic districts. The temperature dropped ten degrees. This was a good thing considering that the air conditioning in Lindsey's old Honda Prelude had seen better days. On the north edge of Palmcroft, I sat through the long wait at the Seventh Avenue light, brooding over what had happened. Then I crossed into Willo, past the old fire station, and headed home. A right on Fifth Avenue and a left on Cypress. The street was quiet and most of the houses were dark. Normal people had gone to bed. My house was dark and not inviting. I vowed again to get some lights on timers and drove on.

At the Sonic on McDowell, I ate a foot-long Coney dog and drank a medium Diet Cherry Coke. The bright lights and blaring bubblegum music gave a false sense of protection. The condition of the car gave me no choice but to turn off the engine and open the windows. The climate could thank me later.

An AK-47 was a crappy assassination weapon, so Peralta told me after the cops left. In all but the most expert of hands, it had a tendency to ride up and have bad accuracy. On the other hand, who could miss at that range? Smith/Zimmerman/Patterson had pulled onto Grand and another car came alongside.

Did he recognize the car and stop to talk to its occupants? Did the encounter have something to do with the phone call I had seen him making?

Peralta didn't offer any theories. He did say, "Somebody who uses an AK that way, it's his preferred weapon. He likes it."

I ate the wonderful crunchy Sonic ice, marinated in cherry, and took a little comfort that I was the only car in the place. A little comfort.

Oh, I wished Lindsey would call and ask, "How are you, Dave?" and being Lindsey she would know from my voice that I was not fine, nowhere near it, not even in the same state as fine. But my cell phone was silent.

There was nothing to do but go back to the house, which I did after driving around the block four times.

The 1924 Spanish Colonial on Cypress was lovely and forlorn. The old locks and new alarm system were fine, but I still swept through the rooms with my revolver out. The floor-to-ceiling bookshelves that ran the length of the stairway looked at me indifferently. More bookshelves lined the study, books accumulated by my grandparents, by me alone, by Lindsey and me.

Except for the few years I was away, I had lived in this house all my life, and my grandparents before me. Yet the walls silently said, "You are only passing through here. We will remain." The walls didn't care about the tragedies this house had endured.

In the kitchen, I pulled the Beefeater out of the freezer and stirred a martini, the perfect chaser to diet cherry Coke. The only thing I had done to the house lately was to put up new curtains that completely hid the back yard from view when one was standing at the sink. They still did provide privacy, but I couldn't avoid pushing them against the glass as an extra measure of safety.

I have stopped turning on the lights. I have stopped listening to jazz. I have stopped reading books. The outside world holds no appeal, either. I've made myself go to several movies at the AMC downtown at Arizona Center, but I left each one after a few minutes. I couldn't stand any of it. So I sat in silence in the living room, sipping the cold gin, staring out at the street, trying to keep my mind locked down. At least the neighbors had stopped their well-meaning water torture of relentless expressions of sympathy over Robin's death and inquiries about when Lindsey is coming home.

I went to the bedroom and stripped down without turning on any lights. I lay down on Lindsey's side of the bed. It turned into Robin's side, too, bastard that I am. Over on the bedside table sat John Lewis Gaddis' biography of George F. Kennan. I felt all of Kennan's emotional shakiness and had none of his brilliance. My "long telegram" would not be about the Soviet Union but about my own union that was breaking up, if not hopelessly broken. I picked it up and tried to read. Nothing caught the gears of my brain. It wasn't Gaddis' fault. So I tried to sleep. Peralta would be here at seven, packed for San Diego.

Too soon, I found myself on a Central Avenue bus. No, it was an airliner. I didn't recognize anyone around me. But I dropped my cell phone on the floor and it slid backwards. What if Lindsey suddenly called? I got on my knees and found the phone two rows back.

Then I was out on the street. The sidewalk was broken and I had to watch my step. New buildings were going up and others were being restored. Bright paint was being applied. The city had never looked better, with a huge downtown skyline against majestic, snowcapped mountains. I would have to stop criticizing it.

A door was open and I walked in. Instantly, I was in my former office at the old courthouse. The big room was nearly empty and I felt sad, until I saw Robin sitting at the desk. She looked up and gave me that roguish smile. She stood and I took her in my arms, brushing back the long, tousled blond hair and covering her with kisses, sobbing and holding her while she laughed and we talked over each other. She put a finger over my mouth and I was silent, listening to her tell me... Tell me...

Then she was gone.

I was in a hallway painted blood red, looking for Robin. I walked for what seemed twenty-five paces, trying locked doors, and then turned into a narrower passage. I was completely alone. In my pocket, where my cell should have been, was only a wallet. I pulled it out again and it was a pack of Gauloises, the brand of cigarettes Lindsey smoked.

My gut was in full panic gear now but I kept walking, finding new hallways, each one smaller than the one that came before it, turning and turning. Where was I? It seemed as if I was going in circles. There was nobody to ask for directions. My cell phone was gone and my legs moved only with ever-greater effort. I kept going. Behind me was only darkness. Then I could barely make it through the hall; it was so narrow I turned sideways to make it into the next section. Finally, the walls tapered together in a "V" and I was at the end.

I knew by now that I shouldn't push against the drywall, but I did.

I couldn't stop myself.

I always did.

That was when the explosion came.

We were in the back yard on Cypress. Night. Robin was on the ground and I was on my knees, trying to resuscitate her, trying to stop the bleeding. Her blouse was wet from the blood and it was all over my hands.

I looked up and this time the woman with the gun was still standing there.

This time the woman was Lindsey.

Then the dark bedroom greeted me and I was awake, in the dimension where the mountains were low and the city was not reclaiming Central. Where the downtown skyline was still squat, monotonous, and ugly and the only real event of where I had been was Robin's death in the back yard from a single gunshot.

I had this dream nearly every night. I called it my maze dream.

Chapter Six

Peralta slid into my driveway at precisely seven a.m. I walked out with my bag and the surly attitude of a non-morning person, stowing my gear in the extended cab of his gigantic Ford F-150. I would leave the argument about his personal contribution to greenhouse gases and climate change for another day. He surprised me with a venti non-fat, no-whip mocha from Starbucks, my usual drink, and one he has disparaged on many occasions as virtually anti-American. He, of course, was drinking black coffee. We backed out, cruised through Willo and Roosevelt, and then slid onto Interstate 10 where it pops out of the deck park by Kenilworth School. It was only ninety-nine degrees. I was in my tan suit with a blue Brooks Brothers polka-dot tie, about to keel over from heat exhaustion.

Neither of us said a word as the suburbs fell away and the truck turned onto Arizona Highway 85 for the short but dangerous connection to Interstate 8. The state was gradually widening what had been a two-lane highway, but people still drove like maniacs and fatalities remained common. Today, the road was nearly empty. If only my head were that way. Jagged bare mountains rose up on either side. I remembered from Boy Scout days that one was called Spring Mountain. I also recalled it was about 355 miles from Phoenix to San Diego. I adjusted the vents again to get the most out of the truck's air conditioning.

When he caught I-8 at Gila Bend, I made my first attempt to breach the battlements of his stubborn personality.

"What about the lawyer Felix mentioned?"

"I called him. He never heard of any of those names."

I asked him if he had given the lawyer a description and he shot me a cutting glance. I thought about Felix sitting there yesterday, so straight and self-possessed in his expensive suit, French cuffs, tattoo, and prosthetic leg. He was not someone to forget.

"So tell me what again we're doing?"

"Driving to San Diego."

Five more miles brought a passing Union Pacific freight train and flat desert.

"You know what I mean." The mocha was finally cool enough to drink.

He declined to answer, so I settled into the seat and watched for more trains. We rode high and mighty along the highway, a steady eighty miles per hour, dwarfed only by semis.

The retiree tract houses and fields of Yuma trickled out to greet us, hotter than hell, and ugly. We went through a McDonald's drive-through and ate on the road like two street cops as we crossed the Colorado River and entered California.

I tried again. "Why did you give a false report to the police, saying Smith, or whatever the hell his name is, was never in our office?"

"It was easier." And that was all he said between mouthfuls of a Quarter Pounder with cheese. Peralta was the most by-the-book hard-ass peace officer I had ever known. I told him this.

"Don't be so quick to judge, Mapstone." Bite, chew, swallow, steer with one hand. "And don't get grease on that arm rest. As I recall, you did a little selective application of the law after Robin was murdered."

That was true, but I wasn't going to let him get me into that dark alley.

"I'm talking about now. We don't owe this guy anything."

"You wanted to break the law yesterday by tampering with evidence."

He was right. I wanted to see the number Felix had called from our parking lot. I was a long way from being a Boy Scout.

Peralta shrugged his big shoulders. "He put us on retainer for ten grand. Our obligation is to the client, and that includes privacy."

Sand dunes loomed up on the south. I knew that a plank road was built here in 1915. I didn't know anything about being a private investigator. Listening to our conversation made me question myself again about joining him in the rough little building on Grand Avenue. Robin had suggested it. She expected to live to see it. I violently shook my head.

"You have a headache?"

"No." I ate the Big Mac and daintily wiped my fingers to protect his fake leather or whatever the hell it was on the armrest. "What would you as sheriff have done to a PI who pulled the stunt you did?"

"Probably prosecute him."

"But now you're applying situational ethics."

"Don't be using your fancy academic language on me, Mapstone." The burger was gone and now his right hand was grabbing French fries. Peralta always ate one fast-food course at a time. "I'm just a simple boy from the barrio."

I cut him off. "You went to Harvard." He knew very well what I meant. I gave up for the moment.

We were now in the Colorado Desert, a very different place from the lush Sonoran Desert that surrounded Phoenix and Tucson: no saguaros or any of the other hundreds of plant and animal species of my home country. It was sun-blasted moonscape, a sea of tranquility: long vistas, distant mountain ranges, few colors beyond off-white, ochre, and brown—and in this spot it declined into a sink that was below sea level.

We finished lunch at eighty-five miles per hour. I policed all the containers and napkins, and then the flat, green fields of the Imperial Valley surrounded us, all irrigated, quite irrationally, by a canal running from the Colorado River. If not for the geology of the Colorado's delta, the Sea of Cortez would go all the way north to Indio. It was an amazing thing to contemplate. North of us was the Salton Sea, accidentally created in 1905 when the

Colorado, as it would do before being nearly killed by dams, flooded into crude irrigation canals dug to divert water into what had been the dry Salton Sink. The "sea" became a major bird destination, created its own ecosystem. Now it was dying, helped by the Imperial Valley's toxic runoff. I read the other day that the noxious air from a massive fish kill drifted as far as Los Angeles.

We stopped to relieve ourselves in El Centro. No offense to the local chamber of commerce, but that seemed all it was good for, even though the town now had a Starbucks. The air was hot and hazy and smelled of agricultural chemicals.

Ahead were Plaster City and the startling escarpment of the Laguna Mountains. San Diego had one of the finest natural harbors in the world, but the railroads couldn't easily get there in the nineteenth century because of that mountain range. Instead, they went to Los Angeles and that was that. We passed over one track at Plaster City and it reminded me of the railroad that was finally built to San Diego from the east. If memory served, the sugar baron John Spreckles underwrote it, and the San Diego and Arizona line was one of the most ambitious engineering accomplishments of its day. But it never made money and the land it traversed was so harsh, including a perilous crawl through Carrizo Gorge, that maintaining the railroad was prohibitive.

The wall of mountains and its forbidding canyons beyond did not intimidate Dwight Eisenhower's Interstate Highway System. So I-8 was built in the mid-1960s and San Diego finally had its connection to the east. Every year it brought more Phoenicians to the coast in search of relief from the summer heat.

None of this would have interested Peralta.

We started the serious grind uphill and then we were climbing through terrain strewn with giant boulders, the marble game of the gods. Behind us, the Imperial Valley spread below like a dry seabed. The Interstate twisted and curved, an unwelcome intruder. The sun was on his side, glinting off his thick hair and bringing out the aristocratic profile. I knew this highway well, but the majestic land never ceased its ability to move me.

"So we're going to San Diego," I said. "Do we know if anything this guy told us is correct? He lied about who he was. How do we know this Grace Hunter even existed or killed herself?"

"We don't. We'll find out."

Robert Caro writes about how Lyndon Johnson was a reader of men. Nobody could read Peralta, not even LBJ, and certainly not me. Only occasionally did a "word" reveal itself to a careful observer of his professional mask. As I studied him, I could see an unusual determination in the set of his thick jaw. To be sure, "determination" with Peralta was like saying "deep" about the Grand Canyon. It was always there and spectacular to behold, much less try to hinder. Now, however, the canyon of his tenacity was unusually on display. But I saw something else, too, another word. Concern.

I said, "What if we're being set up?"

"Then it's better to take the initiative."

"What if we're being set up by going to San Diego?"

"I told you, you're not going to see Patty."

When I lapsed into silence and he realized his effort to piss me off had failed, he spoke again.

"Whoever did this would expect us to give a full report to the police and lay low in Phoenix. That would be logical. So we'll do what they don't expect. All you have to do is your history thing."

This was what he used to say when he would barge into my office in the old Court House. It became a longstanding joke. But I blew. "What history?!" It was amazing how his luxurious cab absorbed the sound of my tantrum. "The dead man in front of our office didn't have any history! This isn't a historical case."

As usual, my outburst failed to move him. In as soft a voice as he could manage, "Mapstone, everybody has a history. You need to find it. 'The only new thing in the world is the history you don't know.' Saint Paul said that."

"Harry Truman said that."

"Same difference."

I resisted the familiar urge to reach over and try to strangle him, even if I would lose the fight and he would never even swerve out of his lane.

He said, "We have a name, D.O.B., Social Security Number and photo…"

"Right, and she's a sweet girl who went to Chaparral High in Scottsdale, was a student at San Diego State, worked part-time at the Nordstrom perfume counter at Horton Plaza. She had a boyfriend and somehow she ended up at Larry Zisman's condo on the night of April twenty-second."

"See how much you know?" He lazily draped his arms over the steering wheel despite the tangled road we climbed.

I slumped in my seat. "If any of it is true."

"David." He never called me David. "You have a gift for history. I never thought you'd be happy as a professor. You're a cop down in your bones. But you're a historian, too. You look at a case the same way a historian studies the secondary sources and published material on a subject. You talk to the primary sources, read their recollections. Then you apply a historian's skepticism and diligence, come up with new interpretations, dig out fresh facts, add context, shine the light in a different direction seeking the truth. It's what you do."

It shut me up. Even made me feel better about myself for the moment.

When we crested Laguna Summit, he spoke again.

"Here's something else to consider, Mapstone. We don't know why Felix was shot to hell. Maybe it was because of this girl, or something else in his life that made him carry that Desert Eagle that was on the car seat."

He had been there so briefly, it surprised me he had time to notice and identify the gun on the passenger seat of the Benz. But that was Peralta.

"But," he went on, "he might have been killed because he came to see us. And I don't want the word on the street to be that you can kill our clients. It's bad for business. And it might encourage the wrong kind of people to reach out and touch us."

I let him alone. It was a reminder that there were three ways to do things: the right way, the wrong way, and Peralta's way. Soon we would begin the long descent to San Diego, through the lovely little meadows of eastern San Diego County that looked as if they hadn't changed for a hundred years, back up to Alpine at the edge of the Cleveland National Forest, then dropping and curving into El Cajon, massive Silverdome mountain dominant on our right, the cool sea air coming up to kiss away the memory of the desert, the city swallowing us up, the freeway packed with traffic, and the ocean straight ahead. San Diego: my adopted hometown. I would need to pack my emotions tight.

Chapter Seven

Among the benefits of being the former sheriff of one of America's most populous counties was cooperation from other law-enforcement agencies even after you were out of office. An added perk was that Al Kimbrough was a San Diego Police commander. I first met him when Peralta had hired me back at MCSO and Kimbrough had been a detective. He could have stayed and become chief of detectives, but San Diego made him a better offer, one that didn't include 108-degree May days. Peralta scheduled a meeting with him downtown and complained about the overcast.

"It's the onshore flow," I instructed. "The June Gloom."

"It's not June."

I rolled down the window and looked over the bay at one of the aircraft carriers moored at North Island. "It's cool. I'm happy."

He handed me a copy he had made of Grace Hunter's photo. "Why don't you take the truck and go talk to the boyfriend? Here's the address."

I didn't breathe for about five seconds and handed the address back to him.

"What, you're showing off your photographic memory to an old man?"

"No," I said. "I used to live there." I sat for a few minutes in silence as a big jet going into Lindbergh Field rattled the cab.

Sometimes coincidences were serendipity. Not this one. This was creepy. But there was a job to do. "Drop me off at Old Town. I'll take the bus."

"That's nuts."

"I couldn't find a parking place, especially for your beast."

"You can always find a parking place if you're patient."

"Not in O.B."

As I gave directions to Old Town, he shook his head and shrugged. "You're one weird guy, Mapstone."

Fifteen minutes later, I was on a half-full 35 bus, rolling down Rosecrans Street, turning onto Midway Drive for the ride across the hump of Loma Portal and into Ocean Beach. Behind us was the bay, ahead was the ocean. I counted twenty Arizona license tags and quit counting. This time of year, San Diego was Phoenix West. Native San Diegans hated the invasion. When I lived here and rode this bus almost every day, I learned not to let on where I was from. The bus started downhill, with the sun beginning to burn off the clouds behind me, toward downtown. But ahead, it was still gray, the vast expanse of the Pacific a sheet of lead blending into the overcast. The Pacific played a trick of the eye, seeming to rise into the horizon, even though we were merely descending a long slope to the ocean.

If you stay on Interstate 8, you'd run right into O.B. But most tourists didn't. They went north of the San Diego River to Sea World, Mission Bay and the more popular neighborhoods of Mission Beach or Pacific Beach, or they went south on I-5 to downtown. San Diego had changed substantially since I had lived here, but Ocean Beach looked much the same: the narrow streets, quaint and pricey cottages, one-story businesses lining Newport Avenue and the long municipal pier jutting into the ocean. I had lived two lives in San Diego: pre-Patty in Ocean Beach and with Patty in La Jolla.

It reminded me of the old days, getting off at Cable and Newport, and then walking past the business district down to Santa Cruz Avenue. A couple of guys carrying surfboards walked past me, going west. Seagulls passed overhead making their distinctive calls. The old apartment building was still two stories, painted white, and shaped like a U surrounding an interior swimming pool. My unit had been on the second floor. The boyfriend's apartment was directly beside it. I felt an involuntary urge to check my mail, smiled at it, and walked up to No. 205. The windows were open, as was common here, and the drapes were drawn and partly hanging out.

The loud, angry voice coming from the apartment wasn't surprising, either. O.B. was an eclectic place, where CPAs lived alongside bikers. Once I had been kept up all night when one of the latter had engaged in an all-night screaming fight with his old lady. Now I would put a stop to it, but I was different then.

The voice was deep and menacing, the dispute involving a woman, money, and perhaps more. The dialogue was generally, "I want Scarlett, motherfucker, and your white ass is out of excuses. Where is she? I need her ass back out making money," on and on. "You think you can hide from me? Nobody gets away from me. I own her sweet little booty. Now where the fuck is she? Tell me now or I stomp your white ass to death and find her my own self."

My mind momentarily thought of search warrants and probable cause, but, as Peralta said, we weren't the law anymore. When I heard a fist connect with flesh, cartilage snap, and a man squeal, I opened the door.

"What the fuck?"

The voice belonged to a very large man with caramel-colored skin, mustard-yellow driving cap, delicately manicured beard, eyes way too small for his face. A Bluetooth device was attached to the left side of his head. He was my height and about a third wider. He wore a black T-shirt proclaiming RUN-D.M.C. Below his shorts were heavy stomp-your-white-ass boots.

"Who the fuck are you?"

"Life insurance." I smiled.

He raised his shirt so I could see the butt of a semiautomatic pistol in his waistband. Then he advanced toward me, one step, two...

I thrust my hand forward suddenly, open and straight-fingered into the middle of his windpipe. The small eyes burst wide, the cap and Bluetooth flew off, and he was gasping. Both his hands clutched his throat in what we had been taught in first-aid classes was the "universal choking symbol." Done properly, this was a useful move for incapacitating someone. Done wrong, it would kill him, which was why it had been discontinued by police agencies.

My next move, one second later, was to remove the Python from its shoulder holster and level it at his face.

"See, you never know when you might need life insurance."

He staggered back. From his open mouth came the sound of an ailing carburetor. His eyes showed the most primal emotions: surprise, pain, and the sense that he was suffocating. It was a testimony to his size and strength that he was still standing. That made me uneasy.

"Move back, asshole."

He did. When I was all the way inside, I kicked the door closed but made sure I was still facing him.

"Who are you?" This from a skinny, pale kid with bushy red hair, sitting on a sofa. He was probably the only person in O.B. without a tan. He was in pain, clutching his face. Seeing his hands occupied, I ignored him.

"Can you talk now?" I said this to the black man.

"Iiiihhhhhhhhhhh."

I asked him whether he was right- or left-handed. He opened his mouth and showed a gold incisor. He finally managed, "Left."

"So use your left hand and pull out that gun very slowly and hand it to me." I knew he was lying about which hand he favored, or at least I took that chance. After I had possession of the Glock, I shoved him back onto the sofa next to the white kid. Gravity did most of the work. Large human objects are easier to push around when they can barely breathe.

"Should'a known you was a motherfucking cop." His voice was a shadow of its former booming self.

"I'm not a cop." I kept the .357 magnum leveled at his chest. The barrel was only four inches of thick ribbed steel, but the business end might as well have been the size of eternity.

"Now wait a motherfucking minute." He held out two big hands, palms facing me and tried to make himself smaller on the sofa, no easy task. His expression changed. He wasn't worrying about his throat any longer. "Motherfuck! I've heard about you. Big guy with a big motherfucking gun…."

I held up my hand. He stopped talking.

"Did you ever consider that repeating the same profanity over and over deprives it of any ability to shock? You might consider trying out a word such as 'mountebank' or 'scoundrel.'"

He lowered his hands and took a deep breath. "Look, man, I got no problem with Edward, man. I'm completely good with him. Why you think I'm here right now? This is between me and this skinny pale-ass mother…" He stopped. "Scoundrel."

I said, "Who is Tim Lewis?"

"He is." The black guy quickly pointed to the red-haired kid next to him.

"Then it's time for you to leave."

"What about my Glock?"

"Get another one."

He stood without protest, picked up his cap, and hurried out the door, quietly closing it. I locked it, expecting him to at least be muttering indignation and threats as he departed, but nothing. I heard heavy steps thudding along the concrete, down the stairs, and then they faded. The gate to the street clanged shut.

I waited a few seconds and holstered the Python. "Who is he?"

"I think my nose is broken!" His voice sounded like a teary fourteen-year-old.

"So who broke it?"

"You don't know? He knows you." His eyes were curious. "He calls himself AFP."

My mind did a sort: FDR, JFK, LBJ. I asked again.

Through his hands came a nasal response. "America's Finest Pimp."

Get it: San Diego called itself America's Finest City. I didn't smile. I leaned against the outer wall and stealthily looked out the drawn curtain. The courtyard was deserted. Nobody was at the pool that dominated the space. Beyond the fence, nobody was on the sidewalk.

From my pocket I produced the photo and held it out. "Do you know her?"

"That's Scarlett."

I worked hard to conceal my surprise. "Who?"

"Scarlett. My girlfriend."

"What's her last name?"

"Mason. Scarlett Mason. Do you know where she is?"

I nodded, put the picture away, and asked him what problem he had with America's Finest Pimp.

"I'm really hurting, dude!"

I checked him out in more detail. He might have had the kind of face teenage girls consider cute, at least before his nose had been broken, but to me it looked like a comic-book face, a cross between Archie and Jimmy Olsen. His face was so thin, a vein running up his forehead was prominent.

His body looked rangy and underweight beneath a gray T-shirt, droopy Lakers shorts, and teal flip-flops. A flaming tattoo wrapped itself up his left calf. His fingers, long and slender, were oozing bright red blood from where America's Finest Pimp had hit him, and now it was dripping onto his shirt. I walked to the kitchen, grabbed a dishtowel, and tossed it to him.

"Where is Scarlett? Please…" His tone was plaintive enough to be believable. I was about to tell him to get some ice on his nose so we could talk.

The next thing I heard sounded like a cat, until it didn't. My right hand was on the way back to my holster. "Who else is here?"

"The baby."

Chapter Eight

I grabbed him by the arm and pushed him ahead of me into the bedroom. Once I would hide behind books. Now I was using a human shield. Beside a box spring and mattress on the floor was a yellow hand-me-down crib. After ordering him to stand against the far wall so I could watch him, I approached it.

Sure enough, inside was a baby, incredibly tiny, with a tuft of brown hair and a very soiled diaper.

When I looked back at Lewis, he was kneeling, his head pointed down. "I don't feel good…"

"How long has this baby needed changing?"

"I don't know. AFP was here for couple of hours, waiting for Scarlett, telling me he'd kill me if I didn't give him the money she owed him…" He was sobbing. The vein up his forehead expanded. "I think I have a concussion. I'm dizzy. Can you change him please? I didn't mean to leave him back here alone."

I filed the money part away and let him alone. He was useless. I looked around for supplies. All I saw was a television, along with a video-game box and a cell phone sitting atop a plastic crate that doubled as a bedside table. Opening the closet, I found a shelf with a box of Pampers, wipes, and baby powder.

Back at crib-side, I felt pretty useless myself. As a young deputy, I had delivered a couple of babies in the backs of squad cars. Otherwise, I had spent a lifetime staying as far away from them as possible. At least until a year ago, I figured that would always be the case. But as I beheld this tiny, helpless creature,

I was nearly overcome by a hurricane of feelings and instincts. The bracing stench coming from the diaper brought me back to reality. It wasn't as bad as a dead body left for a week inside a house during high summer in Phoenix.

I pulled out a clean diaper and slid it under the baby, who was squirming with more energy and squalling like a siren. Maybe I was painting myself into a very messy corner, but it was worth a try. Then I set the wipes on the mattress and gingerly undid one tab. The stench grew worse. Thankfully, the window was open and a faint sea breeze was coming in. So far, so good: I pulled the other tab, folded it in on itself, and lowered the front of the soiled diaper. Immediately a little fountain of urine shot all over my tie and shirt.

It was a boy.

Pleased with himself, he kicked and flung his arms. Back to it, I used wipes to clean off his front, between his legs, and under his scrotum, wadding them up and putting them on the soiled diaper. Feeling pretty good about myself now, I folded the diaper in on itself to provide a clean surface, lifted his legs, and cleaned off his backside. That took another four wipes. Then I slid out the bad diaper, rolled it up, and, voila, he was safe and sanitary on the new one. I hooked the tabs and lifted him into my arms, which did nothing to stop his wiggling and crying.

"Better?" I smiled. The big baby head stopped crying for a moment, then started squealing again as if I were torturing him with hot pokers.

Instantly, the silent-but-deadly cloud of odor hit me. The new diaper was heavy again and I felt something oozing out onto my hands.

"Well, hell."

I know a few things: the socio-economic issues of the Progressive Era, the revisionist arguments regarding the causes of World War I, how to prepare a class syllabus. I have some skills, including reloading the Python under pressure, properly tying a necktie with a dimple in the center, and effectively swinging a hammer. I know how to make a dry martini and make love to a woman. Here, I was over my head.

Muttering a lesson in profane oaths for the young master's linguistic instruction, I carried him into the bathroom and deposited him in the sink. The din of his crying was magnified by a power of ten.

So much for my clever first attempt, filled with hubris and baby-shit.

It took another fifteen minutes, a facecloth protectively placed over his dangerous little penis, much clumsiness on my part, and two diapers, but the baby was finally clean, powdered, and back in his crib. I put a rattle in his hand and shook it. He looked at me with a surprisingly grown-up expression, dropped the rattle, and conked out. After what we'd both been through, it seemed like a good idea to me, too.

I wished that Lindsey's face would stop flashing across my vision.

After I washed up and cleaned my tie, I retrieved Tim Lewis, who had slumped against the bedroom wall, silently watching my learning curve.

"Get up. We need to talk."

"Have you been crying, dude?"

"No."

"Thanks for the help."

I said nothing.

A few minutes later, he was back on the sofa and I was sitting across from him on a dining chair.

He stared at me over an icepack that I had improvised for his traumatized nose. A nasty black left eye was also materializing. He started shaking.

"Are you going to kill me?"

That's me: the diaper-changing, first-aid-giving hit man. I said, "I will kill you if you abuse that baby."

"I take good care of him! I love him! AFP wouldn't let me go back and change him. Since Grace left..."

He blinked and I knew he was hoping I hadn't noticed his slip.

I said, "So who was this Scarlett?"

He cursed at himself. "That was Grace's business name. Her brand."

I pulled out the photo again, turned it toward him, and tapped my finger on the pretty face.

"Her name is Grace Hunter," he said.

"Is that her baby?"

"It's our baby." Somewhere under the icepack, I heard a long sigh. "This has gone so wrong."

"What, that you're living with a prostitute?" I was careful to keep Grace in the present tense.

"She's not a prostitute." His face flushed with anger.

"Then what do you call it when a woman works for a pimp?"

I waited and he told it. It wasn't easy telling.

They had started dating as freshmen at San Diego State. He was studying theater and she was a business major. She had wanted to be in theater, too, but her father demanded that she declare a more practical major. Specifically, business. If she wanted money, he said, she could start her own business the same way he had done. Grace moved in with Tim. They were poor and not happy, working part-time at restaurants, already facing big student loans. They broke up. It was a big campus, so he didn't see her often. He dated some other girls but kept wishing he could get back with Grace.

Three years later, he saw her at Comic Con, the huge comic-book gathering at the convention center downtown. But she wasn't dressed like a nerd. She was in a tight but very expensive-looking mini-dress and on the arm of a guy in a suit who was old enough to be her father. He later learned that the man was a producer in Hollywood. She smiled and waved at Tim, and a week later she emailed him to get together.

Tim learned how much had changed in the time they had been apart.

Grace Hunter's entrepreneurial inspiration had come soon after their breakup. One night she went out and got drunk. An older man hit on her, she went back to his hotel room with him, and spent the night. When she woke up, he was gone but on the bedside table was a thousand dollars cash. Whatever weeks or hours of moral wrestling she did with herself, she realized that San Diego was full of male tourists and businessmen, almost all of them dreaming of a night with a California girl. And they would pay quite well.

She drew up a formal business plan on her laptop: her market was affluent, older married men, the startup costs consisted of the right clothes—bikini for the strand, nice dress or suit for a hotel—and her competitive advantage was that she didn't look like a call girl. The tax exposure was zero. Her brand was Scarlett.

For more than two years, she succeeded brilliantly. The men were usually nice, often terribly lonely, some wanted only to talk, and all were willing to use protection. Not one beat her up or even made her feel creepy. Once a month, she had herself tested for STDs and was always clean. That checkup report would ensure top dollar. She gathered regular clients and her discretion gained referrals. Thanks to her patrons, she stayed at the best hotels and resorts in the area. A few times, men paid her to be with them on more lavish adventures.

"Did she do kink?" I interrupted. "Bondage?"

"No," he said. "That doesn't sound like her at all."

I wondered how much he really knew her, but shut up and let him continue.

The money she earned was awesome. The Great Recession didn't hurt her profits. This sure beat taking on more student debt. She set up small accounts at banks around town, depositing cash as if it were her tips as a waitress. Over time, she consolidated them into a smaller number of bigger accounts. She took out loans from her father and paid them back, telling him that she had a job helping a woman stage condos and houses for sale. Her father's checks were clean to deposit. It was a crude way to launder money, but it was good enough.

The only thing Grace Hunter hadn't assessed for her business plan was the competition. And one night she was kidnapped, beaten, and raped by America's Finest Pimp. He told her that he ran the hotel girls in America's Finest City. He would control her liaisons and take seventy percent of her gross earnings. If she held out on him, he promised, he would beat her to death and take her body out on his boat, feeding her remains to the sharks. For the next three months, she lived in constant fear.

Then she saw Tim again.

He took off the icepack and shook his head. "We thought we'd be safe in O.B. She had money saved. Then she got pregnant and the baby came along. We were happy. She just got a job at Qualcomm and I was going to be a stay-at-home dad when I graduated. I guess she decided to leave me. But I can't understand how she could leave our baby."

Lindsey's face again, whose eyes were such a deep blue that in certain light and certain mood they appeared violet. I thought about the new life I had held in my hands, minutes after gripping the potential death of the Colt Python in the same hands. It was a corny thought, to be sure. But Lindsey's voice burned like acid on my face: *You did this!*

Focus, Mapstone. "Why didn't AFP get her addicted? That's the usual M.O. for a pimp."

"She convinced him she'd be worth more clean. She was good at convincing people. AFP sees himself as a businessman. She paid him straight, every week, until she disappeared and came to be with me."

"Did it bother you that she'd fucked all those men?"

I phrased it as crudely as I could and he stared at the carpet. He was a natural suspect. Jealousy was always a prime motive, wronged spouses and boyfriends always prime suspects.

"All those men, their dicks inside her." I spoke tawdry fluently. "It would sure bother me. It would bother me to find that my wife had been fucking even one man other than me."

Trust me. Only every second, splinters under my skin. But the splinters didn't want to make me kill her.

I said, "I know you're a nice guy, Tim. But didn't it get to you? Did you ever think about killing her when you thought about all those men…"

"No!" His face flushed apple-red.

I took my time, studying his expression and body language, and letting the silence work for me, having watched Peralta interrogate many suspects.

Finally, Tim drew up his wiry frame. "That was in the past. She regretted it. I loved her. I'd rather die than hurt her."

I believed him. He didn't have murder in him.

"Did she ever talk about a man named Larry Zisman? He used to be a pro football player. Owned a condo downtown."

"Was that one of her clients?"

I didn't answer.

"The name doesn't sound familiar," he said. "And she didn't talk about those men. I didn't want to know and she didn't tell me."

"So you guys lived alone here. What about friends?"

"We'd say hi to neighbors. It's that kind of place. Grace stayed in touch with Addison…"

"Who the hell is that? A man or a woman?"

"A woman. She was her best friend."

"Did she visit?"

Tim said that Addison had visited several times, but they never left O.B.

"Addison didn't know anything about Grace's, you know, business."

"I need her contact information." Then I asked when he had seen Grace last.

"The morning of April twenty-second. I had classes. When I came home, she was gone. I never even got a text goodbye. All her stuff is still here. It doesn't make any sense."

"Are you afraid she's gone back to the life?"

He shook his head. "She said she was done and I believed her. She got rid of her old phone, even. We were good together." He sighed. "I wanted to save her from the past."

Tim Lewis looked like a weak reed of a white knight, but his sincerity was obvious. I had gone through my white-knight phase. Now I was covered with tarnish. I made him go through the day she disappeared in detail. He had gone to classes at eight-thirty that morning. Grace was with the baby at home. When he returned around three that afternoon, she was gone. All she took was her purse and cell phone. She always carried pepper spray and a knife in that purse. Nothing had seemed unusual in their apartment.

"Why didn't you go to the police?"

"I filed a missing person's report the next day. The cops made me wait twenty-four hours and even then they didn't take me very seriously. I could tell. They thought she'd left me. They said she was an adult and there wasn't much they could do unless I had evidence of foul play. Of course, I couldn't tell them she used to be a call girl." He shook his head. "Anyway, AFP pays the cops off. Grace warned me. I was sure I'd eventually hear from her. I called hospitals for a week. Nothing."

Grace would have been dead by the time he went to the police. But things fell through the cracks in every police department.

"Where's her family?"

"They lived in Arizona."

I asked him to get me their address and he did.

"What about a brother? Big guy? My size with close-cropped hair and a prosthesis on his lower leg?"

"She was an only child."

I looked at the skinny kid with the cat crawling up his leg: I thought, *dear old dad*. I said, "Who is this Edward that the pimp was talking about?"

"I have no idea. I swear!"

So I told him she was dead and waited as he cried. It was a long wait. He said over and over that Grace would never kill herself, especially after the baby came.

Finally, I asked if he had any place he could go.

"My parents live up in Riverside. It's a boring hellhole."

"My advice is to go there. Right now. And stay awhile."

He nodded, but it was obvious he was descending into a fog of grief, in addition to being beaten up. I made him repeat what he would do.

Go.

Now.

I handed him my business card.

"Private investigator," he said quietly. "Are you trying to find out who killed Grace?"

"Yes."

"I want to hire you."

"We already have a client."

He repeated his request. "I've got to know what happened to Grace. And I want the bastard who killed her to burn." Misery shone in his watery, pale eyes.

"Okay."

He reached under the cushions of the sofa and I tensed.

"Here's five hundred." He handed me a wad of cash. "Is that enough for a start?"

"Sure. But I'll do this pro-bono."

"No," he said. "I don't want your charity. I want you to work for me, and cash talks. Grace taught me that."

I realized it might be good to have a living client, especially because the man who had hired us yesterday was dead and Peralta had lied to the Phoenix Police, saying he had never even come into our office. I took the cash and wrote out a receipt for it on a blank sheet of paper.

He rooted around in the kitchen and returned with a flash drive. "This has her client list. The regulars."

"Have you seen it?"

He shook his head. I could understand why he wouldn't want to look.

I took it and told him we'd be in touch, but that he should call me when he got to Riverside.

His voice stopped me as I was halfway out the door.

"Thank you again for changing the baby. Do you have kids?"

I didn't answer.

"They totally change the way you look at life."

Chapter Nine

Personal history: the day I arrived in San Diego to take an Assistant Professor of History position at the same university that Grace Hunter would later attend, I drove all the way to the end of Interstate 8. It put me in Ocean Beach. I had never been there before. Unlike today, when I was growing up Phoenicians didn't go to San Diego every summer by the tens of thousands. I had visited the city a total of one time before, staying at Hotel Circle in Mission Valley. I had no idea of this magical enclave called Ocean Beach.

But that day I had taken the freeway as far as it would go. After growing up in the desert and then spending several years completing my Ph.D. and teaching in the Midwest, it was as if I had landed in my own little paradise. Ocean Beach immediately felt like home. That evening I walked the 1,971 feet to the end of the municipal pier, turned around, and looked at the neighborhood as it rose up to the spine of the Point Loma Peninsula. The lights in the houses looked like Japanese lanterns and I made a vow out loud:

"I'll never leave."

A few hours before, I had rented my apartment a block-and-a-half from the ocean. I was neither a surfer nor much of a beach person. As a native Phoenician, the idea of tanning went along with the promise of ruined skin soon and melanoma later. But I loved O.B. The only thing that could pry me out was that I loved Patty more.

Patty.

I met her at the ugly main San Diego State University library. We both reached for the same book at the same time, Paul Fussell's *The Great War and Modern Memory*. She was an English professor and, with the Sharon Stone jaw line, classic Wayfarers, and lush wheat-yellow hair, you might mistake her for another shallow Southern California beauty. With the millionaire developer father and house in La Jolla, you might assume she was spoiled, too.

I never made that mistake. I judge a woman by the books she reaches for.

My life was so unfurnished when we met. I had a fairly new doctorate in history, boxes of books, and the old house in Phoenix that had belonged to my grandparents, now rented out. I happily let her help make me the man I became, in all good ways. She taught me how to open a Champagne bottle like a man of the world. Opened my ears to jazz.

Patty appreciated my love of history, ability to dress well, being "debonair," as she put it, for turning out well-balanced and kind, despite having lost my parents before I could even remember them. She called me a *mensch*, one of the best compliments I ever received.

It pleased her that I loved ethnic food and had a very dry sense of humor and possessed an eclectic past that included working for five years as a deputy sheriff trained by a tough older cop named Peralta. I had published my first book, *Rocky Hard Times: The Great Depression in the Intermountain West,* and it had been favorably reviewed. This also pleased her. We made a sophisticated, good-looking couple. But I knew I was marrying up.

She spoke French well. Not well enough to satisfy the most obnoxious waiter in Paris, but her French was better than my Spanish. Thanks to Patty, I learned fun and useful phrases: *cherchez la femme,* which proved to be true in cracking one cold case. *Dragueur*, a skirt chaser. *Terribles simplificateurs*: the world was full of those, Arizona especially. *Billets-doux*: love letters, the writing of which she excelled. *La petit mort*: orgasm. The vocabulary she had taught me was coming back now with the sea breeze.

It was things like this that made me cluelessly happy being with her.

I was one of the few who were allowed to call her Patty. To the rest of the world, she was Patricia. She teased me about spray-painting her name on a wall of I-5. For a long time, I wondered if we would have stayed together if I had committed that simple act of vandalism, decorating the concrete spaghetti with eight letters, leaving drivers to wonder what passion had stirred a man to do such a thing?

A man who would have done that could have kept up when she got on tenure track at the University of California at San Diego, an infinitely more prestigious appointment. He would not have been content being a good teacher, nor would he have bridled at the intentionally dull and social-science-y conventions of academic historiography.

He would have realized that even if *I* didn't feel in competition with her, *she* expected me to overachieve, as her father had demanded of her. The impetuous one with the spray paint would have done more than appreciate, support, and learn from her seemingly infinite avocations, from cooking to film history and painting. He would have tried harder to match her imaginative gift giving even though it couldn't be done.

That man sure as hell would have focused on publishing more so as to ensure tenure at second-rate San Diego State.

Who knows? I can argue this history one way and then the other. Participants don't usually make good historians. Even Churchill had his flaws. As for Patty, she was needy and broken, too. She was as insecure as I was. Our insecurities together acted as an accelerant to burn up our marriage. I taught her things of the world, too, made her happy for a time. The collapse of our marriage wasn't all my fault. Just mostly my fault.

I am too close to the events to recount them dispassionately.

I do know two things. One is that we married too soon. We weren't the people we would become. And I know a simple, transcendent fact...

Chapter Ten

She was the Glory Fuck of My Young Life.

Chapter Eleven

Now I stood at the end of the same pier, the longest on the West Coast if I remembered correctly. A man fished off the south side and pairs of lovers strolled out toward me. My chest was tight and I could feel my heart trying to make its escape, my throat tightening. It was merely a panic attack. I knew that now. They never came in situations where a normal person would panic, only when I was quiet and alone. If I couldn't stop them, at least I could get away from other people so the attacks wouldn't cause me to do something inappropriate. Like tell the truth. Whatever.

I thought again about Patty. Contrary to Peralta's baiting, I wasn't afraid of seeing her. It would be nice, actually, to know she was happy.

As for my native prudence, that had gone away in the preceding months. Now I had barged into a stranger's apartment and assaulted a man with a move that could kill, and I wasn't even a cop anymore. Get me a can of spray paint.

I wondered if she remarried and had children.

Now it was hard to imagine that lost love as even real, especially after Lindsey.

I remembered the Fussell book Patty and I had both been reaching for. Writing about World War I, he meditated about how our age couldn't understand why hundreds of thousands of British soldiers had gone "over the top" to certain death from German machine gunners for something as abstract as *honor*.

But for them, that sense of honor and obligation was as real as our age, drowning in illegitimacy and irony, is for us.

What a pity. *Quel dommage.*

I had brought Lindsey to O.B. exactly once, when we had first become a couple and I worried that I was falling for her too fast, this magical younger woman with the fair skin and nearly black hair. She had browsed the postcards and made fun of the tourists. The memories caused me to pull out my iPhone and text her:

"I'm in San Diego with Peralta, on a case."

It was a fool's errand. She wouldn't respond. I didn't say I loved her, even though I did. Why set myself up for the disappointment of her silence? She wasn't wearing her wedding ring now. I still wore mine, even though I operated heavy equipment: large-caliber firearms. I studied my ring and my hands that had changed the baby. I didn't even know the baby's name, but I remembered his tiny hands and arms struggling against me, struggling against a world of trouble.

This little soul who hadn't asked to be brought into that world. I didn't even know his name.

That tattooed kid who was his father had better be on his way to Riverside.

Lindsey had worried whether she would make a good mother.

Now this child's mother was dead. After meeting America's Finest Pimp and learning about Grace's venture as Scarlett, I wondered if the man in our office yesterday had been right to question the circumstances of her death. He hadn't said a word about Grace being a call girl. Had he not known? Hell, I didn't even know who he really was.

The pimp had mentioned a big man, an enforcer, someone he was afraid of enough to clear out and leave us alone. Was that the big man from yesterday, assassinated on Grand Avenue? And who was Edward, someone else the pimp feared?

Too damned many questions and barely twenty-four hours into our first case. I felt only my lack of ability. This was not what I had done as the Sheriff's Office Historian. It was no cold case but was uncomfortably warm. Maybe I should have chucked

Robin's fancy that I be Peralta's partner and found some community college where I could teach.

The idea of coming to San Diego wasn't unpleasant because of Patty. It was bitter because San Diego represented my spectacular failures.

Looking up the hill at O.B., I remembered that I had broken my vow. I had left my little paradise.

The phone buzzed in my hand. The screen read: "Peralta."

I gave him an abbreviated report over the comforting noise of the surf. The beach wasn't crowded and the onshore flow was still keeping things soothingly cool.

"I went to Balboa Park," he said. "Really beautiful."

I agreed. It was a very un-Peralta like thing to do.

"It was where they held the 1915 Panama-California Exposition," he went on.

Yes, I knew that, but quietly noticed his uncharacteristic interest in something that didn't involve law enforcement.

"We're checked in to the Marriott on K Street. Know it?"

It was in the Gaslamp Quarter which had been built long after I had left, but I knew how to get there.

"Your key is at the front desk."

My own room. I wouldn't have to listen to him snore. He hung up before I could ask how his end of the investigation had gone.

"Mister?"

The small voice behind me went with a small, slender girl with long brown hair that looked as if it hadn't been washed in a week.

"Do you want a date?"

I told her I didn't.

"I'll suck your cock for twenty bucks."

She was jonesing from whatever she was addicted to, visibly shaking, looking like a drowned kitten. I asked her how old she was.

"Eighteen," she said. "I'll suck your cock for twenty bucks. I need to get something to eat. I know a place we can go."

She looked sixteen at the most, probably younger. I asked her if I could call a shelter for her, told her she didn't have to live on the streets. She asked if I was a cop.

"Not anymore."

"I'll suck you for fifteen."

I left her there and walked off the pier and up Newport Avenue to catch the bus back downtown. My heart decided to stay inside me, at least for a while.

The phone buzzed again. Lindsey had actually answered me. Her text read, "Be careful, Dave."

Chapter Twelve

San Diego had changed extensively since I had lived there, and, unlike Phoenix, mostly for the good. It was a major high-tech center now, not merely a tourist-and-Navy town. It had less population than Phoenix but surpassed it in almost any measure of quality. About the only thing that seemed the same was the mediocrity of the newspaper, formerly the *San Diego Union-Tribune*, now under new ownership with its name contracted to U-T. It sounded like a far campus of the University of Texas, but I'm sure a consultant charged big bucks for a new "brand."

Downtown, thrown away in the 1960s and 1970s, had made a stunning comeback, including the Gaslamp Quarter with its lovingly restored historic buildings and Horton Plaza urban mall. Nobody would know it used to be skid row. Walking to the Marriott, I was struck for the gazillionth time how Anglo the city seemed, even though it sat right on the Mexican border. The barrios south and east of downtown had been carefully tucked away and so it remained.

I showed my driver's license at the front desk and got my key card to a room on the eighth floor. Before going up, I went into the business center and booted up the computer. I am a lifelong Mac user and couldn't understand why anyone would use Windows. So I waited, and waited.

Then I plugged in the flash drive and clicked on the icon.

A window popped up and the screen went blank. Then Grace Hunter was talking to me.

"Hi, babe. I bet you'd like to know what's on this drive. But if you don't have the code, too bad."

A white box appeared and I had nothing to enter. The screen went dark again. But for a few seconds she had been alive. I could see her allure with her wide smile, the elegant movement to push her hair out of her face, the sexy taunt in her voice. I popped out the drive and stuck it in my pocket.

When I stepped out of the elevator, a woman was walking toward me: black, shoulder-length hair, attractive if older, elegantly dressed. As she came closer, I was sure I was wrong. I saw plenty of ghosts in my dreams.

But, no...

"Sharon?"

"David!"

She ran to me and gave me a long hug.

Her face was flushed and, up close, her usually perfect hair was mussed.

All I could do was sputter words. "What? Why?"

She grinned at my discomfort.

"What's wrong?"

Where to begin? She was Peralta's ex-wife. She had moved away to San Francisco in as final a breakup as I could imagine. I had known both of them for most of my adult life. And here she was, having obviously been in his room. But it was none of those things. I felt the embarrassment of nearly coming across my parents having sex.

"It's all right, David." She laughed that full-out laugh that always put me at ease. She studied me. "You've lost weight."

Her eyes held concern rather than a compliment. I knew the suit was now almost hanging on me.

I said, "So you're why he went to Balboa Park. I thought something was odd."

"Maybe he can grow a little after all," she said. "I was down here for a conference, so..."

So, indeed.

She hugged me again, made me promise we would get together for drinks or coffee before we left, and disappeared into the elevator.

After a minute to collect myself, I knocked on his door. He greeted me in a bathrobe.

"Why are you blushing?" he demanded.

"I got too much sun at the beach."

"Why is your shirt and tie a mess?"

"A baby peed on me, okay? You change and I'll come back."

"I'm fine," he said and walked inside, leaving the door open. I reluctantly followed him.

He plopped down on the unmade bed. I sat on a sofa and filled him in on Tim Lewis, the baby, and Grace Hunter's small business. He closed his eyes and grunted after every few sentences, taking it in as he always did. He offered no more reaction when I showed him the flash drive. We would have to find someone to break the code.

The room was too warm for my suit.

I wrapped it up. "Tim Lewis has parents in Riverside. I told him to take the baby and go there today."

"Did you get their address?"

"Yes." I said it a bit too testily.

"What's wrong?" His Mister Innocent voice. Then, "Look next to you, on the desk. It's the entire case file on the girl's suicide."

I swiveled to see several thick folders bound with a large red rubber band.

"Man, you have the pull," I said. "How is Kimbrough doing?"

"He's happy." He slurped on a Diet Coke. "I'd like to say it was my pull, but remember that suicide in Coronado? The girlfriend of the millionaire from north Scottsdale who allegedly hanged herself?"

I remembered. It had happened at the Spreckles Mansion in the rich, idyllic town that sat on a spit across from San Diego. The rich guy had purchased the iconic house. As I recalled, he made his money from acne products and cosmetics. The girlfriend, young enough to be his daughter of course, had been alone when his young son had tripped and fallen over a balustrade in the mansion. The child had died.

The next day the girlfriend had been found hanging from a second-story balcony, naked, a cloth in her mouth, and her hands bound with rope. As with Grace, the authorities had pronounced it a suicide.

Peralta shook his head. "I can see your mind making connections, Mapstone. They're not there. It has nothing to do with our case. Bill Gross is a good friend of mine." That would be the San Diego County Sheriff. "His department was called in because Coronado PD doesn't have the expertise for a complex death investigation. The media put Bill through hell on this one. News choppers overhead got pictures of the body and pretty soon it was on the Internet. Everybody became an amateur sleuth. They even got Dr. Phil involved."

He shook his head. "But the woman in Coronado really did kill herself based on the evidence. Hell, the sheriff's department even put up a special page with the information on their Web site. Kimbrough said his chief didn't want Grace Hunter to turn into another media circus. So we lucked out and have copies of everything."

"So what about our young woman?" I asked. "Suicide?"

"You'll have time for light reading." He pointed at the stack of case files, in case I had forgotten. "The short answer is they believe it was a suicide."

"What do you believe?"

He shrugged the big shoulders. "I'll wait for your report. Kimbrough brought along the night detective who was the first to respond to the call."

"Night detective?"

A quarter of one side of his mouth attempted a smile. "I'm showing my age, Mapstone."

I looked at the rumpled sheets and doubted that.

He continued, "Departments used to have night detective bureaus to cover the late shift, so the investigation into a major crime could begin immediately. Now it's almost all in-house with each unit, so, for instance, homicide has its own people on call. That's the case here. I was using old-time cop talk. Did I ever tell you about the night detective I met when Miranda bought it?"

He was being so uncharacteristically loquacious, and actually talking about himself, that I stifled my impatience.

"It was 1976, and Miranda was out of prison. He actually went around signing Miranda warning cards. Somewhere I have one he signed for me. Anyway, I was a green deputy and was serving a warrant down in the Deuce. The old La Amapola bar. Means 'little poppy.' I must have gotten there the second after Miranda got in a fight and was stabbed. People were scattering. The first PPD unit was a night detective. This tall guy named Cal. They called him the Red Dude on account of his hair. He marched my ass out in a hurry. We became friends later. Never did find the suspect I was trying to arrest."

If I had my geography right, the bar where Ernesto Miranda died was located where the Phoenix Suns arena now stood. Mike Peralta, historian. It made me wish he would talk more about his past, but we had business and he moved right along. I tried to imagine a time when he had ever been a rookie and uncertain of himself.

Night detective. It had a nice ring.

"Anyway, I talked to the detective. You would have liked her. First name Isabel. Cute little chica. Make you forget about Patty."

"Will you stop that shit!" I pulled off my suit jacket and threw it on the floor. It would have to go to the cleaners anyway.

His eyes followed the garment's flight, then fixed his gaze on me again. "Grace's body was found on the concrete by the pool. It was a straight fall and she landed on her head. Massive trauma, loads of blood. She was handcuffed from the back, nude, and no real note was left, like our guy said in the office yesterday."

"What do you mean 'real note.' "

"I want you to read the reports. Hang with me and I'll give you the overall run-down. So the uniforms that initially respond go upstairs and the door to the condo was locked. The manager lets them inside."

He folded one brawny brown calf over the other and told me the cops found no sign of a break-in. The lock was a deadbolt, so nobody could simply close the door behind them and cause it to automatically lock. It had to be secured from the inside, as if Grace had done it, or from the outside with a key. The only ones with keys were Zisman and his wife. She wasn't in San Diego on the twenty-second. There were no signs of struggle. Grace's purse was there with a hundred dollars in it, her keys, and a brand-new cell phone.

I said, "The handcuffs didn't arouse suspicion?"

"Sure. But sometimes people who want to kill themselves bind their hands so they can't change their minds. I've seen those calls in Phoenix. That was the case with that girl in Coronado, although she used rope and not cuffs. SDPD thinks the same was true here. Kimbrough had Isabel demonstrate how a person could do it. Then walk to a balcony and go over."

"Where'd Grace get the cuffs?"

"Apparently the former quarterback likes bondage. They used them during their playtime."

I tried to ignore his bulk in a bathrobe lying in a bed where he had had some "playtime" of his own. This was something I did not want to visualize or even contemplate.

"Does he own this condo?" I asked.

"He did. It's for sale now. He was away at his boat when Grace killed herself and the alibi's good. The owner at the slip next door saw him there during the time of the suicide. Zisman told the cops she was his girlfriend and she'd been feeling depressed, but he had no idea she might do something like this, yada-yada-yada."

"And they believed him?"

"Zisman is a reserve police officer in Phoenix," Peralta continued. "He showed his badge and identification. That might have bought him a little professional courtesy the night Grace died. He cooperated fully. I'm sure he was scared shitless this would make the papers or television and the missus back in Arizona would find out."

I told him newspapers usually didn't report suicides out of concern that there might be copycats. Grace had died at night, with no television news choppers in the air.

"So Zisman walked?"

He nodded. "There was no evidence of his involvement. No probable cause to hold him, much less get an indictment. If they arrested every Arizonan who had a mistress stashed in San Diego, they'd have to build a new jail."

Chapter Thirteen

It was nearly five but Peralta wanted to go out again. He had scheduled a meeting with a real-estate agent to see the condo.

I changed into casual clothes, a light-blue shirt and cargo shorts. The Python was too big to carry, which was why I had invested in a Smith & Wesson 340PD Airlite, an eleven-ounce, snubnosed .357 magnum that slipped easily into the right-side pocket of the shorts. I stashed the Glock that I had confiscated from America's Finest Pimp in a drawer. Who knew how many unsolved shootings or homicides it was connected to? I would deal with that later. Peralta was out of the robe, thank goodness, and in tan slacks, dress shirt, and blue blazer.

We walked ten blocks down Broadway toward the waterfront. The condo was hard to miss: more than forty stories, right across from the beautifully restored railroad station, with its blue Santa Fe railroad sign on the roof. In the lobby was a watchful concierge and, sitting on the edge of a chair with perfect posture, an auburn-haired, middle-aged woman who exuded perkiness. The Realtor. We made introductions and she took us up the elevator to the nineteenth floor.

We must have looked like the oddest gay couple she had ever dealt with.

"I have so many clients from Phoenix," she chirped. "This is the place to be."

The deadbolt turned with decisive effort and opened onto an empty living room. The condo hadn't been staged for the sale.

What most stood out was the handsome hardwood floor. And then the view, of course. Asking price: $599,000.

I let her walk Peralta through the rooms and wandered off by myself to the balcony. It was amusing to hear her calling him "Mike" in nearly every sentence. Nobody but Sharon called him Mike. But he was as convivial as could be, a skill he had learned over the years while wooing voters. Not that he had needed to put on a front. His record as sheriff was spotless, with crime down, jail conditions excellent, response times across the county top-notch, and his history professor solving high-profile old cases. All that didn't matter when his opponent ran against him claiming he was soft on illegal aliens. I pushed that out of my mind, opened the glass door, and stepped outside.

The view of downtown and the harbor was not as stunning as you could get for one or two million bucks on the upper floors, but it would do. If you had the money to escape the summer hell and dust storms of Phoenix, San Diego would be about as close to heaven as you could get.

The sun had burned off all the clouds and was now angled to throw the city into enchanting relief. The water was flawlessly blue and full of pleasure boats, which were dwarfed by the carrier at its mooring on North Island. The Navy kept the Nimitz-class carriers there because they wouldn't fit under the bridge that connected San Diego to Coronado, even though it soared 1,880 feet, a blue arch, across the channel that led to the Pacific Fleet's base.

I drove that bridge many times but was glad not to be going over it this trip. I was glad not to make connections between Grace Hunter and the suicide at the Spreckles Mansion. As I got older, I didn't like heights, didn't like bridges. I didn't like being on this balcony with the restless wind, distorted and accelerated by the other skyscrapers, flapping against my shirt. San Diego didn't really get earthquakes. A small fault line ran through Rose Canyon east of La Jolla, but otherwise it was pretty safe. That made me happy, nineteen stories over downtown.

At the edge, I looked down on the pool. A party was going on and the people looked very small. As I recalled, a body fell at thirty-two-feet-per-second, accelerating as it went down. It was a long damned time to contemplate death, to wonder if you'd made a big mistake.

What desolation must this young woman have felt to want to kill herself, sure that the terror of the fall and the pain of impact would be brief, and then nothing, comforting oblivion. If that was what really awaited us. Who really knew? I reached under my shirt and ran my finger along my totem, Robin's cross.

"Hey, babe…" The video of Grace on the flash drive was vivid in my mind. The confident, teasing voice and smile. It fit perfectly with Tim's description of a young woman who started her own business, however illicit, and was the consort of men who would pay thousands for her company. Would that same woman commit suicide?

I stared down at the concrete for a good five minutes.

The railing was at my belly button, but I was about ten inches taller than Grace Hunter. If I were suicidal and athletic, I was tall enough to hike one foot to the top of the railing and launch myself off. No fuss, no time for second thoughts. Grace couldn't do that. Based on the description of a five-foot-four woman, her legs weren't long enough. Handcuffed, she would have had to do a bit of a gymnastics move to go head first. Or maybe she hopped up on the railing backwards and pushed out into the sea-kissed air.

I was gripping the railing so hard my hands started to hurt. Making myself stop, I ran them along the smooth metal. The balcony was secluded, so nobody from an adjoining unit could see what was happening there. Other condos, offices, and hotels were too distant to give a detailed view, so witnesses were unlikely, especially after dark. I'm sure the cops had checked that out.

Such a lovely place to stand. How could you look out on this city and see anything but pleasure and hope? I knew better. *"Et in Arcadia ego…"*

The Latin phrase came into my mind. "Even in Arcadia, I, death, hold sway."

If she didn't kill herself, who did? Not America's Finest Pimp: he was searching for her, didn't know she was dead. Zisman? It still couldn't be ruled out. Alibis can fall apart with a little push. I wondered about this Edward that AFP had mentioned with dread. I wondered more why Grace, safe with Tim in Ocean Beach, with a new baby and seemingly much to live for, had gone to see Zisman.

"David, I see you like the view!" the agent chirped behind me. Her voice gave me a start. "Oh, I'm sorry!"

"David is a little jumpy," Peralta said behind her. Two beats later, he asked, "Was this the condo where that girl fell from?"

She quickly herded us back into the living room. "Yes, it was a terrible thing. A suicide. Young people have such a hard time…"

After a few minutes more, she loaded us with marketing materials and we left, walking in silence. Peralta wanted to eat at the Grant Grill in the restored U.S. Grant Hotel, so we waited in the bar, me with a martini, him with a Budweiser, surrounded by tourists. Only three people came up to say hello to him and say how much they wished he were still sheriff. They meant well. It made me angry.

After two more martinis and a fabulous supper, I felt better. Peralta and I went back over what we knew as we ate. He wanted to visit Grace's parents. I wanted to check out the list of regular clients. It had only taken me a day to go from not wanting to take this case to full buy-in. I had even landed another client. Was this Peralta's usual ability to rope me in, or had I done it myself? Better to follow this case than to sit at home alone with only my thoughts, memories, and regrets. My mind was a bad neighborhood. I didn't want to wander around there alone.

"If we visit her parents, maybe they'll agree to become our clients," he said, polishing off the king salmon. I wondered if he was joking. It sounded a bit like a used-car salesman on the make.

I told him about Tim Lewis hiring us and said we didn't have to worry about having a real, live client. His expression was unreadable, but I didn't think he was happy about my effort at business development. He was not worried about spending our dead client Felix's money at this posh restaurant, however.

I used the silence to fold and refold my napkin. I reached in my pocket and slid out my iPhone, slid it back. Then: "So you don't think it's a suicide?"

"I want you to read the reports and give me your opinion, Mapstone. But, based on what you've told me, what she was into, and the cops didn't know about it…" His voice trailed off, his meaning obvious. He ate and chewed, thinking.

He said, "I don't know why SDPD wouldn't have had Grace in its computer when her boyfriend filed the missing person's report. Maybe a lag. Maybe a system glitch."

"Maybe somebody paid off."

He poked his fork at me. "Why do you keep checking your phone? If you want to call Lindsey, call her."

"Like you called Sharon?"

He smiled slyly. A rare, actual smile.

But my phone-checking wasn't about Lindsey, to the extent that anything I did wasn't about Lindsey.

"It's past nine now," I said. "Grace's boyfriend ought to be in Riverside. He ought to have been there hours ago, even with the worst traffic jam in California. I told him to call me, and I've heard nothing."

He stared past me in thought.

"Maybe a careless kid. He's there and safe."

"At first he was afraid I was going to kill him," I said. "I don't think he would space this."

I told him I wanted to go back to O.B. and check.

"Want me to go with you?"

I told him no. "*Sauve qui peut.*" Every man for himself.

"Why are you speaking French, Mapstone?"

I smiled. "Memories." To be a show-off, I added: "*Pourquoi pas?*" Why not?

"*Bonne chance*," said the simple boy from the barrio.

With that, I walked out front where I gave the U.S. Grant Hotel doorman five bucks to hail me a cab.

Chapter Fourteen

The cab let me out in front of the apartment building at a quarter of ten. All the street parking was taken, probably all the way down to the business district, if not beyond. Your own parking space was a precious thing in O.B. I stood there as a black Dodge Ram truck slid by on Santa Cruz. The truck had a tag frame that read, "I (heart) Rancho Bernardo."

I shook my head. "Good luck finding a parking spot this time of night, suburban boy."

Then I was alone. When I lived here, O.B. had been dimly lit by yellow streetlights, a program the city had begun to cut the light pollution and protect the Palomar Observatory. Now the streetlights looked new and were definitely brighter, reflecting off the gray ceiling of the returning clouds. It was probably bad for the astronomers but good for me. I could see that the sidewalks were deserted, a good thing because I felt itchy with anxiety.

With all the windows open, I could hear televisions, a couple making love, and the subtle resonance of the surf a block and a half west. It brought back memories of the rare nights when there was fog and I would hear the foghorn coming from down by the pier. Tonight, it was so still I could hear my steps on the concrete.

It was ten degrees cooler than downtown. For a few minutes, I let the temperature help me feel normal again instead of breathless from the Phoenix heat. Then I walked to the gate and stared up at the apartment. The windows were closed, curtains open, and lights off. The tension that had been swelling for hours in my middle relaxed. The kid was gone and had forgotten to call me. He was mourning. He had a baby to take care of.

I thought about walking down to Newport and taking the bus downtown, but it was better to be sure. The vocal passion coming from the southeast apartment had subsided, so the gate loudly protested against me pulling 1950s metal hinges against each other. It put me on guard, but no curtains parted to see who was coming in. The pool was deserted and the water sat perfectly still and inviting.

When I looked up this time, I could see Tim's door was partly ajar.

The dread wouldn't let me go. Sure, there was a chance he was sitting inside, enjoying the breeze through the cracked door, playing a video game on headphones while the baby slept.

But only a fool would believe that.

I took the stairs two at a time, careful to keep my footfall quiet.

By the time I reached my old unit, I had the lightweight Smith & Wesson in my right hand. The windows to Tim's apartment were on the far side of the door so I couldn't see what was inside the apartment. I tapped lightly on the hollow door and called Tim's name. The door was open three inches. Beyond was darkness. Now it didn't seem like such a good idea to have come alone. Second-nature almost got the better of me: I almost called, "Deputy sheriff!" but I pushed the door all the way open and stepped silently into the room.

I moved to the side, to avoid providing a backlit target.

The outside light streamed in through the windows. Tim was sitting upright in the dining chair I had used earlier that day. It was directly facing the door. His face was tombstone white and the blood from his slit throat had flooded his T-shirt. There was no point in checking for a pulse. His dead eyes stared at nothing and his hands were in his lap, bound with handcuffs that glinted from the ambient light. Something like a big, curved bar of soap was in his lap. It had probably come from the kitchen.

Tim was gagged with a dish towel wrapped with duct tape. My eyes were drawn to his hands. Every one of his fingers had been broken. They had tortured him before they slit his throat.

The killer had also tossed the place. Clothing, food, video games, books, cushions and the flotsam of daily life were strewn around. Every drawer had been pulled all the way out and turned over, in case something had been taped beneath it. The pillows had been slit open and their stuffing pulled out.

Why didn't you leave when I told you? I forced back that thought. Right now, I had to secure the scene and observe, even if I wasn't the law anymore.

There was enough blood to do finger painting on the south wall of the living room. The red characters were uneven and drippy, but the words were familiar.

PERALTA AND MAPSTONE, P.C.
PRIVATE INVESTIGATORS

The moron had left his fingerprints in Tim's blood.

A closer look would have to wait.

I hurried into the bedroom and swept it with the barrel of the revolver, fearing what I would find. No bad guys. And no baby in the crib. I quickly checked the bathroom and the closet. No baby. I felt my own pulse slamming against my temples. The bedroom had also been thoroughly gone through. Whoever had done it, and taken the baby, hadn't bothered with the baby supplies.

I pulled out my phone to call Peralta and then the police.

Then something clicked in my brain. I dropped the phone back in my pocket, barely feeling my hand.

The object in Tim's lap was not a bar of soap. And it had lettering that suddenly opened a file in my vast memory of trivia.

The lettering carved into the object said,

FRONT
TOWARD ENEMY.

"Oh, God."

I heard a voice say those words. It was my voice, but my mind was desperately processing my options. I don't know if I made a conscious decision because my next memory is reaching the walkway outside the door and letting adrenaline heft my right foot to the top of the railing, balancing myself with my left hand. Then I was midair headed down for the pool.

Hoping that I remembered which side was the deep end.

The smooth surface came up suddenly and next I was underwater, surprised by the liquid cold, my terror-filled muscles acting in concert with only one goal: dive deep. I touched the bottom and started counting but only got to three before feeling a sharp concussion overhead. It popped my ears and pushed me violently against the far wall of the pool. I swear my brain felt about to burst. Something large and heavy missed my head by no more than six inches. It was half of a cinderblock.

When I came up, gasping for air, Tim's apartment was gone and the smoke made it difficult to assess the damage to other units. The surface of the water was coated with glass fragments, burning drapes, a can of Pringles, papers, the debris of daily life—and little metal balls. Those had been ejected from the Claymore anti-personnel mine that had detonated. Robin's cross floated on the surface, glinting under the light, still attached to the chain around my neck. The revolver was still in my hand.

Something soft bobbed against my arm.

It was Tim's head, face up, hair like seaweed, staring at the overcast.

Chapter Fifteen

We started back to Phoenix at dusk the next day, driving through the desert at night the way people used to do, before advanced automobile cooling systems. Back in the days when only a fool would cross the wilderness without an adequate supply of water.

Before we left, Peralta found a deserted space where he could park and get into the steel storage compartment that sat in the extended cab behind our seats.

It was a gun case.

"Time for heavy metal," he said, and I didn't think he was about to break out some Black Sabbath CDs.

Ten minutes later we were speeding east on I-8. I had received a tutorial on a Kel-Tec RFB assault rifle, "a bull pup," he called it. Barely more than two feet long, it was black and homely. But with the fire-selector capable of semiautomatic and a twenty-round box magazine, it didn't need to win a beauty contest. I slid it beside me, barrel down, safety on. Peralta slid an assault rifle into the well between his seat and the door. It looked a little like an M-16, but it was matte black with a retracting stock and a rough-edged thing on the barrel that might have been a flash-suppressor or a hand-guard—or not. He didn't bother to explain besides telling me it was a Colt AR15 Magpul Special.

"A good truck gun," he said.

My world was still a little blurry from the blast. My stupid question: "Why?"

"I want to have an edge," he said. "Are you steady enough for this?"

"Yes."

The question irritated me, but I had no time for that. I had no time for sentimental thoughts about departing from my second hometown as we climbed out of Mission Valley into El Cajon and began the long uphill grind—away from Ocean Beach, away from my other life in this beautiful city and its balm of cooler weather. I opened the glove box, pulled out the gun-cleaning kit, unloaded my Airlite, and began cleaning and oiling it to avoid any trouble from its contact with the pool. My hands shook.

"Sorry you didn't have any time for fun here," Peralta said, trying his best to sound sympathetic. "I should have at least set up drinks for you and Isabel, the night detective. To talk over what she found. Anyway, she was cute."

"You're trying to set me up? You're the one who keeps saying Lindsey will come back."

"You need to get laid, Mapstone. It'd do you a world of good."

"Like it did you." I heard my voice, joyless and raw.

Grace, Isabel the detective, Grace's friend *Addison*. Oh, I felt old and in a foreign country. The young women's names sounded either like they belonged to old ladies or unfeminine and strange. I shouldn't have been so judgmental.

But I was particular in my female names. I liked boomer names like Susan, Amy, and Karen. Pamela: three syllables of sexy. Lisa and Linda were nice. And Patty. I had preferences for Generation X names, too. Heather and Melissa. And Lindsey. And Robin. *Addison*? No. Leave it to me to start categorizing and analyzing even small things. Maybe it was a good sign. Or maybe I was leaking blood inside my brain from effects of the explosion.

I wanted to take a nap. But then the dreams would come.

This was the first time we had spent alone together since the blast and I briefed Peralta as much as I could. My head hurt despite nearly overdosing on Advil, everything felt slowed down, and concentration was difficult. My shoes, the only casual pair

I brought, were still soggy. The one constant thought I could hold was the missing baby.

I did my best to brief him.

He immediately interrupted. "You're one lucky bastard. The kill zone of a Claymore can be fifty meters. It's a shaped charge, meant to explode in the direction that it's pointed. You might have been better off running to the bedroom and getting under the bed. That way you wouldn't have been directly in front of it."

"Trust me, there wasn't anything left of the bedroom, and there was no bed frame." I started to zone out a little. "Hell, I don't know. I reacted with instinct. How did they detonate it?"

"Could have been anything nowadays: timer, laser, plus the good old fashioned wires." One big hand was enough to handle the steering wheel. "We used to set up Claymores to ambush NVA columns. They'd come down a jungle trail and we'd let the gooks get well inside the kill zone. Then we'd set off one at the front of the column and they'd naturally run backwards. That's when we'd set off the Claymores from the back, going forward." He laughed malignly.

"Sounds like fun."

"You don't know. You weren't there." He said this without irony.

"Thank you for your service to the country, sir. Now, may I fucking continue?"

"Sure," he said. "But how did you realize it was a Claymore?"

"I read about it in a book."

When my eyes were closed, I started to get dizzy. When I opened them, the car lights from the freeway hurt. Looking off to the shoulder, I was overcome by the fear someone would suddenly step in front of us. So I stared into my lap.

After the explosion, I pulled myself from the pool. My cell phone was ruined, of course. But my gun was fine. It wasn't needed. No bad guys were there to finish the job. Instead, people were shouting and screaming. I went from apartment to apartment, getting people out, sending them to the street until the fire department could arrive. That seemed to take forever. One man living in my old unit looked badly injured. I found him last, under the remains of a heavy desk that probably saved him, and I stayed with him until the first cop came in the door with a flashlight and a gun.

It was a miracle that the damage wasn't worse. One person in critical condition, two more suffered less-serious injuries. It helped that the people directly below Tim's apartment were gone; the same with the residents of the unit directly to the south. No fire followed the explosion and the emergency crews quickly shut off the gas.

I remembered choppers overhead and a bright beam from the sky.

Then, after a cursory checkup by the paramedics, it was all cops, all the time. I never got a chance to have coffee with Sharon. Nor did I have time to order a new cell phone. Instead, I spent the hours telling my story to seven different San Diego cops, including Kimbrough, who was not at all happy to see me. Then ATF showed up and took me downtown to talk more. What sleep I got came from leaning my head against a wall while waiting for the next round of questions.

I was fortunate for a law passed after 9/11, giving retired police officers in good standing the power to carry a concealed firearm in any state. Otherwise, things could have gotten very disagreeable. Somehow Peralta had pulled some levers before he left office and I was able to "retire" with a combined fifteen years service to the Sheriff's Office. The pension was shit, so don't judge me as a greedy public employee. But the conceal-carry benefit probably kept me out of jail.

The cops and feds didn't think I did it—"it" being called a "possible act of domestic terrorism" on the television crawler I saw while waiting in one of the fed's offices. But they didn't like that I was in San Diego as a private investigator and that my client was dead. I wondered if they'd force us to stay in town for further questions. Instead, it was a wonder that we weren't escorted to the city limits. I thought momentarily of my unread George Kennan biography and how he had been declared persona non grata by Stalin, his ambassadorship to Moscow cut short. I was persona non grata in San Diego at the moment and for better reason.

An Amber Alert was issued for the missing baby. Detectives had called Tim's parents in Riverside and assembled more information: a photograph of the now-orphaned infant and his name.

His name was David.

"I should have gone with you," Peralta said.

"You couldn't have moved as fast as I did."

"I wouldn't have mistaken a Claymore for a big bar of soap."

He had me there. I went on and tried to tell him everything, step by step.

"Did you tell them about the pimp?"

I said yes.

"Did they believe you?"

"They did when I gave them the Glock I took off him."

I had no doubt that America's Finest Pimp was now sitting in one of America's Finest Interrogation Rooms, but I didn't make him for the killer. He had been too unnerved by my arrival and my assumed connection to the unnerving Edward to return to the apartment. Anyway, the pimp didn't strike me as the throat-slashing kind and certainly not as a bomb maker. But I didn't even know his name. The cops told me nothing. There was no professional courtesy to give to a private investigator.

When the de-brief had exhausted me, I asked Peralta a question. Did it pass the smell test? The rich guy leaving a thousand dollars on the nightstand for Grace, and then her setting up a business based on that kind of sum? Not a twenty-five-dollar blowjob from a hooker on Van Buren, but hundreds, even thousands of dollars.

"Sex is big business," he said. "Don't forget Eliot Spitzer. Didn't he pay four or five grand every time? I've seen plenty of investigations into high-end prostitution. We took down a county supervisor while you were away teaching, for putting hookers on his county credit card. The single-girl-on-her-own part of it is unusual, but she eventually got caught by a pimp. That sounds real."

I put away the gun-cleaning kit, reloaded my revolver, and slid it back into my pocket.

"If you'd gotten gun oil on the carpet, I would have killed you," he said.

I ignored him. "Why would a man pay for sex, especially when there's so much free stuff around? Especially why would a rich man do it?"

"Tiger Woods spent something like four million bucks a year on prostitutes."

"Your mind is an amazing thing," I said, repeating a phrase he usually applied to me. Having my brain rocked like a Jell-O salad had addled my mind at the moment.

His big shoulders shrugged. "What can I say? I'm a golfer."

"Do you spend four million…? Never mind." I really did not want to know.

Even in my driest spell, in my twenties when young women weren't drawn to a guy who read books and talked about history, I didn't contemplate going to a prostitute.

"Sharon could tell you the psychology," he said. "With a young woman and older man, it's called the Lolita Complex, I think. Some men are drawn specifically to prostitutes. Rich men want the privacy that the right prostitute can provide. Most of these guys are married, remember, and they don't want their wives to divorce them and take half of their wealth in a community property state. Politicians are willing to take the risk. A prostitute never says no, never has a headache, and she'll do kinky stuff the missus might not do."

"And it's a huge human trafficking problem."

"That, too."

Back in El Centro and the heat, we went through the Wendy's drive-thru and pulled to an empty part of the parking lot to eat.

"So," Peralta said, "what didn't you tell the police?"

He had parked the truck so we could see anybody coming into the lot and escape through two different driveways. His caution was good.

"Fuck!"

My concussed brain coughed up something essential.

"I forgot the flash drive. I forgot to give them the flash drive."

Peralta was silent.

"I've got to get it to them."

"Anything else?"

Yes, there was. I unpacked another chamber of my addled brain and told him about the writing on the wall: our names written in blood. Of course this critical piece of evidence didn't survive the blast.

He paused mid-bite. "How would the suspect know about us?"

"I gave Tim our card."

Peralta was silent and it was a long time, for him at least, before he resumed eating. About fifty seconds.

Many things about this case were unknown, but one was becoming clearer. The killers weren't only after our clients. They might be after us. I stroked the ugly little rifle beside me, glad that Peralta was into this kind of heavy metal.

"What should I do about the flash drive?"

"Keep it," he said. "Let's see who's on it."

We finished our meal and stopped at a truck stop, where I bought a cheap cell phone to get me by until I could order an iPhone. Then we returned to the Interstate, one of America's great accomplishments of the past century. Today the nation refused to do great things but that didn't keep people from crowing about our "exceptionalism." I had bigger problems than the fate of nations, but I let Peralta mind the rearview mirror.

Who knew how many killers roamed the anonymous Interstates of America tonight? How many truck-stop prostitutes would disappear tonight, meeting terrifying deaths, mourned by none? Except for the infrequent tractor-trailer rig, I-8 was mostly empty and carbon dark, as though the moonless night was trying to steal the beams our headlights threw ahead. Above was a vault of stars that most urban humans rarely saw in person. In my grandparents' generation, it had merely been the night sky. Against it, my problems seemed very small. We were only here for nanoseconds of cosmic time. Inside the cab of Peralta's super-truck, there was no song of the wind or moan of the engine, no sense that our onrushing feet rested only a few inches above the pitiless land.

Chapter Sixteen

Back in Phoenix, our office was in what passed for perfect shape. Every tube on the neon sign out front was operating flawlessly. The house on Cypress appeared safe, too. Even the air was better, the smoke from the forest fires clearing out while we were gone. Nobody had left a message on the answering machine. A neighbor had neatly stacked the newspapers beside the front step. Only the *New York Times* was on my daily routine now.

I couldn't stand to read the *Arizona Republic* any more, the stories about the antics of the new sheriff and the other buffoons that had taken over state politics. I didn't like the way the writers referred to the place as "the Valley," using the touristy Valley of the Sun, not even the geographic Salt River Valley. Here we had one of the most magical city names in the world: Phoenix. And yet the suburbanites insisted on "the Valley." Silicon Valley? The Red River Valley? Shenandoah Valley? And these were the same people who moved from suburban Chicago but said they were "from Chicago." It drove me nuts. The local papers went straight to recycling.

Then I unpacked the flash drive and plugged it into my Mac laptop to see Grace tease me again. The ghost in the machine.

Lindsey could get into the drive but Lindsey was gone.

In the living room, I laid it behind a volume of Will and Ariel Durant's *The Story of Civilization* on the top bookshelf by the staircase. It wouldn't survive an extensive search of the house, but this dusty spot would do for now.

In a few months, I had gone from a deputy sheriff with a clean record to a civilian, a "private dick," as Robin teased me with her delightful lascivious smile, concealing evidence. The top of the book held a sheen of dust. I didn't blow it off. This had been part of my grandparents' library passed on to me. When I was gone, it would be broken up in an estate sale or tossed in the dump.

After lying awake a long time, I slept badly with two guns to keep me company. Many dreams interrupted my sleep but the details were gone after I opened my eyes. If Tim and Grace had shown up as new dramatis personae, I couldn't recall. Robin was there. I couldn't remember what she said. I got up in the night to check the Amber alert and the San Diego media Web sites several times. Nothing was new.

By half past seven Sunday morning, a hitherto ungodly hour for me, I opened the automatic gate and pulled into the office, then shut it behind me. The high temperature was only supposed to be in the nineties today, the old normal for May when the dry heat was bearable and even pleasant in the shade. At this hour, the air was cool. No bad guys were waiting inside, merely a stale odor and the same old furniture. I dropped my briefcase on the floor and my Panama hat on my desk, crown down, and flopped onto the sofa to drink my mocha and eat a bagel. Remembering Sharon's reaction to my gaunt appearance, I tried to make a commitment to eating more regularly.

Peralta arrived fifteen minutes later wearing a Stetson and jeans. He peered at me over his sunglasses, surprised that I had beaten him into work.

"How ya feeling?" He tossed the cowboy hat on his desk, letting it fall where it landed.

I told him San Diego had been a blast. He didn't smile, disappearing into the Danger Room to either bring out more weapons or admire his prizes or whatever he did in there. How was I? I hurt like hell and the tension inside me was thrumming like a tuning fork. Otherwise, I was great.

When he returned, he leaned against the doorjamb, all six-feet-five of him. Maybe half of a supermodel could have squeezed through the remaining space.

"I'd like to bring Sharon into our practice. Is that all right with you? What the hell are you smiling at?"

That last part was more like it. I wasn't accustomed to Peralta being solicitous of my opinion. In the old days, he barked orders and made demands, alternating between the "good" Peralta who was a natural leader and inspiring peace officer, and the "bad" Peralta, who could be manipulative, micromanaging, and Vesuvius when he didn't get what he wanted.

In my office on the fourth floor of the old courthouse, I had been somewhat insulated from the worst of his personality. Getting laid had obviously done him a world of good. And his term "our practice" sounded both professional and ironically on target. We were definitely practicing. I told him none of this. Why was I smiling?

"You," I said. "Of course, great if Sharon joins us. I love Sharon. Why would she want to work with us?"

"We need her expertise. She's been consulting for San Francisco PD, you know."

I didn't. I knew she had moved there to be closer to their grown daughters. She had stopped her popular radio show and quit writing the best-selling self-help books that had made her a wealthy woman.

"So you don't mind?"

"Of course not."

"We can put Lindsey on the payroll when she comes back, too."

That should have made me smile. We had no payroll besides the ten grand from Client No. 1 and Tim Lewis' five hundred. Outside of business cards, our practice was only getting started. But I didn't smile or answer directly. Lindsey wasn't coming back, except to get her things and move away permanently to be with her lover or lovers to come.

"Are you and Sharon getting back together?"

He evaded.

"Now I want you to think about this, Mapstone. Every police agency in Southern California is looking for that baby. It's a big deal and we're going to get in the way. The feds are investigating the explosion, who got his hands on a Claymore, and if we get in their way, we could compromise an undercover operation."

"We have other strands we can follow," I said. "Grace's friend and parents. Her list of johns. Tim's parents. Larry Zisman."

He nodded. "But we're going to make enemies if we get on the wrong side of law enforcement. We might get prosecuted. Are you sure you want to stay on this case?"

I was momentarily confused, recalling his insistence that we couldn't allow our clients to be killed. But it didn't last long. "I do."

"Why?"

I repeated his rationale back to him. Then, "I remember our names painted in blood on the apartment wall. Whoever set that Claymore was counting on me coming back. They watched me go into the apartment and get well inside it before they set it off. So we've made enemies whether we want them or not. Then there's the little matter of withholding evidence. You didn't tell the Phoenix cops about our client. I didn't tell the San Diego cops about Grace's business, or about the flash drive."

"You gave them the pimp."

"Sure, but only that he was a guy threatening Tim when I showed up. I told them that's all I knew. Seems to me, if we're not pro-active, the bad guys will come to us, and if we don't solve the case, the good guys could come to us, too, and not in a good way."

He sighed. "I guess my point is, that I can take this one, if you want to bow out."

Now he hurt my feelings. It was that petty and selfish on my part.

I said, "No way."

"Are you sure you want to do this?"

I told him that I was sure.

He strode over to his desk and picked up his hat.

"Then bring your breakfast and saddle up." He pointed to my desk. "You might want to leave your fancy headgear here."

Chapter Seventeen

Up Grand Avenue, we had a fast ride cutting northwest through the checkerboard street grid of Phoenix and Glendale.

"So where are we going?"

"To see a guy I know," Peralta said.

"A guy you know?"

He nodded. It was going to be that kind of day.

"I want to talk to Larry Zip," I said.

"Not yet. Read the report. Then I want us to strategize before we interview him."

With that, he fell into his customary silence. What he was feeling from the contradictory events of the past few days, I wouldn't hazard a guess. Peralta's emotions were a deep ocean trench where leviathans stirred.

I distracted myself with the ritual obligation of memory.

I remembered when produce sheds and the remains of icing platforms for refrigerator railcars lined the Santa Fe railroad that ran parallel to the highway. I remembered passenger trains. Farm fields separated Phoenix from what was then the little town of Glendale. In grade school, we rode the train to the Glendale station. I even recalled one or two dilapidated farmhouses sitting right across the tracks.

Now it had all been filled in. Although the railroad was still there, the area around it mostly consisted of tilt-up warehouses, along with anonymous low-slung buildings, most with for-lease signs, and a gigantic Home Depot. Passenger trains were long gone. So, too, was the agricultural bounty that the Salt River Valley growers sent back east by rail. The children and grandchildren of the farmers who owned this land were living in places like San Diego thanks to the profits made selling it for development.

The road soon clogged up and stayed that way for miles. Much of Grand Avenue in the city of Phoenix had been turned into flyovers, back when the planners, such as were allowed here, thought about turning it into a freeway to Las Vegas. Like so many Phoenix dreams, this one didn't work out.

As a result, when we reached the "boomburbs" of Peoria, Sun City, Sun City West, and Surprise—yes, that's the town's name—Grand hit a six-point intersection at least every mile and other stoplights in between. And nearly every light was red. Traffic was miserable. The built landscape was new, cheap, and monotonous—made to speed by in an automobile. Smog smudged the views of the mountains.

Most of these had once been little hamlets on the railroad, but now they were home to hundreds of thousands populating the subdivisions that had been smeared across the broad basin that spread out from the actual Salt River Valley toward the White Tank Mountains and was labeled, incorrectly, "the West Valley." They came from the suburban Midwest or inland California and most thought life couldn't be better.

The metropolitan blob was slowly working its way northwest to Wickenburg, a combination quaint former mining town and home to celebrity rehab centers. I loved Wickenburg. It was authentic and charming, everything suburban Phoenix wasn't. As a young deputy, when I was working my way through my bachelor's and master's degrees, I had worked a patrol beat out here. The state had about four-and-a-half million fewer people and the land was empty, majestic, and mysterious. Wickenburg and the other little desert towns huddled to themselves. A lone deputy had many square miles to cover, usually alone, and traffic stops were always risky. So were family fights, where a husband

and wife that had been trying to kill each other a few moments before were suddenly united in trying to kill you.

But we weren't going as far as Wickenburg today. Peralta turned left into the shabby little desert village of Wittman and drove west. After five miles or so and several turns, the last remnants of settlement were gone, the roads turned to dirt, and we were surrounded by desert. The smog hadn't reached this far north today, so the Vulture Mountains stood out starkly ahead. Go far enough and you'd find the fabled and long-ago played-out Vulture gold mine and who knows what else hiding in the desert. We bounced over the bed of the meandering Hassayampa River, dry this time of year. As a Boy Scout, I had learned the legend that if a person took a drink from the Hassayampa, he would never tell the truth again.

Immediately ahead, the country turned hilly and rugged, good terrain for saguaros. I was glad I brought two frozen bottles of water. But even in the air-conditioned truck cab, they were already half melted. It was only ninety-eight degrees outside. Inside my body, I was sore everywhere from my dive out of the apartment. Even my face hurt.

The bare impersonation of a trail appeared on the right and Peralta took it. Another mile and we reached a rusted metal gate. Peralta honked six times: three short, three long.

"Get down in the seat," he commanded.

"What?"

"You heard me."

I did as I was told as he shut off the engine, opened the door, and stepped out. He raised his hands high and his voice boomed. "Don't you shoot me, you paranoid son of a bitch. We need to talk."

This didn't seem promising.

The longest pause came to an end with a shout from the distance, "Go away!"

"I'm coming in if you don't come out!"

"Is that you, Peralta? Go back to your lettuce field, beaner! I'm done with the law. Got nothing to say."

Peralta shouted back: "Why aren't you on your reservation and cleaning toilets at a fucking casino, bow-twanger? Get your redskin butt down here!"

"If I do, it's only gonna be to kick your wet-back ass!"

"Good luck trying, wagon-burner!"

"Watch me do it, spic!"

"Bring it on, breed!"

It was, needless to say, not faculty-lounge language. And although Peralta was my least politically correct acquaintance, the outburst seemed out of character. Suddenly the yelling stopped. After too long a silence, I reached for the Colt Python and prepared for the worst. But when I rose up, the gate was open and Peralta and another man were shaking hands and embracing.

"Who's the white eyes?"

"David Mapstone, meet Ed Cartwright."

The shorter man beside Peralta was stocky in jeans and a Western shirt, with a long mane of lead-colored hair pulled back in a ponytail. His face looked like the Indian in the environmental ad way back, with a tear running down his face from the damage we had done to the land. He was tearless in appraising me. When we shook hands, I noticed the pistol on his belt. He handed me a business card with only his name and a phone number. I gave him one of my new private detective cards. The ones I once carried, with the gold badge, were only for my scrapbook.

I followed the two of them as they walked through the gate along a rutted, dusty trail to an adobe house that sat on a rise maybe a quarter of a mile away. Beside it, in a carport, was a restored Chevy El Dorado with a bumper sticker that read, AMERICAN INDIAN AND PROUD OF IT. The sun was frying my skin and I wished we could have driven the distance.

"Still waiting for the apocalypse, Ed?" Peralta asked.

"Yup."

"Show Mapstone your bunker."

That didn't sound like a good idea but pretty soon we were trekking off into the desert while Peralta stayed behind. The land was lush with sage, prickly pear, thick stands of cholla—jumping cactus—and ancient, towering saguaros with four and five arms. Those saguaros had watched the procession of humanity through this land for hundreds of years. Unlike their brothers in places such as Fountain Hills, they had avoided the bulldozers, at least for now. The silence was surreal and healing, except for the temperature and the fact that I was on high rattlesnake alert, walking heavily so the vibrations of my tread would give the poisonous snakes plenty of time to get out of our way. Cartwright was spry and walked fast. I worked to keep up and the muscles in my legs and back burned with pain.

Before we reached another hill, he led me around a lush palo verde tree. Beyond was a well-concealed cut that was obviously man-made. It led down until it was below ground level and zigzagged. It reminded me of the way trenches had been constructed on the Western Front in World War I. They zigzagged so an enemy soldier couldn't stand above the trench and take out an entire company with his rifle. We were on the verge of the hundred-year mark of that cataclysm that changed the world, but few Americans paid any attention to the past.

Cartwright broke my reverie. "Peralta and I were in 'Nam together. The sheriff's a good man in a shitty situation."

I agreed that he was.

We zagged to a stop. Cartwright hefted away a tumbleweed and unlocked a door that blended perfectly with the tan soil.

"This was an old mine," he said. "There's probably hundreds of them out here."

Now I was really worried about rattlers. But beyond the door, I could see only bright lights and a clean concrete floor.

Getting inside required another sharp turn beyond the entrance. Nobody could open the door and start shooting at the occupant of Cartwright's keep. We walked down a long flight of concrete stairs and made an abrupt turn into a short hall. He unlocked another door, metal and heavy, and closed it behind us.

We entered a space that looked about twenty feet long and wide enough for two men to stand comfortably. The ceiling was a foot above my head. On both sides, shelves rose six feet high holding meals-ready-to-eat, canned food, water, first-aid supplies, and ammunition. Boxes and boxes of ammunition for several calibers of firearms.

Beyond this supply area, the shelter opened up and held a bed, two chairs, and a desk with exotic radio equipment and other electronics. A well-stocked gun cabinet took up one wall. An American flag was posted to another. It was a forty-eight-star flag, the way it would have looked after Arizona was admitted to the union in 1912. Beside it were highly detailed U.S. Geological Survey maps of the area. The map fiend in me wanted to study them, but I felt mildly claustrophobic and unsure of my host.

"Ventilates to the outside," he said. "But I've got filters against fallout and biological attacks. I can air-condition it, if I need to. Got two generators and plenty of fuel farther back into the mine. Redundancy on everything. There's an emergency exit that comes out half a mile on the other side. I built it all myself."

He was plainly proud of it and I suppose there were worse retirement hobbies as long as he didn't wander down Tegner Street in Wickenburg and start mowing people down with one of the M-16s in that gun cabinet. The place was surprisingly free of dust and noticeably cooler than the outside, but I could feel myself only a few internal degrees from heat exhaustion.

I tried to be convivial, in an end-of-the world way, complementing his bunker. He seemed amiable enough, for an armed survivalist vet who might suddenly snap and kill me, stuffing my remains somewhere back in the old mine as varmint treats.

"Were you military, son?"

"No."

I could have let him judge me in silence, but I made an effort to keep the conversation going. Get people to talk about themselves, as Grandmother always advised.

"So this is where you ride out doomsday?"

"You bet your life. We came within an ass-hair of blowing up the world in 1983. The Soviets picked up a launch signal from the continental U.S. Their computer system said it was an incoming American missile. It was a glitch, but they didn't know this. They always expected an American first strike, and their strategy was launch on warning, so our missiles would hit empty silos."

He jabbed a finger my way. "If it hadn't been for a Russian colonel who suspected it was a false alarm and refused to send on the alert, they would have fired every ICBM they had over the pole at us and adios, baby. Hardly anybody knows how close we came."

"Stanislav Petrov," I said. That was the Soviet lieutenant colonel who perhaps saved us all.

"Very good. Don't think it won't happen again. All those missiles are still sitting there, waiting to be used. Damned Russians are building an underground city that's as big as Washington. You look on the Internet. Israel and Iran. North Korea. China's got miles of tunnels to hold their nuclear forces. Hell, we're even allies with Hanoi now against China. Makes you wonder why anybody even wants to live."

His agitation grew as he talked and he paced over to the gun cabinet and I placed a hand on the butt of my Python. My spinal cord was filling with ice.

"We got seven billion people on the planet, climate change, ebola and diseases we don't even know about that can't be killed by antibiotics. Your people did this." His expression was accusing, his voice angry. "Couldn't leave well enough alone. Had to conquer nature, but she won't be conquered, kid."

He sighed. "Anyway, it might not even go down that way. You take away the power and gasoline from five million people in Phoenix in high summer, and watch what happens. I'll be fine."

I had no doubt.

Chapter Eighteen

After fifteen minutes of this cheery conversation, we arrived back at the adobe, where Peralta was standing under the shade of the porch, smoking a cigar, and surveying the jagged treeless mountains on the horizon.

"You got another Cuban, Sheriff?"

Peralta produced a cigar and Cartwright ran it under his nose, inhaling like a connoisseur. "You people wouldn't even have tobacco if it wasn't for us."

"Apaches didn't have tobacco," Peralta said.

"Well, then we would have killed the Indians that did and taken it. Thanks for the cigar. Now I don't have to kill you." He carefully slipped the stogie into his front pocket. "I see the kid here is a revolver man." He pointed to the Colt Python in the Galco high-ride holster on my belt.

"He doesn't trust semi-autos, thinks they might jam." Peralta raised an eyebrow, an act of raucous comedy coming from that face.

"It can happen," Cartwright said. "May I?"

Every instinct told me to decline, yet I handed the heavy revolver over, butt-first. He opened the cylinder, dropped out the six rounds in his left palm, and dry-fired it against the wall: click, click, click.

"The Combat Magnum. Listen how clean that action is." His tone was that of a wine connoisseur. "It was the first gun to be bore-sighted with a laser, you know. Finest mechanism you'll ever find in a revolver. Tight cylinder. Highly accurate." He handed the gun and ammo back. My pulse pulled off the fast lane. I was fortunate that the house was air conditioned and dark inside, to cool me down and conceal my apprehension.

The living room was furnished with handsome leather chairs and sofas. Books were everywhere: in floor-to-ceiling shelves, on tabletops, and sitting in stacks on the hardwood floor. They were not of the *Anarchist's Cookbook* genre. Instead, literature, philosophy, poetry, political science, and, of course, history filled the room. Classics and new, important works. I'll admit it: I took stock of a person by the presence of books and their titles, and I almost started to let down my guard. I could see no television or newspapers. He might not even know that Peralta was no longer sheriff.

Cartwright returned from the kitchen with bottles of Modelo Especial and we sat.

"What brings you out to my humble outpost, Sheriff?"

"One guy shot and killed earlier in the week with an AK-47." Peralta took a swig and a puff. "Then my partner here almost bought it with a Claymore."

Cartwright made a tisk-tisk-tisk kind of sound. "Walk down memory lane, eh? Did you tell him about the way we used Claymores to ambush the slants back in the day?"

Peralta nodded. "Whoever did the shooting with the Kalashnikov was damned good. Pumped ten rounds into the victim sitting in a car. The shooter was in another car. Only one shot failed to hit the target. And this was daylight, right on Grand Avenue down in town."

"Sounds interesting."

Peralta waited.

Cartwright sighed. "I'm retired, Sheriff."

"Bullshit. You know things. You know more than me when it comes to assholes seeking illegal weapons."

"Is there such a thing as an illegal weapon in Arizona anymore?"

"If there is, you're selling it," Peralta said.

So he was an arms dealer.

"Not true," Cartwright said. "Drive back to Wittman or Circle City or Mesa for that matter and you'll find guys who can fix you up with anything you want."

Peralta sat back, wreathed in cigar smoke, his expression losing its amiability.

He said quietly, "They can't fix you up with a Claymore."

Cartwright spoke softly, too. "I'm not a rat. Never have been."

Peralta had handled the tribulations of the past several months better than me. Of course, some of them hadn't affected him quite so personally. Still, I was the one who seemed angrier about his loss of the election and the ugly, racist campaign that preceded it. He had turned philosophical and, if such a word could be applied to him, mellow.

But watching his face now, I could see the flickering of the old anger and impatience. Cartwright spotted the launch signal, too, and knew it wasn't a glitch. Still, he tried to escape.

"You know I'm not in the game anymore. Give an old man a break. I'm tired now. I need to rest."

"You were up to your ears in Fast and Furious," Peralta said, referring to the federal operation meant to disrupt the flow of guns to Mexico that had gone horribly wrong. It had cost the U.S. Attorney his job, brought hearings in Congress, and even become an issue in the presidential campaign.

"My part worked." Cartwright glared back at him.

The two dark stone faces faced off. Cartwright's was cut with gullies in geometric precision, while Peralta's aging congregated around the crow's feet beside his eyes. His hair was still naturally jet black. He was actually better looking than he'd been at thirty-five. He wore distinguished well.

Neither seemed willing to give. I tried to imagine them as young infantrymen, fighting for a country with a poor record of treatment for Apaches or Mexican-Americans and yet there they were, brothers in arms, in Southeast Asia. That bond showed in their expressions, too.

Finally, Cartwright stood and walked slowly at first, as if his hip hurt. Then he strode out of the room. In five minutes, I heard his tread and something landed in my lap. It wasn't as heavy as I imagined.

"Your boy's pretty cool," Cartwright said.

Peralta watched me. I can't tell you why I didn't make the jump of the startled or run screaming from the house once I saw he had dropped a Claymore on me. Instead, I carefully studied it: "FRONT TOWARD ENEMY" the same as the one in Tim and Grace's apartment, two sets of extendable legs, and a small housing on top where wires, or another kind of detonation mechanism, could go.

Cartwright eased himself into a chair across from me. "You're lucky to be alive, son."

He hefted an AK-47 in his hands. "Mikhail Kalashnikov's baby. Cheap to make, easy to use. One of the first true, mass-produced assault rifles. Seventy-five million of 'em all around the world." He quickly field stripped it and put it back together, his pudgy fingers working expertly. Anybody who watched television had seen AKs in the hands of freedom fighters or terrorists, take your pick.

"How do you know your guy was killed with an AK? Was the weapon recovered?"

"No," Peralta said. "I heard it."

Cartwright nodded. He understood.

"Anybody can buy an AK. You know that. Using it with such precision is another matter. And why would you want to? There's too many good, modern weapons available. Maybe your suspect has a thing for the gun? Maybe it's his bad-ass signature. You should run that through ViCAP." The FBI's violent criminal database. "It's probably not some disgruntled 'Nam vet. We're getting too damned old. But the older we get, the tougher we were."

He chuckled. Peralta didn't.

I was half-listening to the ordnance talk. The Claymore sat a few millimeters from my genitals. I kept looking at the instructions stamped on the front. Such a funny thing. So you don't forget and aim it wrong. I shouldn't even be here right now. Why did I get over that apartment railing and into the pool with only seconds to spare, when Robin hadn't been safe in our back yard? Contingency was the god damndest thing. Robin would have made the better mark on the world if she had lived and I had died.

Peralta tapped an inch of ash into an amber glass ashtray. "I've thought about all that, Ed. Quit stalling."

"The Claymore is a different matter entirely." He cocked his head. "Is this connected to the explosion in San Diego on Friday night?"

So much for being cut off from the world.

Peralta said, "You know it is, so quit playing games."

To me, he said, "How far did you get into that apartment before you realized you were in the danger zone?"

I told him.

He let out a long whistle.

"So you see," Peralta said, "This is personal and it might get a hell of a lot more personal."

Cartwright set the rifle in his lap.

"Do you know how far my ass is already in a sling even by talking to you?" he said. "Even by you being here?"

"I don't care." Peralta swiveled his head.

"So give me something to work with?" Cartwright folded his hands over the assault rifle. "Who was killed with the AK?"

"Anglo, thirty-five or so," Peralta said and went on to describe our first client including the expensive prosthetic leg and the multiple names and identifications.

"Nobody I know," Cartwright said.

I said, "He had yellow eyes. Very well dressed. And he had a silver Desert Eagle on his passenger seat when he was killed."

Cartwright shook his head slowly, but I caught the involuntary tic of his left eye.

"Didn't do him much good," he said. "You're probably lucky he got killed when you weren't in the line of fire. One less dirtbag in the world and the kid here survived. What's not to like? Now I need to take a nap."

Suddenly, a fury rose in me. Tim Lewis' face hovered in my mind. And the baby I had held in my arms.

Cartwright asked me what I was doing.

"How do you set this thing off?" I was fiddling with the Claymore.

"You can't." He smiled at me like I was an idiot. "It's disarmed."

That did it. I threw the Claymore straight at his face. When he reached to catch it, I was up, crossed the eight feet separating us, and picked up the AK-47 from his lap.

"What the…" He let the dummy Claymore fall. It clattered on the wood floor. Next he reached for the pistol on his belt.

I chambered a round in the AK-47, although I didn't aim it at him. Yet.

Peralta said, "I wouldn't move, Ed. Mapstone here had a run-in with Los Zetas where they tried to put a hand grenade in his mouth, so he's PTSD'd to the moon."

Through his teeth, Cartwright said, "Why is he alive then?"

Peralta spoke softly. "That's why I wouldn't move."

He spoke quietly, "How do you even know how to work that thing, kid?"

"A million child soldiers in Africa can work it. Want to take a chance that I can't?"

He studied me through angry but uncertain eyes, his hand still on the butt of his sidearm.

If Cartwright had even started to pull the weapon, I would have pumped several shots into him before anything like judgment could have caught up with the rage I felt. A savage stranger's voice started speaking. It was coming from my mouth.

"You listen to me, old man." I spat out the last two words. "I've got two young people murdered and a missing baby. Now I've got an armed whacko survivalist sitting in front of me who thinks he can get off a shot before I send him to hell. Who knows how many weeks before they find your body? What I don't have is time to waste finding that baby, and that means you don't have time."

"All right, son. Please calm down."

I swung the barrel to his chest.

"Now you have ten seconds less time."

He saw my finger was on the trigger and a sheen of sweat appeared across his forehead.

"A dozen Claymores went missing from Fort Huachuca last month," Cartwright said.

Peralta shook his head. "That's an intelligence installation. What are anti-personnel mines doing there?"

"The military has this stuff everywhere. Makes it hard as hell to track. Who knows how much walks away from bases and nobody ever knows?"

I wanted to know who took it.

"Word is, soldiers."

"Active-duty soldiers?"

He nodded. I didn't lower the weapon.

He swallowed. "White supremacists are in the military. That's not new. You remember a guy named McVeigh in Oklahoma City. Now there's more of them. We've spent more than a decade at war, and we're sending home killing machines." He sighed. "Anyway, the word is, that's who took the Claymores. I don't know if it was to sell or to use."

"What about prostitutes? Are they involved in running high-end whores?

"That's all I've heard, son," he said. "Do what you please."

He closed his eyes and in the terrible silence that followed he put his hand in his lap. I lowered the assault rifle.

Peralta said, "Give me that and wait for me at the truck."

My blood was still up but I did as he asked.

Before I walked out, I heard Cartwright's voice.

"You have an unusual name, kid. I read a book by somebody with that name once, about the Great Depression."

"He wrote it," Peralta said.

"It wasn't bad," he said. "But you should have written more about the effect on the tribes."

He was right. I closed the door behind me.

Half an hour later, we hit solid pavement and Peralta spoke for the first time since he had returned to the pickup truck.

"There was a day when he would have killed you."

I let my breathing return all the way to normal before speaking.

"Ed? As in Edward? America's Finest Pimp thought I was the enforcer of some guy named Edward. He was afraid of Edward, and he didn't strike me as the kind who was afraid of many people. The man he described as Edward's muscle sounded a hell of a lot like Felix."

"That's not this Ed," Peralta said.

"How do you know? Did you see the 'tell' when I told him about Felix? He was lying."

"He had a loaded AK-47 being held by a crazy man, Mapstone. That's not a 'tell' you can trust."

"Maybe. His name is still Edward."

"Ed was a decorated FBI agent before his end-of-the-world fetish got him in trouble and he was fired. Only that's not the whole story. He's quietly enjoying his FBI pension and an honorable retirement."

"So tell me the whole story."

"Being known as a disgraced, bitter former special agent gives him cred. He deals guns to skinheads and bikers, cartels, Mexican Mafia, whoever pays. Gives 'em training, if they need it. And any takedowns happen so far down the line that nobody suspects crazy old Ed Cartwright."

"I never heard of him."

"You wouldn't," Peralta said. "He doesn't work for the FBI, doesn't work for Alcohol, Tobacco and Firearms. He reports to higher authorities. Maybe where your wife works, Mapstone. Nobody else in Phoenix law enforcement even knows about him, except as another reclusive old coot living out in Wittman with his guns. That's the way it's supposed to work."

"Why would white supremacists deal with somebody who has brown skin?"

"They must dig the whole Apache noble savage thing."

My breathing return to normal. It would have helped if Peralta had given me the whole story before we went visiting, to know what his play was. That kind of non-disclosure was like the old Peralta. It would have helped if Cartwright could have done a better job of connecting the Claymore to an apartment in San Diego, a young woman's fall out of a condo tower, and her boyfriend's violent death. Was he her boyfriend or husband? I didn't even know. How nuts was that?

"We've got white supremacists in the armed forces," I said. "I thought that was the least racist institution in America."

"Not after you break the force in two long wars," he said. "And drop recruiting standards. And have a black guy as commander in chief, which has brought out all the whackos. You remember the group they arrested in Georgia? Five soldiers were stockpiling weapons. They wanted to poison the apple crop, set off bombs, and overthrow the government? Thank God for stupid criminals."

"Until some smart criminals show up," I said. "So I assume Cartwright's bosses will be on this."

Peralta shrugged and we rode the rest of the way in silence back through the antic monstrosity of the suburban asteroid belt and into Phoenix. It might have been quicker to take the Loop 101 down to the Papago Freeway but Peralta stuck to surface streets. What were all these people doing out? Driving was the local sport.

Outside the office, he shifted the truck into park and turned to face me.

"Mapstone, I know you're not yourself, but…"

Peralta's voice trailed off. He set his jaw and turned forward. I got out. He drove off.

Chapter Nineteen

A few minutes later I returned home, eating a Popsicle to cool down and brooding. For the first time in my life, I had come close to being the worst thing possible in law enforcement: a hot dog. Cartwright was Peralta's play and I should have stayed in the shadows, let him handle it, and listened. I had allowed Cartwright and my anxiety over the baby to strip away my professionalism, send me into a tantrum with a loaded gun. He was going to get the idea that he couldn't count on me, never a good place to be with Peralta.

But the reality was that Peralta wasn't getting anywhere and Cartwright was holding back. Now I knew about the stolen Claymores but the connection from there was tenuous. The idea of white supremacist cells in the military was frightening. Some future Gibbon would write about that. For much of America's history, the nation had frowned on large standing armies. Now it was part of our economic policies and if you didn't "support the troops," you were a commie. And how all this tied in to Grace, Tim, and baby David, I did not know.

I was still running out of time. Sure, every law enforcement agency in Southern California would be working this case. But it was on me. That, at least, was how my concussed brain parsed it.

I checked the Amber Alert for the tenth time that day. The baby was still missing. He hadn't been in the apartment when I went through it. That much I was sure of. I was also certain that this was no child-custody issue but a kidnapping. Soon the FBI would come knocking. I was, after all, not merely a washed-up historian of cold cases. I was an expert on lost children.

But there would be nothing helpful I could tell them. My lost child was the one conceived with Lindsey. The child that never made it past four months in her womb before the miscarriage. Lindsey fled to the job in Washington, insisting that Robin continue to live here. Her only demand of me was that I keep Robin safe, a task at which I had failed. Now they were all gone and a house I had expected to be filled with unaccustomed baby sounds was silent. There was no Amber Alert for our loss.

These were thoughts I had become a master at stuffing in a closet of my brain and locking away. Patty had complained that I lacked the discipline to write serious history. She didn't know how disciplined I could become. I hardly cried now. It helped that I had hidden away all the photos of Lindsey and Robin. I didn't speak of it. No pity party for me. I didn't want Sharon Peralta to shrink my head, get me in touch with my feelings. Those would kill me. I was not special. The world was a planetary engine fueled by loss. Some things could never be made right.

At the Sheriff's Office, one of the cardinal rules of "incident command," say a hostage situation, was "stay in your own lane." One of Peralta's commandments was to avoid what he called a jurisdictional goat fuck. We were gone from the Sheriff's Office, and yet I knew he still thought that way. So I tried to choose a lane to make my own, take one of the many strands that had dropped on us in the past few days and follow it.

That would be the suspicious death of Grace Hunter.

Putting the Mac to sleep, I moved over to the leather chair, the police files of Grace Hunter's death on my lap. My body gradually cooled off from the hike through the desert to Cartwright's bunker. From the study, I could see the big picture window of the living room and I dawdled, staring out at the lush shady landscape of the street. Phoenix had done so many things wrong as a city. One of the things it had done right was preserving some of the old neighborhoods such as Willo.

I meditated on all the things I had done wrong in San Diego. Whores always lied. This was something I had learned as a young deputy. Most had drug habits. Most had children. So much could go wrong in their lives. Telling the truth was an occupational hazard. I should have interrogated Tim in much more depth. Who knew if Grace was even telling him the whole story? On the other hand, I had never dealt with high-priced call girls. Yet something told me the same operating procedure, the lying, applied. Many of them were victims. Some were not. None had a heart of gold, whatever Tim's conviction that she wanted to leave the life and be a mommy in Ocean Beach.

I should have gotten much more information about both Tim's and Grace's pasts, should have asked to see her computer and especially her emails. When she didn't come home that day, did he try to call or text her? I failed to ask. Did they have any friends in town with whom they socialized, besides her girlfriend Addison? Had any new neighbors moved in, or were there folks they had recently started to hang with, and had any taken an interest in Grace? I didn't know.

I had assumed we would have more time for a follow up, a foolish supposition considering that our first client, the one who had launched us on this quest, had been gunned down outside our office. Most of all, I should have waited until Tim was safely in his car with the baby and driving out the alley and toward the freeway to Riverside and his parents' house. I was not at the top of my game.

The police files had a familiar feel. Every department used standardized reporting now. But the information from my first spin through the paperwork showed me I wasn't the only one who had made mistakes. I pulled over a legal pad from the desk and started making notes.

On April twenty-second, the first emergency call came in at 11:54 p.m., a woman had fallen or jumped from a condo balcony. It was placed by another female who had been with her boyfriend in the Jacuzzi by the pool. Grace landed no more than twenty feet away and the caller was sure she had come off the nineteenth floor. The woman lived on twenty and her balcony was distinctive because of its hanging plants.

The first units to arrive, three minutes later, were a fire department engine company, then, five minutes after the first call, a paramedic unit. Grace was obviously DOA. All the witnesses agreed she was nude and handcuffed from behind.

Unfortunately, the building's night concierge was there, too, and opened the condo door for the firefighters. And they walked right in, finding the place empty, and the door leading to the balcony open. Uniformed police got there six minutes after the call, which had originally been routed to the fire department as a medical emergency. That's not surprising. The woman in the Jacuzzi was probably hysterical when she made the call and was perhaps assuming, with the hope of the traumatized, that Grace was only hurt. But it was several minutes before the officers could secure the condo.

That meant the first investigator to arrive, Isabel Sanchez, the "night detective" to use Peralta's lingo, was already facing a contaminated scene. I thought about Peralta telling me she was a looker, how it would do me a world of good to get laid. What would my opening line be? "Hi, I'm David and I'm concealing evidence. What's your sign?"

Back to work, Mapstone. At least two firefighters, the night concierge, and perhaps some curious civilians had been in the unit before the uniformed officers ran them out. The "fact" that the condo had been locked with a deadbolt also came second-hand, from the night concierge.

The inventory of Grace's belongings was minimalist: one pair of jeans, a cotton blouse, bra and panties, and black sneakers. But the clothes had not been neatly folded. The blouse was draped over a chair in the living room and the bra was two feet away on the floor. The jeans and panties were in the bathroom, again on the floor. There was a small amount of standing water on the bathroom floor, but the towels were dry and the shower hadn't been recently used. One sneaker was in the hallway leading to the bedroom. The other was in the kitchen.

Her purse was on the living room sofa, a small black satchel, tipped on its side. Inside were a wallet, cell phone, tissues, keys, sunglasses, and hand lotion. I studied the photos of each. No pepper spray or knife, which Tim had said she always carried.

A cynical street cop would say Grace was wandering the condo, stripping down as she cried or raved or hallucinated. Maybe she splashed water from the sink onto her face—and onto the floor—trying to make herself snap out of it. But then she found the nerve, walked to the door, opened it, and stepped out on the balcony. Next, to make sure she couldn't change her mind again, she handcuffed herself.

It might have gone down that way.

Wide-angle shots of the rooms showed nothing to indicate violence. Lamps were in their place. A big, fragile piece of pueblo pottery was undisturbed on a table nearest to the glass door. The bed was made. The kitchen looked as if no one ever cooked in it. The floors were clean except for the discarded clothing.

Another photo showed the inside of the front door. Writing in red said, I AM SO SORRY. It jarred me momentarily, bringing back memories of the wall in Tim's apartment. But it wasn't blood. A lab report said it was lipstick.

My cynical street cop, who had spent so many hours filling out paperwork for successful and attempted suicides, said to me: "See, she offed herself. Leave it to a Southern California airhead to have no writing implements other than her lipstick."

The only problem was that the inventory showed no lipstick, no cosmetics of any kind. I did a grad-school speed skim of the rest of the incident report, supplemental reports, and Detective Sanchez's case notes. No lipstick tube.

Sanchez tried Grace's keys on the condo door. None fit. Her driver's license had an out-of-date address. But her parents' names and phone number were in her wallet, and they were the ones Sanchez called to notify. They flew over and identified her remains. If Grace's wallet also had baby photos, they weren't listed in the inventory. There was no mention of a baby anywhere.

The medical examiner rushed through the autopsy and toxi-cology reports, the cops no doubt being mindful of the Coronado case. Its findings were what you would expect from a fall of at least one-hundred-ninety feet onto concrete. Massive head trauma, burst organs, collapsed lungs, and dozens of fractured bones. "The cause of death was the fall," one comment noted. Her bloodstream contained neither drugs nor alcohol. Her wrists showed abrasions where the handcuffs had been placed, but this could be consistent with a falling person's panic. She had semen in her vagina.

I got up and returned to the laptop, using Google to search for keywords about what happened that night. Not one story appeared. I remembered what my friend Lorie Pope, once a reporter at the *Arizona Republic*, had told me: that newspapers had reassigned or pushed out the old-time police reporters, the ones who went on calls and formed close relationships with the cops. That was how she and I had first met, me a deputy, Lorie working the police beat on the city desk. Now the newspapers only wrote up what the police public information officers told them. Crime upset readers, or so the editors thought. Television was a different matter, but only if they had "visuals," and no station seemed to pick up on the action that night. It was nearly midnight when she fell, after the end of the eleven o'clock news. If SDPD feared another suspicious death circus, they didn't need to worry.

The death and autopsy photos were what I expected. About all that was recognizably left of Grace Hunter was the butterscotch hair with blond streaks.

Larry Zisman returned at one, a little more than an hour after Grace's long dive. Sanchez initially interviewed him downstairs in the owners' lounge. Then she took him to the station to sign statements.

Zisman and his wife had owned the condo for six years. They often spent the summer months there. His wife worked for Intel and sometimes traveled, so Zisman was frequently there alone. Zisman described Hunter as his girlfriend and begged the police not to tell his wife. They had five children. He had never been unfaithful before. The usual routine. He also referred to Grace as "Scarlett," a discrepancy Sanchez noted and questioned him on. "Subject states that he only knew deceased as Scarlett, a student at SDSU."

He had met her three years before at a convention and they became occasional lovers. He denied giving her money, only some presents. As for the handcuffs, they belonged to Zisman, the reserve Phoenix police officer. He said they used them for light bondage during sex.

Zisman said they had a fight the night of her death. She wanted to see him more regularly and demanded that he leave his wife. She became hysterical and was generally "emotional" and "high strung." It did not become physical, according to Zisman's statement, only shouting and tears. "Subject stated that he left the condo at approximately 2230 hours with Hunter still there, to let the situation cool down."

According to Zisman, they did not have sex that night.

Zisman said he went to his boat, which was moored at a marina less than a mile away, and stayed there reading until half past midnight. Coming and going, he talked with a couple that owned a craft at the next slip. This checked out.

So if Zisman left the condo at half past ten that night, Grace was alone for little more than an hour before her death. If she was, in fact, alone.

I thought about what Tim had told me. He had gone to classes that morning and not returned until after three. Grace was gone. So even if she went out right before three, it left many unaccounted hours before her death. I found nothing that gave an indication of how they might have been spent. Grace had a new cell phone and it had no information on it, no calls, no texts, either incoming or outgoing. Would the mother described by Tim simply walk out of the Ocean Beach apartment, leaving the baby, and not even check in?

If Sanchez asked Zisman the last time prior to that night he had seen Grace, or Scarlett, it wasn't in the report. If he hadn't seen her for, say, eighteen months, then Tim's story might be accurate. If he had been with her four times that month, Tim had been betrayed. Unfortunately, after my encounter with the Claymore mine, I didn't think Isabel Sanchez would tell me diddly.

If Tim was telling the truth about them hiding out for more than a year in O.B. as Grace gave birth to their baby, one of the most important questions remained unanswered: why Grace would have gone downtown to meet up with a former john?

I had to hand it to Zisman. From the case notes, he came across with exactly the right mixture of distraught, surprise, and forthcoming. And maybe all that was genuine. But he was also in law enforcement. The only ones better at lying than whores were cops.

Then there was the missing lipstick tube.

I walked around the house and returned to the chair, spending two hours reading in more detail. This didn't change my initial impression. The man with the prosthetic leg had been right.

This was not a suicide.

Chapter Twenty

Back at the desk in the study, I wrote a report for Peralta. This was my element, as it was back in the days at the Sheriff's Office, where I was his in-house egghead clearing cold cases. In thirty minutes, I had shot all the holes I could find in the shoddy and rushed work of the San Diego cops, and then I printed out the report.

A few seconds later, the house phone rang. We had cordless phones in other rooms, but the phone on the desk had belonged to Grandfather, with a real dial, now a retro amenity, and the old-fashioned ring that could put a nail of dread into your brain. As in the old days at the Sheriff's Office, I would answer and he would announce one word, "Progress?"

Only it wasn't Peralta.

"Doctor Mapstone." It was an average voice, neither young nor old, lacking any accent, be it from the Midwest or from the heart of Mexico. An unfamiliar voice. And he was using Doctor Mapstone, exactly as Felix did—the inflection even reminded me of Bobby Hamid, the gangster that Peralta sent to prison for life. I was easy to find. I was in the phone book of whatever company currently owned the former Mountain Bell. I switched on the recording device that Lindsey had added.

"Yes."

"How could anyone fail to get tenure at San Diego State University?"

"I always surprise. Are you calling to offer me a job?"

"Perhaps. In a way."

"Go on. I need options."

A fine laugh followed, not villainous at all. The kind of laugh you could have a beer with. "I bet you do. You have something that I want."

"What would that be?"

"Don't fuck with me." No emphasis or emotion entered his voice. He might as well have said, "Excuse me."

He went on, "You have something I want, and I am willing to give you something in return."

"Did you make that same offer to Tim Lewis when you were breaking his fingers one by one?"

"Yes, I did."

At least that was settled. I wasn't talking to the tenure committee, calling to say they had made a mistake and wanted me back as a professor. I was talking to a stone-cold killer. Caution flooded my nervous system: he had the baby. I had to be careful not to bait him into further death. I wasn't sure one could negotiate with a man who would slit Tim Lewis' throat and paint the wall with blood, but I had to try.

"He claimed that he didn't have it. So I can only assume that you do. But you present a bigger challenge because of your law-enforcement connections. I have to take a different approach."

"I bet. You're a murderer and I'm coming for you."

So much for David the Negotiator.

The voice remained steady and calm. I hadn't gotten under his skin. He sure as hell was under mine. Smooth and calm and very sure that I wasn't tracing him. He seemed in no hurry to hang up.

"I know you want to come for me, Doctor Mapstone. I learned how you settled your Mexican trouble. Impressive. I don't underestimate you."

"I didn't have Mexican trouble. I had criminal trouble. You're no different."

"You're wrong there. We might even be on the same side, using different methods."

"I don't think so."

He cleared his throat. "If I told you we were in a battle for this country, for whether it can remain a white nation, you'll dismiss me as a racist nut. You work for a Mexican. And you're an academic. You've been brainwashed. Samuel Huntington has it right about the clash of civilizations, but it's happening in America. In fact, it's killing this country. You don't want to face the facts."

He was mighty chatty and had done some reading. I said, "I'm not sure Professor Huntington would agree with you." God, I wish I were tracing the call.

"David," he switched to the familiar, "I don't want to kill you. I had a chance already. I didn't take it."

I wondered if he even had the ability to change baby David's diaper and feed him. I asked him about that chance to kill me that he didn't take.

"The apartment. You're very physically impressive for a man your age, getting out the way you did. But I helped you by waiting to detonate the Claymore. Do you have a new cell number since your old phone went with you into the pool?"

A man my age? Fuck you.

I said, "So you were watching."

"How do you think I gave you time to get out of the apartment? Now answer my question because I won't give you time ever again."

I gave him the number of the temporary phone I had bought at the truck stop in El Centro.

"Drive to the Park Central parking lot. Be on the south side of the lot in five minutes. Come unarmed. Wait and I'll call. Stay in your car. If any police are with you or near you or I even suspect you're fucking with me, you won't get what you want."

Even the profanity was said with a businesslike calm.

Then the line went dead.

I switched off the recorder, checked my watch, and called Peralta. After I gave him a quick update, he told me to get moving, follow the caller's instructions.

"Where are you?"

"Camelback Mountain."

"It'd be nice to have some backup."

"Get moving, Mapstone. I'll get there when I can."

Wondering what he was up to, I pulled the heavy Python and its holster out of my belt and set them on the desk. The freshly cleaned Airlite .357 magnum slid into my pants pocket and was barely noticeable. I added a small Ka-Bar "last option" knife, with a serrated blade, inside my waistband. As the name implies, it is for use if you get in a fight for your weapon and are afraid you'll lose. I further armed myself with a bottle of frozen water.

Halfway to the car, I stopped, turned around, and went back in the house. In the office, I rooted around in Lindsey's tech drawer and found a blank flash drive. If I had to trade, at least this might buy me some time to assess the situation. If the mystery caller actually made contact with me, I could show it. Then he would have to show the baby. Then things would get interesting.

Less than three minutes later, I pulled into the bland assortment of low-slung buildings that was Park Central.

When I was a child, it had been the first shopping mall in Phoenix, a sweet, modest, open-air affair on the site of an old dairy. For the past two decades, since the Midtown skyscraper boom collapsed with the 1990 real-estate crash and retail fled toward Scottsdale, it had been mostly offices. Most were medical-related, tied to gigantic St. Joseph's Hospital and Medical Center to the west.

Local wags were calling St. Joe's "Mr. Joe's" now, after the bishop had withdrawn its Catholic affiliation because an abortion was performed to save a woman's life. It was a mere kerfuffle in the many local rows of the moment. Even without reading the newspaper, I knew Peralta's successor was doing "sweeps" to pick up illegal immigrants and holding news conferences to trumpet this as a huge triumph of justice. The Legislature was an insane asylum. Nobody in power was talking about anything real or important.

Like almost everything in Phoenix, Park Central was surrounded by a large surface parking lot. In Phoenix, the word
"park" often doesn't mean a recreational space but an asphalt
place to leave your vehicle. Those were among the reasons why
the weather kept changing for the worse. Today the lot was
nearly empty, except for cars near the popular Starbucks on the
southeast corner of the former mall. All of Midtown Phoenix
was virtually deserted on Sunday. I eased the Prelude in that
direction, hoping to find some shade from the skyscrapers lining
Central Avenue.

The best I could do was to catch a little relief from the sun in
the shadow of the Bank of America building. Nothing looked
unusual: nobody following me, nobody sitting in a car waiting.
A light-rail train slid by, its electronic bell penetrating the sealed
passenger compartment of the Prelude. Across the street were two
mid-century towers, one tall, one short. The tall one once had
an outside glassed-in elevator, which, I am told, was a popular
spot for a quickie before it reached its only stop at the top floor.
The short tower had been the site of the Phoenix Playboy Club.
Back in the day, Midtown Phoenix could swing.

Ten minutes later, the phone rang. It made an annoying
xylophone sound. I listened on my headset.

"You've done well so far. Go through the Jack in the Box and
get something to eat from the drive through. There are only two
cars in line."

The incoming call readout said, UNKNOWN.

I sped a hundred yards over to the Earll Drive exit, drummed
my hands on the steering wheel for the light to change, and
turned north on Central. It was so nice that he was concerned
about my eating. Sure enough, only two cars were ahead of me.
I checked the mirrors, craned my neck around. Nothing.

My destination put me more on edge. The drive-thru was
hemmed in on one side by the restaurant and on the north and
east by the fancy One Lexington condo tower and its swimming pool. I had heard stories about those pool parties. Maybe
the caller had a different party in mind for me. If he wanted to

trap me from behind, then walk up and spray the Prelude with machine-gun fire, this would be the ideal place.

"Welcome to Jack in the Box, would you like to try two Jack Tacos for a dollar?"

The disembodied voice startled me. I said two Jack Tacos were fine and waited for the line to move, my hand on the Airlite. Did I want to add an order of curly fries? Hell no. So far, no car pulled behind me. An ancient Toyota Camry was belching fumes ahead, two young children yelling and beating on their mother's shoulder with shopping bags.

He might have been sitting under one of the umbrellas outside the Starbucks across the street, but no—he couldn't have seen the Jack in the Box line with such precision. The caller was mobile. He implied that he had something I wanted. That could only be the baby. And what I had was the flash drive. How did he know I had it? Torturing Tim Lewis would easily have given up that answer.

I got my order and pulled to the edge of Central. The phone rang again.

"What?"

"Drive north to Indian School. Go the speed limit. I'm watching."

"I want to hear…" I wanted to hear the baby's voice before continuing, but he didn't give me a chance to finish. Now would be a really good time for Peralta to show up. But he didn't call, and I didn't dare tie up the phone calling him again.

So I did as told. I let a few cars pass. Nobody goes the speed limit in Phoenix. Aside from people waiting at the light-rail stations in the middle of the avenue, I could count the pedestrians on one hand. One was a man in a red cap running south with six dogs on leashes in front of him.

Once upon a time, the city's leaders had intended Central Avenue to be Phoenix's version of Wilshire Boulevard in Los Angeles. It didn't work out. The old corporate headquarters, banks, and shops that made Central the most important business location in town were bought or closed or lost in the savings-and-loan crash. Much of what remained moved out to Scottsdale or other suburbs as Phoenix became a back-office town, heavily dependent on population growth and real-estate hustles, and then the Great Recession had cleaned our clock.

As a result, this part of Central held an assortment of bland skyscrapers with massive parking garages behind them. A few quirks of the older city remained, such as the curved "punch card" building that was once the headquarters of Western Savings. When the thrift went bust in the savings-and-loan scandal, the tower went mostly empty. A pair of domed, two-story circular buildings complemented it. They had been retail bank branches and their mid-century appeal endured. I recalled that inside, each building had a sunburst skylight. In a healthy city, one such as San Diego, they might have been remade into a jazz club or a restaurant. Instead, both sat empty, the blinds hanging as if the savings and loan had closed the day before.

Other Central landmarks passed by as I drove north: an inverted pyramid and Macayo's restaurant, whose façade was meant to resemble an Aztec temple. And much empty land.

Somebody had bought it long ago, gotten the City Council to zone it for high-rise, and cleared the old single-story buildings or bungalows. But development never happened. Speculation and flipping did. Because it was zoned for high-rises, no developer could afford to do less than build towers—for which there was no demand. So the land stayed bare, aside from an occasional plan that went nowhere.

Farther north, back in the 1980s, somebody had promised to build the tallest building in the country. That site was still bare. Absentee owners were banking it on their asset sheets for someday, even as decades went by. This was the heart of the nation's sixth-largest city, but these parcels might as well have been World War II Dresden after the debris from carpet-bombing had been carted away. I had read that forty-three percent of the city of Phoenix was empty land. What were a few art projects on vacant lots against that?

Hardly anyone knew what had been lost, first by the sky-scraper rush, then by the mass abandonment. But these blocks had once held hundreds of bungalows and adobes of the same kind that were now protected and coveted in districts such as Willo. These had been neighborhoods people cared about.

Back in the 1940s, most of Central had been lined with queen palms and handsome haciendas, irrigation ditches, and citrus groves. When I was young, most of these had been replaced with shops and businesses, but it was a vibrant street. "Cruis-ing Central" was an essential tradition on Friday and Saturday nights until the police banned it.

Now the most influential people rarely if ever saw the torn heart of the city, much less gave a damn. It was the only place I felt at home. I drove the streets and the history of the place formed the effortless backbeat in my mind, memory stitching together memory. I was helpless against it.

Half a mile later, I reached Indian School Road and he called again.

"Go into the park and wait."

Steele Indian School Park stood on part of the grounds of the old Phoenix Indian School. The choice acres facing Central had been given to a big developer and, naturally, sat empty. The rest, meant to be a grand central park for the city, wasn't much. The imposing brick entrance signs were the most impressive features. Otherwise, it lacked the shade trees of old Encanto Park and the city never seemed to have the money or vision to make it into anything beyond sun-blasted grass with a couple of historic buildings saved from the Indian school and plenty of hot concrete sidewalks.

Today, it was nearly empty. A Hispanic family was having a picnic under an awning. I put the car into park and munched on a Jack Taco, waiting, watching. No other cars came or went. He could see me from the parking lot of the VA hospital to the east. Note to self: keep some binoculars in the car. Lindsey's Prelude smelled of fast food. My watch ticked around to five minutes, then ten, fifteen, twenty.

At twenty-one minutes, he called again and ran me around. My efforts to start a conversation were immediately cut off. I followed the instructions and drove east on Indian School to Sixteenth Street, south a mile to Thomas, and then back west into the core. Traffic remained light. If someone was following me, he was doing a very good job staying hidden. I thought about pulling off into a sidestreet, backing into an alley, and seeing if I could catch him behind me. But it was too big a chance. I stayed with his itinerary.

Another call: "Go to the McDonald's on Central. Pull into the parking lot facing east. I'll be there in a few minutes."

This next leg took me about five more minutes, back the way I had come before, a few blocks north of the punch card building. I drove to the east end of the long lot and waited. Ironically, the FBI offices were in my view to the northeast. Otherwise, it was acres of empty blight, adorned here and there with a dead palm tree looking like a giant burned matchstick. During the 2000s boom, before the biggest-ever collapse of Phoenix's only real industry, real-estate speculation, these lots facing Central were supposed to become twin, sixty-story condo towers. I don't think anybody ever believed it would really happen. It didn't.

As I drank cold water, the airplane came in low from the east, a small, single-engine private craft. It was flying very low. Dangerously low. Immediately before it passed to my right, it jettisoned something. That something fell straight down and landed in a plume of dust on one of the empty lots. I didn't need a phone call to make me speed a block to the landing zone. If I had that pair of binoculars, I might have gotten a tail number, but probably not. The airplane pulled up and disappeared into the sun.

I slammed the gearshift into park and sprinted into the empty lot. It was a stupid thing to do, but I was powered by a panicky instinct, adrenaline, and dread. Dust was still in the air as I approached a parcel little more than a foot long wrapped in brown paper and tied with twine. Something red was leaking through. My chest felt as if all its bones had suddenly collapsed.

That stopped me enough to return to the car for the evidence gloves that I had always kept there from my time as a deputy. I got the gloves and scanned the side streets: nothing. Then I saw him: a man was walking toward the parcel. He was tall and thin with stringy hair the color of urine.

"Stop!"

He ignored me. He looked like a homeless man, but I had my hand on the revolver as I walked back across the empty ground.

We faced off.

"My stuff!"

Was he really a street person or a watcher? I decided on the former.

"This is police business."

He looked at my PI credentials, not too closely thank goodness, and shuffled quickly toward Central.

I watched him go, then pocketed the wallet and pulled on the gloves. *Call the police, call the FBI*—this was what my interior voice was saying. I ignored it, dropped to my haunches, pulled out a small knife, and cut the twine. *It might be another bomb*, came the interior governor that had saved me so often in the past. I ignored that too, and carefully unwrapped the parcel.

It held a baby doll, covered in blood. It looked as if a plastic bag of stage blood had been inserted into the package so it would burst on impact.

"Hey!"

I looked up and the homeless man was fifty yards away, a maniacal look on his face. "You see me comin' on the street, it's lights out!"

I waved. My stomach felt as if it was going to climb out of my throat. Yeats was running through my brain, *I have walked and prayed for this young child…*

The doll's plastic smile mocked me as I pulled it out of the blood, seeing if the package contained a note. But there was none. The sun beat down on me as I realized the real baby was dead. An entire family wiped out on my watch. It was always going to turn out this way. The baby was going to die. Why did I think it could turn out otherwise? You can't bargain with kidnappers.

There had always been a chance to save the baby? Hadn't there? That we could rescue this child while the bad guys kept it alive and either bargained with us or prepared to sell it on the adoption black market? Hadn't there been a chance?

No.

I banged my fist into the dirt, catching a bunch of burrs that punctured through the latex into my flesh.

I had not reacted as a professional, but as a hysterical civilian. Now I needed that professional core to return and save me.

Scooping up the fresh evidence I was about to conceal, I carried it to the car and laid it in the trunk. I peeled off the sweat-filled, blood-and-burr covered evidence gloves and tossed them in, too. Then I waited in the car, blasting the air-conditioning on my face, for another half hour. The cell phone didn't ring again, no matter how loudly I shouted at it. Not one car appeared on the sidestreets. Finally, I pushed the anger inside and felt very cold. I called Peralta but went to his voice mail. Two things seemed clear: more than one individual was involved, the man who called me and at least one more piloting the airplane. And I needed to get into Grace's flash drive, find out what was so valuable.

There was nothing more I could do but drive back home, Yeats still in my ears, his great gloom in my mind.

An intellectual hatred is the worst.

I would find who did this.

And then kill them all.

The chilled numbness I felt deepened on the doorstep. The door was unlocked. I had gone off in such a hurry that I hadn't even set the alarm. If they were looking for the flash drive, they had come to the right place. I could walk back to the car and get help, but didn't. If they were careful, they had already seen me through the picture window. I had five bullets on my side against their automatic weapons or Claymore mines. Maybe they weren't careful and I would catch them searching. We would settle accounts.

I stepped inside. Heather Nova was on the stereo. I thought about Frank Sinatra's quip about committing suicide listening to Sarah Vaughn. Heather wasn't bad background music to die by.

"Is that you, Dave?"

Lindsey Faith Adams Mapstone was in the kitchen, on her knees scrubbing the floor in front of the refrigerator, her brown-black hair in her face. She rose and hugged me, and, after a long time, I put my arms around her, too.

Her voice was a whisper in my ear. "I have messed up so bad."

"Me, too."

Chapter Twenty-one

I heard the engine of Peralta's truck roaring up Cypress before he walked in the door without knocking. He hugged Lindsey and I took him outside to the Prelude.

"I told you she'd come back," he said.

I ignored that and told him about the call, the runaround, the airplane, and its bombing run. The caller had referred to me as "Doctor Mapstone," exactly as Felix had done. He knew about me, the failed historian and the failed lawman. The newspapers had written up some of the big cases I had broken, but this wasn't an innocent informed reader. He had done some homework. On top of that, he admitted that he had set off the Claymore. All I needed to tie it up in a bow was for him to confess to killing Felix. Unfortunately, the only bow I had was the twine from the package with the bloody doll.

I opened the trunk. Sheltered by the shade, the heat left us alone.

Kicking at the driveway, I said, "The baby's dead."

He slipped on a fresh pair of evidence gloves and carefully examined the bloody doll.

"Let's not get ahead of ourselves." He leaned in, reading off the brand of the doll, noting the quality of the wrapping paper and twine. "Where's the flash drive?"

I told him about the hiding spot in the library.

"It must have something important if he's willing to put on this show," Peralta said.

I told him about my inability to get past Grace's pre-recorded greeting.

Half of his upper lip tilted up, a wide smile for him. "Lindsey can take care of that."

"Tell me we'll find these guys."

He raised up and studied me. "We will."

I followed him back to his truck, where he produced a garbage bag, then we returned to the Prelude, where he slid the evidence inside. I didn't want Lindsey to know about this bloody baby doll and what it implied. Anyway, was she visiting? Was she back for good? I didn't know. This case could only deepen her grief.

"Should I call the FBI?"

"No," he said. "In an hour, you'll have twenty agents setting up shop in your living room. Any chance we have will be lost."

"We don't have a chance. The baby is dead."

"No," Peralta said. I took no comfort from his tone of certainty. He went on: "If the baby was dead, he'd have nothing to bargain with. He did this as a warning. He wanted to throw you a scare in the most dramatic way possible. He'll call again. You ought to check out historic cases and see about bodies being dropped from airplanes."

Now he was trying to distract me.

As I leaned against the fender, which had cooled off enough that it didn't burn me, I thought about being eight years old, coming home from Kenilworth School full of joy to be free, catching the limb of a small tree outside, and getting stung by a bee. As Grandmother removed the stinger, I thought it was the worst thing that could possibly happen, it hurt so much.

Now that same tree was grown tall but my branch was sawed off. It was a long time coming. I was a surprise baby and then my parents died before I even knew them. No brothers or sisters, no aunts or uncles. So many times at the Sheriff's Office, I had eluded violent death. It was something our unborn child couldn't do and saving Lindsey's life meant we couldn't have another.

"Mapstone." Peralta knew I was too deep in my head. "I'll take the package to a private lab and get a workup. Let's go inside."

"What about Cartwright?" The thought had just come to me.

"Stop obsessing about the Edward thing."

"That's not what I mean," I said, unaware of any irony involving a man I was prepared to shoot the day before. "He might be dead or in danger. They're playing us, jerking us around. They kill people we talk to, but they won't come straight for us."

His heavy hand guided my shoulder toward the front door. "Ed will be fine, whether it's nuclear war or some dudes coming onto his property. If anybody was stupid enough to make a move against Ed, he'd have them buried in the desert within the hour."

Inside, he slipped on the pair of Bose earphones that Lindsey had gotten me for Christmas five years ago and listened to the voice on the recorder. He replayed it several times. Then he settled into the leather chair, put on his reading glasses, and studied my report on Grace Hunter. Lindsey was still cleaning the kitchen.

He folded his glasses. "I agree."

"Why would she leave her baby and go see Zisman?"

He ticked off scenarios on his fingers. She received a call like I had, perhaps threatening to kill Tim if she didn't go. Maybe not go to Zisman's condo. Maybe instructions to go to the corner to meet someone, and she had been taken.

Or Zisman himself had coerced her with some form of blackmail or reward.

Or an abductor had gained entry to the apartment and made her leave with him. A gun at one's back is a good persuader—could even make a mother leave her newborn baby.

Or she had gone willingly because she and Zisman were still lovers and Tim Lewis didn't know it, but something had gone wrong, and he had arranged to have her killed while he was on his boat.

"The last one seems improbable," I said. "She wouldn't leave the baby."

"We used to see that all the time," Peralta said. "Mother abandoning a baby so she can go party. Leaving them inside their cars in the summer while they go shop. Remember the mother who drove off with the baby still on the car roof?"

"It doesn't fit Grace, and not only the woman described by Tim Lewis, but the woman's actions. She started her own illegal business, where it required discretion and care. She did it for some time without attracting a pimp, and then she eventually gave him the slip. She wasn't an airhead."

"That's true."

When I waited in silence, he continued. "I was talking to her father."

"I'm surprised he would talk to you."

"I didn't give him much of a choice. When I went to his place, the housekeeper told me he'd gone hiking. He's one of these idiots who climbs Camelback every day, even in the summer. So I got a description and waited at the Echo Canyon trailhead for him. Someday Phoenix Fire will have to airlift him off if he keeps this up. He was so heat exhausted that I didn't have trouble getting him into the cab of the truck."

"You shouldn't have gone alone," I said.

"Why?" He snapped it out in a harsh tone. "I can take care of myself."

"That's not my point. We've had two clients killed and the murderer is at large."

"I'm not an old man, Mapstone. You handled the kidnapper's call on your own. I did this. We don't have an entire department backing us up any more. Sometimes we have to work separately to get results in a hurry. I sure as hell can take care of myself."

I shut up. It was the first time I had sensed that he was not as philosophical about losing the election as he appeared. My concern about him going alone, and my frustration that he hadn't been around to back me up, came off as questioning his abilities.

When he cooled down, Peralta described Grace's father: a self-made man, owning a successful company in Chandler that sold garage-door mechanisms. In a metropolitan area where big garages were almost as sacred as unlimited gun rights and red-light running, it was a very good business. The daughter he described to Peralta was smart, a National Merit Scholar finalist, but a young woman with a rebellious side. Her father had wanted her to attend Stanford, so of course she had chosen San Diego State. In retaliation, he had made her pay her own way.

"They didn't get along?" I asked.

"Didn't sound like it," he said. "The guy struck me as a prick. Chip on his shoulder. Sense of entitlement. And he's got a wife half his age, so he's desperately trying to stay in shape and be the extreme athlete, totally focused on trying to be her age. He's had work done, I could tell."

"She's not Grace's mother…"

"No. They divorced when Grace was a freshman in college and her mother found out dad had a girlfriend on the side that was his daughter's age. He said Grace blamed him for the divorce, but the parents had been fighting for years. Grace couldn't wait to get out of that house."

"The dad told you all this?"

"No," he said. "The housekeeper did. I don't know whether she's legal or not, but let's say she was a fan. 'My Sheriff,' she called me. She was happy to help."

"Where was the new wife?"

"Where else? The spa at the Sanctuary."

After the divorce, Grace had come home to the Phoenix less often, and had visited her dad less still. She hated the young woman who, in her eyes, had broken up her parents' marriage, and refused even to see her.

So her father was surprised and proud when Grace asked him for a loan to start her own business in San Diego. He was even happier when she paid him back.

"How did he seem to be taking her death?"

"Like a tough guy," Peralta said, "but I could tell it's eating at him."

"Did he bring up Zisman?"

"No, but I did. He claimed he didn't know Zisman. Grace never mentioned the guy to either parent."

"Or what her real business was."

"Right. But Grace had no known enemies and she was emotionally stable, even the housekeeper backed that up. She said Grace was the only nice person in the family. No history of suicide attempts. Later, I talked to her mother on the phone and it all jibed. The mother moved back to Iowa and hadn't seen Grace for a year."

"Do they think it was suicide?"

"They don't know what to think. The dad wanted to know who hired us, and of course he had never heard of Felix Smith. They didn't know about her boyfriend, either."

"And they didn't know they were grandparents?"

He shook his head.

Her mother last spoke to her on the phone the day before she died and Grace said she wanted to tell her some good news. She said it was a complicated story. But her mom was at work, so they decided to talk about it the next day. But the call never came."

That made me even more suspicious: additional witnesses that Grace was not depressive, not suicidal. And a phone call promising good news: I assumed that meant telling her about her new baby. This was not a woman who killed herself.

"We have missing time to fill in," I said. "On April twenty-second, Grace was gone when Tim returned at three that afternoon. She didn't die until nearly midnight. None of that time was spent calling her mom in Iowa. So what was she doing?"

I also didn't like the cell-phone situation. Someone Grace's age couldn't live without constant texting. And yet she had a new cell with nothing on it. I looked once more at my phone, willing Mister UNKNOWN to call again. He didn't.

"San Diego PD will re-open this as a homicide based on your report," Peralta said. "It will take time, but they can find her other phone records."

"We don't have time." My temples were starting to ache from stress.

"Maybe I can help." Lindsey was behind me.

I didn't know how much she had heard. But I didn't want her anywhere near a case that involved what would no doubt be a dead baby. Yet before I could speak, Peralta said, "That would be great, Lindsey." To me, "Give her the flash drive with Grace's clients. It's encrypted."

"I need to go to the Apple store at the Biltmore," she said. "And a Radio Shack. Then I can get started."

I handed her the keys to the Prelude.

Chapter Twenty-two

By the time Lindsey returned, Peralta was gone. She set a large bag down on the desk where I was working.

"I want to see the garage apartment."

I wasn't sure that was a good idea for either of us. That had been Robin's space, where she had lived with us after coming back into Lindsey's life following a long absence, lived for two years rent-free after she lost her job as curator of a man's art collection. He lost it all in the real-estate collapse and she was looking for her next adventure. I hadn't been up there since her death.

"I want to see it," Lindsey insisted.

I tried very hard not to sigh. We walked up the staircase, bookshelves on one side and a wrought-iron railing on the other, to the landing that overlooked the living room, then across the walkway above the interior courtyard where Lindsey's garden had sat neglected. I fumbled with the keys and opened the door.

Heat greeted us so I turned on the window air-conditioner. It was a simple space, one large room with a bed and a couple of chairs, an alcove for a little kitchen, and a bathroom. A back door led to an outside staircase on the north end of the building. Grandmother had kept her sewing room up here when I was a child. Robin had added several social realism posters—her specialty in art history—and two of her own oil paintings, abstracts with geometric lines and vivid colors, illuminated by the afternoon sun. Her easel stood in one corner, an empty canvas on it.

Lindsey walked around, lightly touching the edges of the paintings. Opening the closet, she examined Robin's clothes, holding a blouse up to her face.

Her dark hair grew fast and it was now down to her shoulders with bangs added. It fell thick and pin-straight. Women would kill for Lindsey's hair. The edge of it brushed around the nape of her neck as she ran a hand against Robin's clothes. They would kill for her fair skin and the lovely contrasts between dark hair, fair skin, and blue eyes. She looked familiar and yet a stranger. In so many ways, I did not know my wife.

So many times, I had imagined what was next for us, wondered whether I even wanted her to come back. It was a terrible thought, but she had left me once before, when we were first dating, and it had lacerated my heart. She had come back on Christmas Eve and that lyrical return had become a part of our story.

This time when she left, after losing the baby and taking the job offered to her by the governor of Arizona who was becoming Secretary of Homeland Security, the story turned darker. I tried to understand her need to grieve. She had to get out of this house, she had said at one point she didn't know if she could ever stand to be here again, and yet here she was. I tried to understand and yet I had been hurting, too. It was our baby that was dead, not only hers. In the blurred months she had been gone, we had talked nothing out and I had given up trying. I didn't know if I wanted her to come back because I didn't know if I could open up to the pain of another abandonment. The fortifications I had built against her were not strong.

She turned and studied me, a big smile playing on her sensual lips. In her eyes was a nothing look that was densely underlain with meaning. It lasted a few seconds.

"Did you fuck her there?"

She nodded toward the bed.

Before I could answer—the answer was no—she strode quickly over and slapped me. The blow was so hard it brought little lighted planets and asteroids to the edge of my vision.

"Did you fuck my sister in that bed?" The smile was gone and her eyes were burning violet with emotion.

She was about to deliver another blow but I caught it. She was strong as hell. With her other hand, she shoved me against the wall and mashed her mouth roughly against mine. You could call it a kiss if you called knuckle-breaking a handshake. I twirled her around and slammed her back into the plaster and our tongues fought. She was making sounds that were half whimpers, half snarls. We were both sweating. Buttons were popping off my shirt. I was jerking her jeans and panties down despite the fact that not a millimeter of space separated our half-wrestling, half-embracing bodies.

We both fell on the floor and the rest of the clothes came off. What happened next was the angriest lovemaking I could ever imagine. The hardness of the floor was apt. A bed would have been out of place. Her hair fell into my mouth.

Usually there was a part of me standing outside every interaction observing. That me fluttered on the perimeter for only a few seconds, managing to remember Chrissie Hynde lyrics about love and hate and the thin line, wondering if I was taking my woman back or she was taking her man back, noticing that my formerly inhibited Lindsey had been practicing moves and not with me, or if any of this even mattered beyond these minutes and that rough floor, and then the observer was sucked back inside our primal bout and lost. She moaned "fuck me" among many untranslatable sounds.

Her orgasm was more intense and longer lasting than any I ever remembered, and finally she collapsed on top of me. The only familiar gesture was her tucking her feet under my legs.

In the silence, I could only hear the fronds of a palm tree brushing against the window. Spasms ripped through my back as my San Diego dive caught up with me, and my face was still stinging from her slap. All other thoughts had been torn away like our clothes.

My shoulder was suddenly wet. And then she started sobbing, in heaving, loud convulsions that seemed too big to be coming out of her slender body. All I could do was hold her and stroke her hair. She initially resisted even as she mashed herself against me, until she finally gave in and held me too. Her arm wrapped so tightly around my neck that I almost passed out. It was a long time before she was simply crying.

Afterwards, we lay side by side, one of her long legs over mine. The room was finally cooling down. Somebody could have come in and killed us right then and it would have been okay.

She retrieved a pack of Gauloises out of her wadded up jeans and lit one, then exhaled a long, blue vapor trail. Tobacco mingled with the pervasive scent of sex.

I followed the smoke out into the room, down her lovely body, past our reddened knees, and noticed the tattoo on the top of her right foot. The word "Emma" was surrounded by brambles.

It made me smoke one of her French cigarettes, too, even though it would probably make me slightly ill. I am an old guy, so in my mental world body art is confined to Melville's whalers, real sailors and enlisted Marines, and trailer trash. It is elitism out of step with the age, but I find tattoos barbarous. And here was one on the perfect fair foot of my wife. True, she had worn a small stud in her nose when we had first dated, but that was years ago and Lindsey was no longer twenty-eight. This made her feel more alien and distant from me.

The tattoo's provenance was no mystery: Emma, at least for Lindsey, was our lost daughter. Emma wasn't a name I would have chosen. We didn't even know the gender of the baby.

It was better to make light conversation as she lay against me, both of us staring at the ceiling.

"How was the Apple Store?"

"I got a new laptop," she said. "And other stuff."

I had never seen Lindsey travel without a computer. "What happened to yours?"

She blew a smoke ring, then a second.

"They confiscated it after they took away my security clearance and fired me."

Chapter Twenty-three

Lindsey dropped me at the office the next morning. Even though it was ten, I had beaten Peralta there again. I was so sore from the various explosions in my life that my first few steps were like an old man's. I wasn't complaining about the ones that involved Lindsey but I was out of practice. The night before, I went to bed while Lindsey worked on her new computer. She had claimed a space on the landing above the living room and sat cross-legged with her back against the wall. When I was a child, the stairs and landing had seemed exceptionally high. Now, having grown to six-feet-two, I could touch the landing with my hand. Such was perspective and context.

Sleep hadn't come easily, so I was still awake when Lindsey had slipped in bed and curled up against me. It was so much like what Robin had done that first night that it kept me awake even longer. At first I thought my dreams had turned into a hallucination. But, no, it was Lindsey. Robin was taller and bustier. We fit together beautifully. Robin was dead.

Lindsey woke me from two nightmares, but when she wanted to know what I was dreaming, I said I couldn't remember. Hearing about other people's dreams was as tedious as watching their vacation videos and Lindsey sure didn't want to know about my dreams lately.

Around five, we had sex again, this time without the anger, but she was as loud as her half-sister, something new about my wife.

We used to play a game over cocktails. Lindsey had been endlessly entertained about my adventures before we got together, but she had drawn the line at knowing about my former girlfriends. It was better for her mental health not to know, or so she had said. As we had enjoyed martinis, I would tease her: "I'll tell you anything, all you have to do is ask."

"No thanks," she would say.

When I had asked about her life, she would say, "I lived a boring life before you, Dave. There's nothing to tell." I had never believed that, even though I was older than she and had lived perhaps more adventures, but she didn't talk easily about herself. I knew she had grown up in chaos, run away to join the Air Force where she had learned computers, and had claimed one boyfriend before me. Perhaps this was even the truth.

Now I wondered how much I wanted to know about the past months of her life. I imagined her boyfriend in D.C. as wealthy, handsome, and definitely better endowed than me. Maybe he was a black guy. Maybe her lover was a woman. And now I knew this person had mined a deeper lode of sexual passion from her than I had ever been able to reach. For that to happen, a woman had to be willing to really let her lover in, really open herself. She had not done that for me. I didn't realize it at the time, but the past twenty-four hours had shown me different. Did I really want to know about those past months?

After we lost the baby, Lindsey could barely endure being touched. That changed yesterday as we bounced the historic floorboards in the garage apartment. My wife, who had never even used the word "ass" before, was now talking dirty during sex.

I supposed I should thank the son of a bitch.

Now I was slipping my report on Grace Hunter into a file folder when the office phone rang and the readout was a San Diego area code.

"This is Detective Sanchez with the San Diego Police," came a pleasant voice on the other end. So Isabel Sanchez was going to talk to me after all.

"How may I help you?"

"How about opening your gate so I can come in."

This was not good. I wished Peralta were here but pressed the button to open the gate.

The night detective was about five-four with a size two figure, dark eyes with long lashes, and long, black hair that looked as if it had caught a gust off the Pacific at that exact second. Her pregnancy was also beginning to show. The man with her was a few inches shorter than me but very buff with yellow surfer-boy hair. San Diego had the best-looking cops in the country.

"This is my partner, Detective Jones," she said. I invited them to sit down, thinking: sure, Jones—he probably had multiple IDs and aliases, too.

"Deputy Chief Kimbrough speaks highly of you," she said.

"That's nice. He's a great cop."

"That's why we're not filing a charge to ask our friends in Phoenix to arrest you on," said the pleasant voice.

So it was going to be like this.

Several charges came to mind, but she wouldn't know about those.

I said quietly, "I was a victim of a crime in your city."

"I can understand how you might still feel badge-heavy, Map-stone," said Jones, who, with his mean little eyes, looked exactly like a badge-heavy cop. "But you're not a deputy sheriff anymore."

We went through this small talk, all designed to get a rise out of me, for about ten minutes. None of it worked. Jones gave me the cop stare. I returned it with the amiable look of a concerned civilian. I didn't even feel the need to bring up their rushed and shoddy investigation into Grace's death. From their attitude, it seemed clear that Kimbrough had already done that, based on my report that Peralta had emailed to him yesterday.

Sanchez said, "Grace Hunter phoned your office the day she died."

I looked at her evenly, which probably made her more suspicious. But this was the way I always reacted to shocking news. It took me a moment to deny it, but then she produced a copy of the LUDs—local usage details—from Grace's phone.

She handed me the sheet. Sure enough, our 602 area code number stood out, call placed at four-ten p.m. on the day she died. The call lasted two minutes. I memorized Grace's phone number to write down once they had left.

"Care to explain?" Sanchez looked at me sweetly.

I cared a great deal and had no explanation. I turned on my laptop and opened up the office calendar. It showed that Peralta had given a speech that afternoon at a law-enforcement conference. We hadn't been in the office when the call came in. No one had left a message. Sanchez walked around, looked over my shoulder, and examined the listing.

"How long did you know Grace Hunter?" Jones asked unsweetly.

"I didn't know her when she was alive. There was no message left here. You can see from the LUD that it was a quick call. It probably rang to the answering machine and the caller hung up."

Jones leaned forward in his chair. "Want to try again?"

"No."

We sat for a good five minutes with only the sound of the air conditioner to keep us company. I struggled to maintain my agreeable, relaxed look, but the reality was that it sucked being on the other side of an interrogation. I wasn't used to it. This would be a good time for Peralta to arrive.

"It seems too coincidental," Sanchez said, walking in a circle around the office, studying the large, framed maps of Arizona and Phoenix that I had bought at Wide World of Maps to decorate the place. "You go to San Diego and find her husband, Tim Lewis, murdered. His apartment blows up. Now we know that Grace Hunter called you before she died."

"If she did, we didn't know that," I said. So they were married. "And Tim was a client. He asked us to look into her suspicious death…"

"We know all that." Detective Jones dismissed me with a chop of his hand. "We found your receipt in the blast debris. Hand written on blank paper and signed by you. Real professional operation you have going here, Mapstone. No answering service. Hand-written records."

It was my turn to lean toward him. "We all have our short-comings, Jones. Like when Tim filed a missing person's report on Grace with your department and nobody made the connection that she was already dead and misclassified as a suicide."

Jones' ears started turning red.

"Wait for me in the car, Brent," Sanchez said. He noisily pushed back the chair and slammed the door behind him.

She leaned against Peralta's desk and watched her partner leave, then turned her head toward me.

"Are you the good cop?" I asked.

"Dream on. So no call from Grace Hunter?"

"We never talked to her."

"But she called you."

"Somebody called here with her phone. She was found dead with a new phone that didn't have any called numbers on it. That was in your report."

Sanchez persisted. "Why would this somebody call here?"

I told her the truth: I didn't know. Maybe it was Tim, using her phone. Considering he didn't know she was dead when I first met him, that seemed unlikely, but no need to tell her that.

I didn't say how this call to our office indicated that whoever killed Grace, set off the Claymore mine, and took the baby had made that call to frame us, or at least slow us down, knowing the police would track the LUDs. This had been planned well ahead of the moment Felix walked in that door.

The only alternative was that Grace herself had actually tried to call us. But why? She didn't even know us.

"I can make your life miserable." Sanchez sat in the chair in front of my desk, crossed her legs, and placed long fingers protectively across her belly. "Losing your license will only be the start of the hurt I can put on you."

"I don't doubt it," I said. "But Kimbrough and Peralta go back a long way, and you've got a bungled investigation on your hands. Let me ask you a question, if you don't mind: you pulled Grace's LUDs. Do they match with the phone found in her purse that night?"

Sanchez deflated by degrees. Even her hair deflated.

"No. They don't match. The phone she was carrying that night was scrubbed clean of recent calls. We traced it to a seventy-year-old woman who lives on Clairemont Mesa. It was stolen from her in a purse snatching at Fashion Valley mall."

"So whoever pushed her off that balcony took her real phone."

She nodded.

"How is the hunt for the baby progressing?"

She forced her expression to harden. "That's confidential law-enforcement information and you're only a private dick."

Robin's words again. I stifled a smile.

"Come on, Isabel. You don't have to mimic your jerk colleague."

Two beats, three.

Then: "We don't have anything. Not a damned thing. If I had known she was married or had a kid…" She shook her head. "The vic didn't have any of that information in her purse. Her parents didn't tell us, either."

"I understand." I thought about the wall with our names painted in blood, information I had held back for our protection, and asked about fingerprints.

"The apartment was destroyed. It could take ATF weeks to sort through things and see if there are any usable prints." She cleared her throat. "What do you make of Larry Zisman?"

I laid out the backgrounding I had done. Among a certain group, people who had lived here a long time, Zisman was still beloved for his college-football days. He was a razzle-dazzle quarterback in the glory years of Sun Devil football. He left less of a mark in the NFL, playing for five teams before being forced to retire early.

Zisman was a native Arizonan, attended the old East High School, and came back here to live after he retired from the NFL. Not only that, but to live year-round, not only keep a casita at one of the resorts for the winter months. He had started a non-profit to fund athletics for inner-city schools. He was in demand to give speeches at Kiwanis and Rotary, but removed enough from celebrity to be under the radar in a city with so many comings and goings.

"Did it surprise you that he had a lover on the side?"

I held out empty hands. "Who ever knows? But, yes, a little. From what I picked up, Larry Zip was so full of clean living that he might have been mistaken for a Mormon."

"Do you think he killed Grace Hunter?"

"He's physically capable of it. Former athlete. As a reserve officer, he would have gone through police academy training."

She made a few notes.

I said, "It would be pretty stupid, though, to push her off his own condo balcony. He'd know that he would be the prime suspect. Better to strangle her and dump her body in the East County."

"Unless," she said, "it was an act of passion and he did it in the moment."

"Right. But then you have the problem of the alibi, of him being on his boat."

I was only trying to be convivial enough to get Detective Sanchez out of the office. This couldn't be a mutually beneficial relationship because Peralta and I were concealing critical information. We had dug this hole a little scoop at a time, for good reasons at the moment, and now we were in deep. Too deep.

She thought about what I had said regarding Zisman, twirling a strand of her hair.

"I think he could have done it."

"You interviewed him that night and cleared him," I said.

"I read your report," she said. "After our ass-chewing from Kimbrough and before we got on the plane, I dug a little more. The man at the next boat is a good friend with Zisman, you know. He's from Arizona, too. You people really need to find another summer escape. The man is a developer who used Zisman as a spokesman for some of his properties. He might be lying for him."

Zisman hadn't figured in any of my theories about the case—not that I had formed many yet. I had been focused on getting out of that apartment before my body was turned into an aerosol state, and then on examining whether Grace had actually committed suicide.

"What about Tim?"

I cocked my head.

She went on. "Maybe he followed her to Zisman's condo and found out she was cheating on him. Oldest motive in the world."

To me, he barely had the guts to change a baby's diaper, much less kill his wife or have the strength to do it in such a physical manner. Sure, people would surprise you, especially if money or sex were concerned. If so, he would have had to do a good job feigning surprise and sorrow when I told him Grace was dead. And been tough enough to slit his own throat and wire his apartment to explode.

I remembered a case in Scottsdale years ago, where a man cut the throats of his family, shot them, set the house on fire, and blew it up. They never caught him.

Detective Sanchez also didn't know that our names had been written in blood on the apartment wall. Tim Lewis didn't do that in the seconds before his carotid arteries bled out. Then there was yesterday's phone call, Mister UNKNOWN saying he had detonated the Claymore and with his aerial theater implying he either had the baby or had murdered it.

"Tim was genuinely torn apart when I told him Grace was dead," I said. "And remember, the pimp was beating him up when I got there. And if Tim was Grace's killer, who took the baby?"

She sighed. "I wish I could keep things simple. Occam's Razor, right? My ass is on the line for this now, and there's a hundred local, state, and federal investigators living in my shit because of that explosion and kidnapping."

I appreciated a woman who could quote the classics, but this was one instance where the least complex hypothesis wouldn't do.

"The pimp is Keavon William Briscoe," she said, spelling the first name. "He's middling, not a big player. This is a guy who provides prostitutes for sailors and Marines on leave and runs streetwalkers, not escorts for big-time executives and legislators."

"He claimed Grace worked for him."

"Maybe she did. It wouldn't be the first time a coed made some money on the side. The reason I don't like Briscoe for this is that he was in jail on the night of April twenty-second, a parole violation. He had a baggie of pot in the car. He'll probably go back to prison but it gives him an alibi for the one-eighty-seven." The homicide.

"How did he find where she lived?"

"That's the thing," she said. "He was cruising O.B. on April twenty-first and said he saw her, followed her home, and was driving around the block for a parking space when a marked unit stopped him and arrested him. His sister didn't bail him out for several days."

"Did you execute a search warrant?"

"Don't piss me off, Mapstone." The dark eyes deepened. "I usually don't fuck up cases. Yes, we gave his place a total colonoscopy and didn't even find a cheap gun, much less explosives. That brings me back to Zisman. If Zisman found out that Grace was tricking on the side, he would have even more motive to kill her. Maybe it's his baby. Maybe he has access to military explosives."

I nodded, but I had seen this so many times: a detective latches onto a theory and does whatever it takes to make it stick and clear the case. Back when I untangled cold cases for the Sheriff's Office, this was often the original sin in what turned out to be an unsolved case, or worse, one that sent an innocent person to prison.

I also appreciated the heat she was feeling from the brass.

Sanchez didn't know the full extent of Grace's entrepreneurship. It sounded as if she was unsure if she had even been a real prostitute or only a wild child.

"What about her friend, Addison?"

"Addison Conway," Sanchez said. "Jones talked to her. She went back home to Oklahoma at the end of the semester. Grace hadn't made a call to her since March."

"So did Zisman and Grace have contact the day of her death?"

She sighed. "It's not in the LUDs. I went back through two years of records and didn't find his number. Grace called her mother on the twenty-first. She received a call from the human resources department at Qualcomm that same day. She called your office on the twenty-second. That's the only call she made on the day she died. The other thing is, the semen inside her doesn't match Tim's DNA. In fact, it shows evidence that she had sex with three different men, but none of them her husband."

The information exchange was definitely working in my favor. I was processing it, thinking out loud. "Grace had gone to a lot of trouble to drop out and get away from guys like Larry Zisman..."

A big smile played across her face. "Until she needed him. Come on, Mapstone, don't be naïve. Babies are expensive and there's college coming right up on a parent. You probably have kids, so you understand. She hadn't even started her job at Qualcomm. Her bank account was drawn way down, only six hundred dollars."

I wondered if they had checked all her bank accounts, but said nothing.

Sanchez continued: "What if she showed up at Zisman's condo unannounced and wanted money? Former pro football player—she's got to figure he's loaded. Pay up or I'll tell your wife. Better than that, pay up or I'll tell your wife I had your baby. Zisman loses it and tosses her off the balcony, goes to his boat, and has his friends cover for him."

"Wouldn't Grace have been seen coming into the lobby? Or him going?"

"The night concierge didn't come on duty until eleven," she said. "Nobody was at the front desk for eight hours that day. They've been having staffing problems. In San Diego, 'sunshine dollars' only go so far."

I thought back to our visit to the condo. "But the building has a card-key entrance. Nobody could get in without using the card."

"Unless somebody coming in held the door for them. Anyway, after the body hit the concrete, the concierge runs out to the pool area. So if Zisman left, nobody would see him."

"Cameras?"

She shook her head. "The lobby cam was broken all week."

It didn't seem so neat to me. But the former football hero was in her radar lock.

"Have you interviewed Zisman again?"

The luminous black hair shook. "He's not answering his phone. But I've got a lot of questions when he resurfaces."

I still wondered about the missing hours in Grace's day. I said, "Why would she leave the apartment without telling Tim?"

She shrugged. "Men aren't the only ones who lie about sex."

Chapter Twenty-four

Peralta still wasn't at the office when I had finished writing up the notes from my meeting with the San Diego detectives, and I was starting to worry, which was silly given Peralta's ability to protect himself and others.

My concern was forgotten when I buzzed open the gate for Lindsey. It closed and locked automatically after she pulled in. Lindsey in a miniskirt would chase away every concern, to be shamelessly shallow about it. She also carried lunch and my new iPhone, which FedEx had delivered that morning. After putting down the bag, she gave me a kiss and a hug that seemed almost normal. Her hand went up inside my shirt across my belly and onto my chest.

"Was this Robin's?" She touched the cross of Navajo silver.

I hesitated, then nodded.

"May I have it?"

"Of course." I removed it and slipped the chain over her head. She bent toward me as if receiving some kind of decoration.

The Order of the Lost Sister.

I pulled the cross around to fall above her breasts and fluffed out her hair.

"Thank you." She was trying not to cry, so she made herself laugh. "This way it won't tickle me when you're on top."

I tried to hold her, but almost immediately she dropped to her knees and started unzipping my slacks.

"Lindsey." I pulled her up and hugged her. "Just be with me."

"Yeah." Her voice was one notch above a whisper but I heard the sardonic tremolo. She was barely with me. Lindsey's body was in my arms but Lindsey was somewhere else. This appearance was conditional. She wasn't wearing her wedding band. It wasn't her fault. All she had of her child was a tattoo.

A few days ago I had nearly died, despite the claim by UNKNOWN that he waited before detonating the mine. I remembered the chunk of wall torpedoing into the pool inches from my head. I was living on bonus time but did she care? She had said that she had messed up, but maybe that meant getting fired, not leaving me. *Lindsey, just be with me.* What a damned fool I was.

I pushed her over to the desk, kissing her, caressing the soft skin beneath the hem of her shirt. After enough kissing to feel her body relax and even wilt, I lifted her onto the desktop, removed her sandals, and slid off her panties. Sitting in the chair, I started sucking her toes and licking her perfect ankles, slowly working my way north with my mouth and tongue. The fabric of her miniskirt tickled the top of my nose. She didn't resist. I held my arms behind her so she could lean back against my hands. She clutched my head with her hands, bent her knees, and rested her warm feet atop my shoulders.

Circles and slides and figure eights. Cheerleader legs. I played her, made it go on a long time, loving being so connected to everything she was feeling, loving giving her pleasure. I even knew when she was ready to intertwine her hands in mine, gripping me for the grand last movement.

Afterward, she slid into my lap and this time didn't resist being held.

"I love you." I couldn't help myself. It came out involuntarily.

She didn't say anything, but nestled closer.

I was a fool. The Bettye LaVette song played in my head: *Everything Is Broken.*

Sex would keep anxiety and time and death at bay. I never have panic attacks if I am getting laid. I had to be satisfied with this eternal truth for the moment. But sex with Lindsey made me lose focus, made me forget, made me fall in love with her again, ensured that I might withdraw my emotional siege machines.

Steps on broken pavement.

The sound was so soft I wasn't sure I had even heard it over the periodic whoosh of cars on Grand. Lindsey noticed my expression and I held up a hand. Someone was walking across the lot, very slowly. It couldn't be Peralta, whose entrance was announced with the alert of the gate opening, followed by roaring engine and bumping suspension. My blood stopped pumping for a couple of seconds. Someone had jumped the fence, no easy maneuver. It could be anybody. The office door was unlocked.

Mail, she mouthed?

I shook my head. The mail lady came later in the afternoon and the gate was locked.

"Get under the desk."

She didn't question me and scrambled into the cave where my legs would normally go. I pulled out the Python, dropped to my knees, and stayed close.

"Are you armed?" I whispered.

She shook her head.

I slipped the Airlite from my pocket and handed it to her.

The only fancy furniture in our office was our chairs and the leather sofa. Otherwise, most of the rest was second-hand, including the two heavy Steelcase desks that looked as if they had once been part of a 1960 secretarial pool. You could fire a rocket-propelled grenade at them and barely make a dent.

I waited for the door to open. Maybe the gate had somehow jammed open, an innocuous malfunction, and the footsteps belonged to a new client, a traveling salesman, or a Jehovah's Witness who would knock and say, "Hello, is anyone here?"

The room was silent.

I didn't dare move to catch a glimpse. The desk sat so close to the ground, I was confident that if someone did come in he couldn't see us. That would change if he walked behind Peralta's desk, or toward the Danger Room. By then, I would have him in my gun sights, unless he was prepared.

If I get hit, come out blazing, I telepathed to the frightened blue eyes watching me.

The floor was old and creaked when you walked on it. The hinges squeaked when the door opened. But nobody tried to enter. The sound of footsteps came again, this time from the carport. Whoever had come into the lot was still out there. The palm of my hand was sweating into the custom combat grips of the Python.

Then, nothing.

I had to let a good five minutes pass before I dared slither out on the far side of the desk, ready for action. But no one was there. Waiting was the safe way. But it also ensured that I couldn't see if our visitor had a vehicle. For that matter, I also couldn't get a license tag number. We waited. Finally, I stood and locked the door. Peering out the blinds, I could see the gate was indeed shut.

Chapter Twenty-five

Not long afterwards, Peralta arrived, sweeping into the room like a parade.

"Lindsey."

"Sheriff."

She was sitting on my desk. I stopped stroking her knees, said nothing, and resolved to avoid his glance.

"Lindsey!" Sharon's voice. I looked up, and she walked in carrying a bag of hot dogs from Johnnie's on Thomas. This was fun food.

As Lindsey and Sharon embraced, Peralta's eyes found mine, and he knew what we had been doing, and his eyes actually twinkled like a tough Saint Nick of nooners. I felt my face flushing.

"We're all here together, like it should be," Peralta announced like the paterfamilias. As if anything were settled. "So let's eat and get to work!"

Lindsey had fixed us healthy salads, to which I added a Chicago dog from Johnnie's.

"He's too gaunt," Sharon whispered to Lindsey.

I told Peralta about the visit from the San Diego cops and the mystery guest who had been in the parking lot but never came in. His forehead tightened as he listened, but he only dived into lunch.

Peralta, with his mouth full: "Sharon talked to Tim Lewis' parents," which I translated from *shawob awked a wimoois barents*. It had taken many years of listening to Peralta over breakfasts at Susan's Diner and lunches at Durant's to master this particular dialect.

I said, "They talked to you?"

"I used my winning people skills," she said, pulling a chair closer to his desk as she ate her salad like a lady. "Empathy, trust, respect..."

"She flashed her credentials," Peralta said, amazingly pausing in his eating. "Show them."

She held a wallet identifying her as a police psychologist for the San Francisco Police Department.

"After being married to him for thirty years, who could be more qualified?" She winked at him.

"Plus, Tim's mother had all of Sharon's books," he said.

"As I was saying..." Sharon reclaimed the floor, and Peralta, uncharacteristically, shut up. "The mother's name is Vicki, father named Mike. They were both there, a nice couple, and were very generous with their time considering all they've been through. They're devastated by Tim's death and sick about their grandson. The police have tapped their phones, but they haven't heard anything, much less a ransom demand. They don't understand why anyone would have killed Tim or Grace."

I actually swallowed my food before speaking. "So they knew Grace?"

Sharon nodded. "They met her when she and Tim first started dating. After they got together again, they saw her more than a dozen times, including at their wedding, which was held in Riverside, and when she gave birth. They loved her. That was the word each one used."

I listened to Sharon and was so glad to see her. She was a couple of inches shorter than Lindsey's five-seven, but was still in great shape with the black hair and angelic face off a tapestry in a Mexican church. In a way words couldn't describe, she centered our world. I had known her when she was a young, uncertain mother, then as she put herself through college and graduate school, not always with Peralta's emotional support.

This had been one of the old battlegrounds between Peralta and me. Then she had hit it big and finally she had divorced him. But apparently "finally" had a second act.

She said what we had heard before: Grace was stable, not suicidal, and had no enemies. Tim's childhood sounded suburban normal, the kind that produced golf pros or lone mass shooters. And Grace had done a very good job of keeping people from knowing how she had made money working through college.

"They didn't have a clue," Sharon said. "But the world of high-end call girls can be very different from the sexual exploitation you find with streetwalkers or immigrants from Eastern Europe who thought they were getting a trip to America for a job in a factory and it turns out to be a very different kind of assembly line. What Grace was doing was even more specialized, working on her own. Most work for agencies. But powerful men will pay very well for the services."

"I bet." Peralta licked his fingers. Sharon shot him a civilizing glance and he stopped, using his napkins instead.

"These men pay for the sexual skills, no question. The more versatile, the better. They think they have a woman in her sexual prime who really wants to have sex and enjoys it. Many of them are narcissists who want a beautiful young woman on their arms. It's a prestige thing. If he's an executive, it's gotten too risky to hit on subordinates. So a discreet hooker is the thing."

Lindsey said, "Is it only about the prestige and the sex?"

Sharon shook her head. "Many of the johns also want an emotional connection that they feel they aren't getting from their wives. If Grace was all these things, plus polished, cheerful, intelligent, sophisticated, and romantic, then she could get top dollar. In San Francisco, I met call girls who were getting more than five thousand an hour."

"An hour?" Peralta raised an eyebrow.

"Yes."

"Considering she was their daughter-in-law," I said, "it's better that they didn't know her past."

I certainly didn't know Lindsey's recent past.

Sharon said. "They liked being a family to her. It sounds as if Grace's mother was totally self-absorbed and her father was even worse. Tim's parents went to her graduation last year. Neither of Grace's parents did. Her father was at a golf tournament with his buddy, some washed up pro football player."

I stopped in mid-bite and pushed the hot dog away.

"Larry Zisman?" I asked.

"That the name," she said. "He was a star for the Sun Devils back in the seventies. I remember."

Occam's Razor, indeed.

Peralta attacked his second chili dog with more aggression than usual. A Scottsdale McMansion of possibilities had opened up. One room contained the obvious, that Zisman was a client. Another held the possibility that Zisman had hit on his buddy's daughter and gotten it for free. The rest of the floor plan was too twisted to think about over lunch.

I said, "Maybe Zisman wasn't her client."

"He wasn't," Lindsey said.

Everybody turned to her.

"It took me about two minutes to break into that flash drive," she said. "It contained an Excel spread sheet with sixty two clients: names, Social Security numbers, driver's license numbers, dates, and amounts. No Larry Zisman."

Nobody took a bite.

I said, "The johns gave her that information?"

"They would have to do that for an escort agency," Sharon said. "It helps ensure safety."

"But," I said, "Zisman knew Grace's father and covered it up."

I could see the slow burn on Peralta's features over Hunter lying to him. Maybe Grace's father didn't know his daughter had been intimate with Larry Zip. That was the most charitable explanation. But he sure knew that Grace had fallen out of Zip's condo, and yet he hadn't admitted their friendship either to Peralta or Isabel Sanchez.

"There's something else." Lindsey nodded toward our front parking lot. "The Prelude has a GPS tracking device tucked inside the front fender. You can buy one in any spy shop."

My legs and feet felt very heavy on the floor.

"What did you do with it?" Peralta asked.

"I left it there." She ate a bite of salad and dabbed her lovely, orgasm-flushed face with a paper napkin. "If they don't know we found it, we have an edge. From what Dave says, San Diego PD has a hard-on for Zisman now that Dave's shown that Grace didn't kill herself. Maybe we can work with them."

"They're not going to work with private detectives," Peralta said.

After a long silence, I looked at him. "These scumbags have had the upper hand from before Felix walked in that door. They placed a call to our number using Grace's cell phone so the cops would be suspicious of us. I'm tired of playing defense. What's our next move?"

He inhaled and rose up in his chair. "I've heard a person's cell phone can be tracked. Not only the calls they make and receive, but the locations of the user at any point. Is that true?"

"Absolutely," Lindsey said. "Wherever you go, your cell phone sends data and it's mapped. And the cell providers keep those records. So somebody could find out Grace's moves on any given date." She paused and looked into her lap, and then she pushed her hair out of her face. "These companies have very sophisticated security and firewalls."

"Can you hack it?"

My appetite fled. I stood and stalked the six feet to his desk. "I can't believe what you asked her to do. That's a federal crime."

He shot up out of his chair and stabbed a finger at me. "What's your plan, Mapstone? Get blown up again? You might not be so fast next time. We've been played for chumps and our clients are dead. Do you know why? I don't. What I do know is it's only a matter of time before we're dead, especially if they get that flash drive."

"Then we'll take them on. Why bring Lindsey and Sharon into it?"

"Because they're already in it with us." He spat the words. "These assholes are cleaning up loose ends. Tim and the baby were loose ends. Why do they have a tracker on your car? Because they're afraid of you? No. So they can find you and kill you when the time is right. Who's going to help you? Your new buddy, Isabel? Not when she finds out you've been withholding evidence."

He wasn't the only one running hot. I went from zero to asshole in three seconds. I barked, "Lindsey could go to prison! Put your own ass on the line. Put mine. But leave her out of it! Let San Diego PD track Grace's movements. Somebody cased our office. My god, are you nuts? We're not safe here. We're not safe at home. You said it yourself. We're loose ends."

So much for our convivial reunited family.

And then Vesuvius went dormant. He sat back in his executive chair and pushed his hair back with both hands. In a conversational voice: "We are safe as long as they are willing to bargain for the flash drive. That's our hole card. They want it badly. If they hurt us or kill us, no flash drive."

"Did the guy in the parking lot know that?" I told him about our visitor.

"Yes. He was probably some vagrant. If not, he was only on a recon mission."

He looked so damned sure of himself.

"Now," he said, "As for San Diego PD, I would leave this to them, David, but I don't know how sophisticated they are or how big their caseload is. They might figure this out tomorrow or next month or never. The more I meddle, the more suspicious Kimbrough is going to be that we're holding back evidence. I would hack those phone records myself, but I don't know how. Lindsey does. She spent eight years in the Sheriff's Office Cybercrimes Unit. She can reverse-engineer that knowledge."

"I know how to be a hacker." Lindsey's voice was small but sounded weightier than our explosions.

It wasn't as easy for me to dial back my anger, but I tried to match her soft voice. "Don't do this, Lindsey, please."

I had just, maybe, gotten her back. Now I would lose her again.

She took in my imploring glance, studied Sharon's practiced calm, and then looked back at Peralta.

"Can you cover your tracks?" he asked.

Her look was that of the old insouciant Lindsey I had fallen for years ago, in her black miniskirt, nose stud, and irreverence that was somehow never cruel. The quarter smile that got the inside joke. The one who would answer him: *They'll never know I was there.*

Now I knew that within my haunted beauty was her mother's voice telling her she was never good enough, her "Linda Unit" as Robin had called it. I had no question about my wife's skills. But the risks seemed intolerable. There had to be another way.

She looked at Peralta. "You always said I was the best."

"Then do it."

Chapter Twenty-six

Peralta took Lindsey and Sharon outside while I called Artie Dominguez at the Sheriff's Office.

"How's the best detective in the department?"

His usual ebullient laugh was subdued. "David. Long time, long time. What's it like working one-on-one with the Big Man every day?"

"You can imagine." I asked him how he was. He snorted.

"He's missed," he said. "I might come be a private dick myself soon. You won't believe how fucked up things are. Let's say command these days isn't very friendly if you have a last name like Dominguez. I used to get the best homicides. Lately, I've been on auto theft."

"No shit."

"Real shit, man. Twenty-five years and this is what I get. They're out there playing Border Patrol and everything else has gone to hell. Response times are way down. Serious cases are going untouched. The jail's a mess. Wait until you read about the El Mirage sex cases we're not investigating. But rounding up the *campesinos* standing outside Home Depot makes the old farts in Sun City and the East Valley feel safer. Sucks."

"Can you run a couple of names through NCIC and ViCap for me?"

"Sure. It'll take a couple of days so I can do it without my new boss asking questions."

I gave him Larry Zisman and Bob Hunter. He was aggravated with me that I didn't have Social Security numbers and dates of birth. That would mean more work.

"If it makes you feel any better, I have a list of about sixty names with SS numbers that I'd like to email you at home and have you check, too. I know it'll take time."

"Damn, Mapstone. We ought to set you up down here with a desk."

"You know how that would go over with the new guy."

He sighed like a martyr.

"I'll owe you," I added.

"I'll add it to your tab. That it?"

Not quite. I wanted him to check ViCAP—the massive FBI database—for suspicious deaths involving young women falling bound from high places. Extra points if they were high-priced prostitutes. And Claymore mine explosions.

After a pause. "Was that you in San Diego?"

"Yep."

"Fuck me," he said. "I thought you guys were going to be peeping on unfaithful husbands."

"You know Peralta would get bored with that in an hour or less."

"True," he said. "Watch your ass, David."

Then I went into the Danger Room to review the footage of the outside security cameras. I backed it up until it showed a new sedan pull in the dirt beside the south fence. It was a white Chevy Impala. A man got out and looked around. He was young and Anglo with a high-and-tight haircut, shaved on the sides with a weed-like tuft on top. Put him in a military uniform and give him a stolen Claymore and things started to come together. He was no vagrant.

I watched as he climbed on the Impala's roof and expertly vaulted the fence, then walked to the carport. Switching to that camera, I saw him open the Prelude driver's door and lean inside. He popped the seatback forward and climbed into the back. Next, he popped the trunk button and went back there.

He was searching for the flash drive. He repeated the move on the passenger side, and then returned to the Impala, looked around again, and got inside.

Switching to the first camera, I saw him back out to leave and expose the license plate. Nevada. I zoomed in, made a screen shot, and printed it out. It was probably a rental car.

Sharon was standing behind me.

"I'm worried about you."

"Me, too." Why deny it?

"You've changed, David. Lindsey feels it, too."

"That's nice. Another excuse for her to leave me."

She's not going to leave you. It would have been nice to hear that, but Sharon didn't say it.

"Mike told me what you went through with the cartels and the old gangster in Chandler," she said. "Nobody could go through that without being changed."

"And Robin being murdered."

Sharon watched me with those big empathetic eyes.

Yes, there was that. And the trial would soon begin. It was another reason I didn't want to read the local newspaper. It wouldn't be covered because the defendant was a drug addict who killed someone. But because the victim was a blond, middle-class woman who lived in a historic district and was the sister-in-law of a former deputy sheriff—that was news. I would have to testify. I dreaded the effect this would have on Lindsey.

"And losing your child," she said. "You two have gone through so much loss in such a short time. But I don't want to see this destroy two people I love. Your child wouldn't want that. Robin wouldn't want that."

I realized my fists were balled up and forced my hands to relax. "We'll never know, now will we?"

"Mike told me how you chose not to kill the woman who shot Robin," she said. "The David I know would have made that choice."

I didn't answer. It was true: I stalked her, found her, but turned her over to the cops. What Sharon didn't know was that I had the woman on her knees with a dishrag in her mouth, and in my hands I held the assassin's .22 caliber pistol with a silencer. I was about to pull the trigger when my cell phone rang and the readout said, "Lindsey." So I didn't pull the trigger. Part of me still regretted it. Nor did Sharon know that the better angels of my nature watched helplessly as I wrapped duct tape around the gangster's mouth and let the Zetas crew carry him out of his Witness Protection Program-funded suburban Chandler house. Or how I rolled the pieces into place for his hit man to be on the receiving end of a hit himself in jail.

I didn't regret those things.

Sharon said, "You have to be willing to give it time. Lindsey loves you. That's why she's here."

Time again. As if I had it.

I said, "I'm really trying."

Sharon hugged me and whispered for me to be good to myself. I didn't know how. We walked back into the office to greet Lindsey and Peralta.

"There's a tracker on his truck, too," Lindsey said.

"She has a very cool scanner." Peralta was like a little kid. He was enamored with gadgets. He was enamored with Lindsey. Who wasn't?

He went on: "It picked the tracker right up. Might be a good idea to check the whole office." He added, "If you don't mind."

Lindsey smiled politely. "This tracking device is identical to the one on the Honda. It's not a logger, the thing people use to follow the movements of a cheating lover. The logger maps out their movements and then you can see where they've been. These are real-time trackers that feed right into a Google map display in a following car. They want to be able to follow at a safe distance and not be detected."

"Are they sophisticated?" Peralta asked.

"Not really," she said. "They're certainly not federal issue. But they're battery operated. The battery might last a month if they track the car an hour or two a day. Less if they track us for more time or the heat really kicks up. Otherwise, they have to replace the batteries." She sighed. "Or they're on a limited timeline so it doesn't matter."

After Lindsey was done, I told Peralta about my review of the security camera. The man with the high-and-tight hair was casing the place.

Peralta sat on the edge of his desk. "It's time to take the war to these assholes."

My anger had been replaced with exhaustion.

"It's over." I held out the truck-stop cell phone. "It's been twenty-four hours since he's called." I was about to say, "The baby is dead," but a look at Lindsey stopped me.

Peralta shook his Easter Island head. "If it was over, that guy wouldn't have been on our property, searching the Prelude. We need to shake things up. Here's how we're going to do it."

Chapter Twenty-seven

An ancient Greek poet wrote, "The fox knows many things but the hedgehog knows one big thing." The philosopher Isaiah Berlin turned that into an influential essay on writers and intellectuals. I was usually a fox. The kidnapping had made me a hedgehog. The single experience defining our lives right now was the kidnapping.

No matter how many law-enforcement agencies were investigating it, I had received the call. I had been bombed with the bloody baby doll—a warning, according to Peralta. It was certainly done in a way that got my attention. The caller told me he had something I wanted. It could only be Tim and Grace's baby. And he said I had something he wanted. That could only be the flash drive. But how did that make sense? He had to know that we would break the encryption and download the client names.

Lindsey wondered if some information was hidden elsewhere on the drive. If so, that could make this particular piece of plastic very valuable, and Mister UNKNOWN was assuming we didn't know the hidden data were there. Finding it was another task for her.

My task was to be bait.

Peralta called the shots. He had investigated hundreds of kidnappings. I had solved only one, from 1940. So I had to follow his lead.

At sundown, I went out alone in the Honda Prelude. Well, not quite alone: for company I had Mister Colt Python and Messrs.

Smith and Wesson with the Airlite. And several Speedloaders of extra ammo for each revolver. I also had two cell phones: my new iPhone was plugged into my ears and the truck-stop cell, whose number UNKNOWN had, was on the seat beside me.

I drove east on Camelback Road, a spectacular orange sunset to my back, maddeningly thick traffic ahead of me. It used to be that if you went the speed limit in the city of Phoenix, you would make every light with only a few exceptions. Now the freeway entrances and a few million more people had complicated that, so I ended up missing almost every light. It gave me a chance to see the massive ugliness of a city that had grown so fast it hadn't had time to clean up after itself. Things would be better in full dark. Phoenix was beautiful at night.

Peralta was on the phone. "I'm about half a mile behind you, giving you plenty of room."

"Where's the tracker on your truck?"

"It's sitting on a table at your house, like a good captured tracker."

That made me laugh. I stopped when he told me Lindsey was with him. Not only did she have work to do, most of all I didn't want her in danger if this excursion went sideways. I kept that to myself.

"Where's Sharon?"

"She's renting us a motel room."

That was new. I decided not to ask questions but to focus on my task.

The real estate got nicer at Twenty-Fourth Street, with its alternative downtown of office towers, fancy condos, and the Ritz Carlton. The magical Biltmore Fashion Park had gotten a facelift a few years back and now looked like any suburban mall. Half a mile north was the entrance to the Biltmore resort. Only a few blocks south, the once solidly middle-class neighborhoods had turned over. Now people called it "The Sonoran Biltmore."

I swam the traffic current headed to Scottsdale. If someone were following me, I would never know it. But I deliberately avoided any cute tactics to lose a tail. I wanted a tail. Camelback

Mountain loomed straight in front, its head rising first. At Forty-Fourth Street, I turned left and climbed gradually into Paradise Valley.

The road turned east and became McDonald Drive. I wanted to look up and see the Praying Monk formation on the camel's head, but too many headlights intruded. Some toff honked at me for not going the mandatory fifteen miles over the speed limit, then sped around me in his BMW. Phoenicians never used to honk. I used to own a BMW. Patty gave it to me. Lindsey wasn't sorry when some bad guys pushed it out of a parking garage three stories down into Adams Street. I wanted to do the same with this prick.

After the big intersection at Tatum Drive, McDonald calmed down. The area became low-density and very expensive residential, with few streetlights, no sidewalks, and plenty of gates. One would never know that a huge city enveloped this blessed precinct on every side. The road ran to the north of Camelback Mountain. Across Paradise Valley was the mass of Mummy Mountain. I never ceased being moved by these works of nature and how they stood out darker than the night sky. For a few seconds my rearview mirror held no headlights. Then some appeared in the distance. My gut tightened.

Bob Hunter lived in a slummy lot for Paradise Valley, meaning his house was a large, perfectly respectable mid-century ranch. But it was definitely lower end than its neighbors. Most of the similar-age houses along Fifty-Second Place had been torn down and replaced by more impressive mansions. Lush desert landscaping predominated and the land was gentle hills. Paradise Valley had filled in since I was young, but it was still low-density. The properties were spaced far enough apart that a neighbor wouldn't hear a gunshot. A prominent doctor and his wife had recently been bound and shot, and their bodies were only discovered because the meth-addicted killer also set fire to their house.

For my purposes, Bob Hunter's house had an added benefit: no gate. I killed the headlights and slowly came to a stop on the concrete circle in front of the house. Lights were on inside, as

well as on a pair of ornamental wrought iron, amber-tinted porch
sconces. If someone had seen me, I would know soon enough.
Either he would come to the door, or, more likely, I would find
the Paradise Valley cops pulling in behind me.

Neither happened. After ten minutes, Peralta called.

"Report."

"I'm sitting here. Nobody has even driven by. The mountains
look beautiful."

"We're cruising," Peralta said. "I don't want to get too close."

I told him it was too bad we couldn't reverse the tracker and
find out if I was actually being followed.

"I didn't bring that kind of technology home with me, Dave."
I heard Lindsey's voice over his speaker. She had said *home*. That
was a good sign, right?

I kept scanning my mirrors and windshield, trying to get as
much of a three-hundred-sixty-degree view as possible. Nothing
was moving behind the ocotillos and, behind a white wall, the
tall stand of oleanders that blocked off the backyard. I tried to
imagine Grace growing up here, requiring a car for everything.
It was so different from the real neighborhood where I was a
child. It was easy to envision her counting the days until she
could get away.

It was harder to put together Bob Hunter with his golf buddy
Larry Zisman, a friend close enough that he took priority over his
own daughter's graduation. San Diego PD had notified Hunter
of Grace's death; he had flown there to identify the body. He
had known where she had died. They would have asked him if
he knew the owner of the condominium from where she fell.
And he had lied, to Sanchez and to Peralta. Why? That he had
been content to allow the police to classify Grace's death as a
suicide ran a dark charge up the back of my neck.

After half an hour, an amazing time for a beat-up Honda to
go unnoticed in Paradise Valley, I slid it into gear and slowly
coasted out onto the street, then turned north toward Lincoln
Drive. I kept my headlights off and drove slowly. Two hundred
yards ahead I pulled on the emergency brake and stopped the

car without showing taillights. And yet: nothing. If anybody was behind me, he was running without headlights, too.

He could also be a mile away, tracking me on a laptop or a tablet. He didn't have to show himself. But it was better to pretend I was worried about a tail that had me in sight. That way, he could continue to assume we hadn't found the tracking device. So I went ahead with the game.

Lights on again, I sat at the intersection of busy Lincoln Drive. I checked in with Peralta who saw no signs of anyone following me.

"Should we call it off?"

"No," he said. "The guy is out there. He's good. Keep going."

Keeping going meant a drive to Tempe, some ten miles away through heavy traffic. Getting over to the Pima Freeway and zooming south would have gotten me there much faster. But Peralta wanted me on surface streets. So I turned right on Lincoln and took it to Scottsdale Road.

If Central Avenue had been the main commercial thorough-fare from territorial days through the early nineties, Scottsdale Road—and miles of loop freeways containing office "parks"—had taken over that title since then. When I was a child, the intersection with Lincoln had been out in the desert. Now it was deep in the metropolitan blob.

Scottsdale itself was a long, narrow slice between the city of Phoenix and the Salt River Indian Community, the renamed and, thanks to casinos and development beside the freeway, very rich rez. But Scottsdale, oh, Scottsdale, sang of new money, especially up north where it spread east into the McDowell foothills and the people bragged of never coming south of Bell Road, much less to "the Mexican Detroit." Meaning, Phoenix.

Scottsdale was exclusivity and championship golf, celebrities in the wintertime and the weirdness that comes with having more money than brains. It was the capital of plastic surgery: Silicone Valley. City leaders would never allow anything as plebian as light rail. As a result, its traffic was a nightmare, even with most of the wealthy hitting the summer lifeboats for their other homes in the San Juan Islands or other cooler climes. And Scottsdale Road was full of the same schlocky development as the rest of Phoenix, only with some expensive façades and more expensively done traffic berms.

Once Scottsdale had been a sweet little add-on to Phoenix, part faux cowboy tourist trap—the West's Most Western Town— part artist's colony. Now it sucked up capital, development, and retail sales from the center city like an Electrolux. Yet it never seemed like a happy place. The politics were poison. Every section and street seemed to vie for the power to look down on everybody else. Scottsdale wanted to be Santa Fe or South Beach, but it was neither artistic nor sexy. Nobody would set a cop show in Scottsdale. A golf or plastic surgery show, maybe.

I suffered the unending traffic jam south past hotels, expensive shopping strips and restaurants, Fashion Square, across the Arizona Canal, and dropping down to Fifth Avenue and Old Scottsdale. Here, a little humanity showed in the scale of the streetscape. A block away was the wonderful Poisoned Pen Bookstore.

South of Old Town, the shopping strips became more downscale and behind them were ordinary tract houses built in the sixties. At Roosevelt, I crossed over into Tempe and the street changed names: Rural Road. It had once been rural. Now all the fields were long gone. The main Arizona State University campus loomed on the right, including the stadium where Larry Zisman had thrown his legendary passes. Then the big new Biodesign Institute. Who knew what they were working on?

By then, I was ready to chew my arm off from the traffic. The average Phoenician made this kind of drive or even longer every day. How did they stand it? The only place I felt comfortable was in the old city. This was my hometown, but it didn't feel like home any more. The Japanese Flower Gardens were gone. The miles of citrus groves were gone. Why did I stay here? I would miss my friends in the old neighborhood, the familiar diorama of mountains, the smell of citrus blossoms in the spring, not much else.

Larry Zisman lived at The Lakes, a series of subdivisions that took over the farm fields south of Baseline Road starting in the seventies. The tract houses were built around little lakes, hence its namesake. Tempe had made a fetish of artificial lakes, most notably Town Lake, contained within dams on the Salt River.

After some wandering along the curvilinear streets, I found Zisman's house. Unlike some of the houses in The Lakes, it lacked any old-growth shade trees. One pitiful little tree was planted on a small, square lawn. Beyond that stood a stucco house with one window, a door through an arch, and the mandatory large garage door and driveway. Above the garage was a second story. The lights were off. Modest and relatively small, it seemed like an odd home for a one-time football star, but maybe he lost most of his money. Maybe he preferred it here, not far from his college glory days. I pulled directly in front, shut off my lights and engine, and checked in with Peralta. My stomach became a sea of acid. This was as risky as Paradise Valley. Everything about Lindsey's old Prelude screamed "Does Not Belong Here." Signs proclaimed a neighborhood watch. I didn't know how long I dared sit.

Not long.

The Tempe Police cruiser slid in behind me and a spotlight swung white light into the Prelude.

I put my hands on top of the steering wheel and tried to mentally untangle my internal organs. The officer or officers would be looking me over, typing my license plate in for wants and warrants, wondering if the driver was armed. That was my first problem. My second problem: if the person following with the GPS tracker had me in sight, he might misinterpret this interaction. He had ordered me on Sunday to bring no law enforcement. Now here I was, with law enforcement come to me.

"Turn on the overhead light please." A female voice. She was right behind me, in a proper protective stance. I flipped on the dome.

"David Mapstone!"

She came into sight and slid her flashlight into her equipment belt.

"Hey, Amy."

Amy Taylor had been a patrol deputy for the Sheriff's Office. I had worked with her on a number of occasions before she left for a better-paying job in Tempe. She looked the same, attractive and strawberry hair in a tight bun. I glanced over at the truck-stop phone sitting on the passenger seat, willing it to not ring at this moment.

"How's the Sheriff's Office?"

"It sucks."

"That's what I hear. What are you doing?" Her tone was friendly.

So I told her part of the truth. I was working with Peralta now as a private investigator. A young woman had fallen from Larry Zisman's condominium in San Diego, handcuffed and nude, and we have been engaged to find out whether it was a suicide or something more.

"Holy crap!" She put her hands on her hips. "Zisman's married. You know he's a reserve officer in Phoenix?"

"I do. He also owned the handcuffs."

A burst came over her radio and she keyed her mic. I was being saved by a call: a burglar alarm a mile away.

She touched my shoulder. "Gotta roll, David. Call me sometime and we'll catch up. Good luck with Larry. Good guy in my view. Not so much his son."

"Yeah."

"I'm surprised the Army accepted him. Don't tell Larry I said that."

All my senses kicked to a higher gear. The Army. "Of course not. Stay safe, Amy."

In a few seconds she was back in the cruiser, where she executed a U-turn over the rounded curbs and zoomed back out toward the exit of the subdivision. I turned off the dome light and tried to breathe normally again.

Chapter Twenty-eight

I drove back to the center city on surface streets, sick that Peralta's plan didn't seem to be working. My phone was charged and had plenty of time left. It wasn't ringing.

Through downtown Tempe on Mill Avenue, across the Salt River, Galvin Parkway took me through Papago Park, the two iconic buttes backlit by the city, preserved desert all around. I thought about what Amy Taylor had said—not the "call me sometime" part, but about Zisman having a son. That was another new angle. Or it was Occam's Razor and Zisman was the john, even if he wasn't on the flash drive, and Grace had tried to blackmail him exactly as Detective Sanchez had said.

But did that explain why Tim Lewis had been tortured, every finger broken? Somebody thought he had information. Information to kill for. If it were simple blackmail, the problem would have been solved with Grace's supposed suicide. "Death solves all problems," said Joseph Stalin, who had yellow eyes. "No man, no problem." Well, no woman, but there was still a problem. Larry Zisman, former football player, could easily have subdued Grace and thrown her over the balcony. The torturing of Tim Lewis had taken a crew.

At McDowell, I turned left and entered the Phoenix city limits, then drove uphill between the buttes and was greeted by the dense galaxy of lights stretching all the way to the horizon. Phoenix was beautiful at night. On the downhill drive, the iPhone rang.

"I think I've got your tail," Peralta said.

My pulse kicked up. "Do tell."

"A truck followed you though Tempe, made every turn, and then kept going as you went up Galvin through the park and turned on McDowell. He's probably a mile behind you. A black Dodge pickup. California plate. He's got a tag frame that says 'I love Rancho Bernardo,' with a heart thing instead of love, you know."

I did know. It was the truck that had passed me the night I got out of the cab in Ocean Beach, the one I thought was simply looking for a parking space.

"Let's box him in," I said. "Do a felony stop."

After a long pause, Peralta's voice came back on. "No."

"Why?"

"First," he said, "because we're not the cops anymore. Second, because when I hired you many years ago, I hired your whole tool-box, not just the hammer. Since a year ago, all I get is the hammer."

Now it was my turn to be silent. His words stung. His words were accurate.

"So what's the plan?" I asked, and he gave it to me.

"Stay on the phone," he said.

I drove back through downtown and went north on wide, fast-moving Seventh Avenue. Numbered avenues and drives run north and south west of Central; numbered streets and places run north and south east of Central. Now you know how to get around Phoenix. I assumed the pickup driver was learning this from our excursion.

At Northern, I turned west again and after about two miles reached the Black Canyon Freeway, which ran in a trench below grade level. A Motel 6 sat a few blocks up the southbound access road. Getting to it required turning north into the K-Mart parking lot, then passing through the Super 8 parking lot, and finally reaching the Motel 6 parking lot. We didn't even need streets with so many seas of asphalt.

I parked away from the motel building and stepped out into the heat. I had a cell phone in each pocket as I walked the fifty

feet to a room on the ground floor right in the middle of the
ugly four-story box. It had none of the charm of the old motels
that had once lined Grand and Van Buren with their Western
themes and neon signs.

Three other cars were parked in the lot, all of them empty.

Precisely as Peralta had said, a key card was slipped into the
edge of the door all the way down at ground level. I retrieved
it, unsnapped the holster holding the Colt Python but, against
my better judgment, left the gun there. I popped the card into
the lock and stepped inside.

Nobody shot me.

Turning on the light switch, I surveyed a cheap motel room
looking like every other cheap motel room in America. It had
been the scene of countless assignations. Bring in an ultraviolet
detector, and the pattered orange bedspread would have revealed
an army of old semen stains, dead in mid-slither.

I spoke into the headset. "Where's my tail?"

"He's backed off. But don't spend too much time there. I
don't have a good feeling about this. Remember, he can track
you on a computer. He doesn't have to see you."

I looked at the bed again. The spread looked ruffled, as if a
couple had finished and moved on moments before I got there.
I sat in a chair and waited for a call on the other cell. The device
was a little Sphinx made in a foreign sweatshop.

Then I saw it, sitting on the low chest of drawers. It wasn't
a Claymore mine, but somehow it stuck a spike of dread into
my throat.

I studied the Zero Halliburton briefcase with its tough alu-
minum construction. Somewhere I had read this was the brand
of case that a military aide carried at all times with the president.
Inside was the "nuclear football" containing the launch codes to
end the world. And this one looked that sinister.

"What the hell is this?" My voice sounded strange alone in
the room.

He knew what I was talking about without describing the
flashy case that looked so out of place in the shabby room.

"Sharon bought it today. Open it up." He gave me a code. I dialed open the lock and unlatched it.

Inside were some men's clothes, legal pads and pens, and a shaving kit.

"Look in the socks," he said.

Sure enough, inside one of the rolled-up pairs of socks was a flash drive.

He was inviting them to steal it.

"Is this the real flash drive?"

"Of course not," he said. "But Lindsey encrypted it so it would take even a good techie hours to break in."

"But..."

"Mapstone, why don't you hang there for a few more minutes, then find a place to stash the case, and call me when you're back in the car." He hung up.

The motel room felt close and hot around me. I used the bathroom, checked to make sure the door was locked again, and searched for some artful spot to place the briefcase. The bed was on a solid wood frame, so that wouldn't work. The drawers would be too obvious: better to make them think I was trying to hide it. So I arranged it under the pillows and remade the bed with military neatness.

Back in the car, sweating and worried, I started to go out to the access road, but changed my mind.

Instead, I cruised north through the alley behind the motel, turned around, shut off the headlights, and slowly drove back the way I had come. I nosed out behind the building in time to see another car: a new white Chevy Impala coming around the front of the Super 8. There are thousands of lookalike Impalas. But this one looked exactly like the one that I saw on the security camera earlier in the day outside our office, right down to the Nevada tag.

Wishing the Prelude were not so damned white, I watched as the Impala sped up to the door I had left minutes before. If he noticed me, it didn't show. He was moving so fast, I thought he might ram through the wall. But, no, he slammed to a stop at the last second. If I had the brake-shop monopoly in Phoenix, I would be a rich man.

I dropped the emergency brake enough to slide another couple of feet beyond the edge of the building. The security lighting on the outside of the motel was impeccable. Back where I sat was relative darkness.

Out of the Impala stepped the high-and-tight haircut who had been searching the Prelude earlier in the day. He was wearing jeans and a black T-shirt, carrying something in each hand. One something was a gun. He headed straight to the motel room door without even looking in my direction. If he were a soldier or a former soldier, it was poor situational awareness, but it worked in my favor.

I relayed all this to Peralta on the iPhone.

"He's also got some kind of a crowbar," I said. It was small and black, easy to conceal, and made quick work of the door. "He's inside. I'm going to take him."

Peralta might have had a very clever plan. But this was as close to the suspect as we were likely to get. I felt suddenly cool and comfortable, my breathing even.

Peralta barked at me. "No. This is not the guy who was tailing you. Don't go back to that room, Mapstone…"

"Too bad." I pressed the little red virtual button on the glass screen that said, "end call," and tossed the earbuds onto the seat.

I mapped it out in my head: twenty quick strides to reach the door, keep the Python down against my leg so it wasn't obvious I was packing, pause, assess, and try to quietly ease the door open. No kicking it down. The crowbar had made that unnecessary. Then he and I could have a civil conversation about where the baby was. That is, unless he raised his firearm.

But with my hand on the Honda's door latch, I hesitated. What if the black Dodge Ram suddenly showed up?

High-and-tight almost immediately re-emerged, carrying the Halliburton briefcase. It gleamed in the light. So much for my clever job of hiding it. He quickly got into the Impala and drove toward the access road. I rolled after him, headlights off.

After the third ring, I activated the iPhone.

Peralta's voice came across: "don't follow him."

"Are you nuts? This is the guy who was casing our office."

"The plan is working, Mapstone. Let the plan work."

All I knew was that I had spent several hours I could never get back driving around Phoenix and had nothing to show for it. Still, I reluctantly swung around the other way, back north through the alley, and turned on my headlights.

As I came around the other side of the motel, two Phoenix Police cruisers were sitting driver's door to driver's door. They might have been talking shop or sports or flirting with each other. Or they were watching me. By this time, however, I was only another law-abiding citizen driving through the night.

The Impala driver was long gone.

I muttered profanities.

"Glad you didn't use the hammer, Mapstone?" I could feel the gloat carried across the cell towers. "Sharon left the briefcase when she rented the room. Earlier today she sewed a small tracking device into it. Two can play this game with electronics and ours are better."

I spoke low and slowly, in a rage. "So explain the next move to me, Sheriff."

"Come down to the Whataburger at Bethany Home. Go through the drive-thru. We're in the silver convertible. But don't come over to us."

I did as told, merging into the concrete river of lights that was the freeway and speeding south two miles. After taking the Bethany Home Road exit, I crossed over and made a quick jog up the northbound access road to the restaurant. The building was separated from the traffic by a faux desert berm with a couple of palo verde trees and some creosote bushes. And the drive through, which ran around it like a letter "C." The entrance was at the top of the "C," so I went that way, noticing Sharon's Infiniti parked in one of the spaces to my left, across a gravel-covered berm.

The bad guys knew his pickup, thought they had it rigged with a tracker. In its place, he was driving a silver two-door convertible, starting price sixty grand.

"You're very inconspicuous in that ride," I told Peralta, "especially in this part of town."

"Check it out, Mapstone."

On the left, immediately in front of the restaurant, a black Dodge Ram was parked near the door. Sure enough, his frame hearted Rancho Bernardo. The windows were tinted dark and I couldn't tell if the engine was running.

Better to not linger: I pulled into the drive-thru, anxiously tapping the steering wheel and wondering about the truck's occupant. His partner had probably told him that he had broken into the motel room and taken the briefcase. Now, what would he think if he saw me pulling in? Maybe he was inside, but I doubted it—he would be tracking me from the cab of the truck.

I didn't understand why Peralta was taking the risk of having me drive here. I hoped he believed in coincidences.

"So what's the plan again?"

"Get your order," Peralta ordered. "Pull around to the front, pull in a couple of spaces apart, and eat it where he can see you. Pretend to be dumb."

That part was easy.

By this time, I was actually hungry. So I got a burger, fries, and Diet Coke. Then I parked three spaces south of the Dodge Ram. The tinted windows made it impossible to see if anyone was inside.

Take small bites in case you get in a gunfight, like your grandma taught you.

I was two bites into the cheeseburger when Lindsey stepped out of the convertible and walked toward the restaurant. She was wearing a short khaki skirt and a tight sleeveless top that accentuated her small, pert breasts and very erect nipples. Her ability to look ten years younger than her real age was not diminished by the harsh lights of the parking lot.

She strutted within inches of the Ram driver's door and went inside.

My head throbbed. Over the phone, I demanded, "Are you crazy?"

"No." Peralta was fully in his Zen master mode. I almost preferred the volcano. He was taking a hell of a chance, assuming that my presence would distract the driver. I prayed he hadn't checked me out in enough detail to realize that the woman with the legs that went on for days was Lindsey Faith Mapstone.

Five minutes later, she walked back the way she had come. She paused in front of the Ram's grille and sipped sensually from a drink, paying no attention to me. She turned back as if she were going to return to the restaurant, and then faced forward again, fellating the straw for the occupants of the truck. If they had missed her the first time, they sure didn't now. She stepped off the curb and walked to the convertible, her skirt swinging saucily.

If the truck door opened on the way to grabbing her and hauling her off for rape and ransom, I was going to control and dominate the situation immediately, badge or no badge.

"Fuck!" Lindsey yelled it.

She had spilled her purse on the asphalt behind the truck. She knelt down and slowly gathered up her stuff. Now she was most vulnerable, but neither truck door opened.

After an interminable time spent picking up the contents of her purse and slipping them back in, cursing all the time, she finally made it around the berm and slid into the passenger side of the convertible. Peralta nonchalantly backed up and drove in the opposite direction from the freeway, toward the Big Lots store, and disappeared.

I was left to eat my meal for as long as it took for the Dodge Ram to leave. It consumed a leisurely half hour. They left after twenty minutes but I waited longer before I dared move.

My pulse gradually went down. I called Peralta and reported in.

"So what next?"

"Next," he said, "we go home."

"I thought you were following them?"

"We are, Mapstone. With you there to help distract him, Lindsey inserted a tracking device inside his rear bumper. She also got a good description of him through the windshield."

I'm not sure he needed me there. Lindsey did a fine job of distracting him all by herself.

Chapter Twenty-nine

I was about to turn south on Third Avenue into Willo when the xylophone sound made me jump. Exactly like before, the digital readout said, UNKNOWN.

I answered professionally. "Fuck you."

There was a long pause and I thought he might hang up. Then: "You think you're clever. You think you're putting the pieces together. But you're wrong. You can't solve this case without my help."

"Why would you help me?"

"I thought we could do business."

The past tense didn't give me hope for the baby.

I said, "You're wasting my time."

"Lose anything tonight?"

I was silent.

"You better check, absent-minded professor."

I didn't say a word. Let him think he outwitted us and found where we were hiding the flash drive, in a motel on the freeway.

Finally, I spoke. "I'm tired of games. Drop a baby doll on me? What does that mean to me?"

I feared what it meant. But I didn't say it. Instead, I pushed on. "I used to solve historic cases for a living. There was a mobster in Seattle who liked to dispose of his victims by having them pushed out of an airplane into Elliott Bay, while he watched from a skyscraper downtown. Unless you're him, this call is over."

"You didn't like the airplane? I wanted to get your attention. To get you in a bargaining frame of mind. Where would the fun have been if I had just left the package in the vacant lot for you to find? Anyway, if we can drop a baby doll out of an airplane, we can drop other things, too. Just a simple civilian airplane can be quite lethal. Wait until we steal a drone..."

Taking a chance that he was full of his own grandiosity, I said, "I'm hanging up."

"Wait."

"For what? I bill by the hour. You're not mysterious. You're not scary. You're an ordinary douchebag. You're wasting my time."

"You put up a brave front, professor, but you know it's over. Because of your carelessness, now you have nothing to bargain with. That's a good thing for you. I'll let you and everyone you love live. I got what I want."

Mustering my best acting, having studied theater under Peralta, I filled my voice with surprise. "You son of a bitch!" As if it was only now dawning on me that I had lost the briefcase.

"Don't hang up," he said. "I want you to think about what I've told you about the country. Don't be a traitor to your race."

"What about Tim? What about the guy you shot outside our office? They were white."

I could feel his shrug. "They were in the way of the greater good."

Now I knew he had killed Felix, too.

I asked about Grace.

"She was a whore," he said. "All I wanted was the information she had. She wouldn't give it to me. So we made her give herself up like a whore."

"You raped her before you pushed her off the balcony."

The rich laugh. "Come, come, Professor. We're both men of the world. I had to let my team have some fun. She sounded like an animal being tortured because they wanted her ass, too. I was above any of that nonsense. But boys will be boys. Afterward, I gave her another chance to help herself. She didn't take it."

I was about to call him a baby killer but he cut me off.

"You think I'm a criminal, a terrorist. That's what many contemporaries thought about Washington and the Founders. Soon enough, you'll know that I'm a patriot. Count your blessings tonight, Doctor Mapstone, and sleep well."

The truck-stop cell blinked off, perhaps for good. I pulled over to write down notes on the conversation. The street ahead and behind me was dark and empty.

Chapter Thirty

Robin and I were staying at a beachside resort. It curled around a cove on the Pacific with magnificent scenery but we hadn't left the room. She had never looked more radiant. She didn't have Lindsey's classic beauty and was always aware of that. Indeed, they didn't look much of anything like each other. But her smile was the better of the two sisters and it brought all her features together. Her hair was dirty blond, its wavy tresses hitting three inches below her shoulders.

At the moment, she pushed it out of her face as she told me something important. She held a baby in her lap.

Then she sent me out for something, I don't remember what, and on the way back I couldn't remember the room number. Lindsey was at one of the bars and swiveled her stool to face me. She reached out and we embraced and kissed. But I had to get back to Robin. She had the baby with her. So I told Lindsey I would be back and wandered through the halls, restaurants, and shops trying to find the corridor that led to our room. I would have to explain all this to Lindsey but that would have to wait.

But I couldn't find the room, no matter how many halls I roamed, or stairs I climbed. The resort seemed to be adding new buildings as I walked. The place was full of people and I had to push my way through crowds. Some people seemed to know me. I fished in my pocket for my cell phone to call Robin, but all that I found was a rubber pad that said, FRONT TOWARD ENEMY.

"Dave…"

My eyes came open in a dark room. Our bedroom. Lindsey was standing over me.

My groggy voice came to life. "Do we have a fix on those trackers?"

"We're following them. Remember, Peralta wants to wait and see where they go to nest."

I remembered. It frustrated the hell out of me, but he was no doubt right.

She set her baby Glock on the bedside table, slid out of her clothes, and lay next to me. The skin-on-skin was sublimely visceral.

"Want to see where Grace Hunter's phone went?"

I did.

She opened her new laptop, the bright screen hurting my eyes. I sat up. The clock on the computer read four a.m.

"Have you been up all this time?"

"I couldn't sleep."

It worried me. I didn't like the idea of her perched on the landing above the living room. True, I had checked from the outside. No one could see her through the picture window. But a fresh memory of Robin shot and dying in the back yard shook me.

"We shouldn't be here," I said. "It's not safe."

I didn't give a damn about the assurance I had gotten from the killer.

She said, "We've got an alarm. We've got guns. And we know where the bad guys are. Peralta says we're safe."

"He's not omnipotent, no matter what he thinks."

She nodded to the computer screen.

"Let me distract you. I went back a year, and Grace Hunter never left Ocean Beach, exactly like Tim told you. She would walk down to the market a few blocks away, here on Newport Avenue. All her calls were to Tim, her parents, and her friend, Addison. Now, check out April twenty-second. At two-fifty p.m., she leaves the apartment and walks north. It's like she was going to the store. Maybe for diapers."

I watched as Lindsey brought up a Google maps display.

"Here, at two-fifty-four, she's really on the move." I watched as the red line ran out of O.B. on Narragansett Avenue, turning north on Chatsworth, and east again on Nimitz Boulevard, heading toward downtown.

"Does she have to be making a call for this to show up?"

"Nope," Lindsey said. "People would freak out if they knew how much data were being collected on them every minute. All that needs to happen here is for the phone to be turned on. But look here. At three-oh-five, they stop. Right here."

The map showed the intersection of Nimitz and Locust. It was a nothing little street right before the big stoplight at Rosecrans on the Point Loma Peninsula.

"And that's it. That's where she stays."

I thought about the missing hours.

"Or," Lindsey said, "that's where the phone stays."

"What do you mean?"

"Grace's phone never made it downtown. At four-ten, at Locust and Nimitz, the call was placed on this phone to your office. Grace might have made it. Or, she might have already been in that condo downtown. But at four-seventeen, the phone was turned off at the same location."

I put my arm around her. "So somebody made contact with her on the way to the store. And she got into a vehicle. Somebody she knew. So she got in with him and they drove toward downtown. Toward Zisman's condo. But what happened at Nimitz and Locust…" My voice trailed off. Things didn't track.

Lindsey shook her head, her voice authoritative. "She had a baby waiting at home. She wouldn't leave him for long. And Zisman wasn't one of her johns. So why would she leave the baby and go to his place? No. Somebody snatched her off the street."

I was fully awake now, the dream almost forgotten.

She opened a file. "Here's where things get interesting. There was a call made from that phone a few minutes before the call to your office."

"The San Diego cops didn't have that on their LUDs."

"They wouldn't," she said. "It was placed to a scrambling device. Very advanced, very expensive. It scrubs any of the conventional records of the call, even an incoming call. Only some government agencies and corporate executives use this. You have to know where to go in the cell-company databank to find the trail, then decrypt. But here it is. The call was five minutes long."

"Are you sure nobody knew you were hacking all this?"

"Oh, somebody knew or will know. But what they saw was a low-end data breach coming from the People's Republic of China."

She opened another file: the list of Grace's clients. "The scrambler call was made to this number. It's his private line." Another screen showed me his face on the cover of *Fortune* magazine. He looked my age yet was making more money in a week than I would make in my lifetime. Why did I need three college degrees?

"He runs one of the top venture-capital funds in the country," she said. "He could afford this kind of security. All these executive types have protection. According to the records, he and Grace saw each other regularly for more than two years."

I took it all in, or thought I did, amazed again at Lindsey's talents.

I stopped myself from tapping my finger on her clean computer screen. "Then the phone was turned off for good, right there on Nimitz?"

"Not exactly. It was turned on again last Friday."

Suddenly, the air conditioning felt too cold.

"Where is it?"

When she gave me the address, I grew colder still. Grace Hunter's cell phone was in evidence storage at the Phoenix Police Department.

She said, "I answered all of Peralta's questions and it hasn't even been twenty-four hours."

I let out a long breath. "You're fast."

She put her hand on my private parts. "I can be."

Chapter Thirty-one

We were at the Good Egg having breakfast four hours later. Like its neighbor Starbucks at Park Central, it was an institution in Midtown Phoenix. Unlike Sunday, the offices inside the nearby towers were open and the restaurant was busy. The morning was cool enough to sit outside, a dry seventy-nine degrees under the umbrellas, not even hot enough to require the misters. A pleasant dry breeze was coming in from the east. Light-rail trains cruised by on Central, clanging their bells. In her round, nerd-girl sun glasses, Lindsey looked like a spy.

Here we are, I thought, easy targets in assassination range. But the tracker on the Dodge Ram was far away and three Phoenix Police units were in the lot out front, the cops having coffee next door. It would take the bad guys at least a little time to break into the briefcase and even longer to figure out the flash drive.

To figure out they had been played for fools.

A pickup truck did arrive: Peralta's. He was in a suit again and gave us a tiny nod as he walked toward the breezeway and the entrance. I knew it would take time for him to get out on the front patio. He was past his period after leaving office where he didn't want to come here, didn't want to see the assortment of politicos and officials who used the Good Egg for morning meetings. He had shifted his morning routine over to Urban Beans on Seventh Street.

But apparently he was willing to be seen again. I looked back and, sure enough, he was working the room, shaking hands, slapping backs, everyone having a great time. Where were they when he needed them? Now they had a sheriff who was a national embarrassment. He had a long conversation with Henry Sargent, who was sitting at the lunch counter. Henry was a retired honcho from Arizona Public Service.

"Lindsey!" Peralta sat down, full of morning pep. "What have you got for me?"

She went through it as the same waitress who had served him for the past fifteen years poured coffee and went off to place his order.

I read his face: satisfied, impressed, interested, troubled, more interested. An outsider would never know this from his seemingly immobile features, ones that could elicit confessions from criminals or compromises from county supervisors—or, this being Arizona, the other way around. But after so many years, I could see the slight rise of the right eyebrow, the tightening of his mouth, and the easing of a frown which didn't mean his mind was easy. I wondered what troubled him. For me, it was the whole thing.

I asked, "When are we going to interview Zisman?"

He acknowledged me for the first time with a glance of disdain at my Starbucks mocha. "Not yet."

"When?"

"Mapstone, you sound like an annoying child on a trip. 'Are we there yet?'"

"Maybe. That makes you the dad who's lost and is too stubborn to ask for directions."

It was only me and Peralta being ourselves. Lindsey interrupted. "Boys. I think the targets are definitely in the nest."

She handed over her new iPad, to which she had added Google maps. Peralta studied it, and then handed it to me. Sure enough, both red dots had converged.

"They've been in this same location for several hours," she said.

I worried that they might have discovered the trackers and discarded them at the spot on the map. But Lindsey said she had modified each to send a different signal if anyone fiddled with it.

"What time did they get there?" Peralta handed the tablet back to her.

"Around two a.m. They spent a few hours at a bar in Sunnyslope before that."

He nodded.

The two red dots had nested less than a mile from the bar.

"Excuse me," he said, and walked back inside the restaurant. The next time I caught sight of him, he was in the breezeway, which once held scores of shops when this was a mall. He was leaning against a pillar, his phone to his ear.

Back at the table, he took his time with breakfast. I had no choice but to do the same, even though I wanted to kick down their door an hour ago.

At last, Peralta gave instructions: take the Prelude home and park it. We would ride with him to greet the kidnappers. I hoped they were good and hung over.

As we left Park Central, he was in the cab of his truck, making another call.

Fifteen minutes later, we were northbound on Seventh Street. Lindsey rode on the jump seat of the extended cab, back with the weapons compartment where he kept his heavy metal. Aside from numbered streets to the east and avenues west, the other easy way you knew your way around Phoenix was to look at the mountains. The South Mountains showed you that direction. The Papago Buttes, McDowells, and, on a clear day, Four Peaks stood to the east. West were the White Tanks. We were driving straight toward North Mountain.

Sunnyslope was one of the few places with soul outside the old city, with a real identity that wasn't subsumed in endless subdivisions. It was located beyond the Arizona Canal and outside the oasis, a desert town, a Hooverville from the Great Depression, and a place that retained its own proud, quirky identity even after it had been annexed into Phoenix in the 1950s. The relatively few natives from there my age and older were "Slopers" first, Phoenicians second. From my perspective, it had some interesting unsolved murders.

The place remained unique even though it had filled in with some of the same fake stucco schlock you found everywhere. A couple of its more notorious biker bars remained. You were aware of being higher than downtown, up against the bare, rocky mountains that shimmered in the sun. If the smog hadn't smudged the view to the South Mountains, you'd see you were at about the same elevation as Baseline Road in south Phoenix, where the Japanese Flower Gardens once stood. From both places, the landscape rolled down to the dry Salt River.

Peralta slowed as we approached the five-point intersection with Dunlap and Cave Creek Road. The parking lot of a shabby shopping strip looked like a used-car joint selling black Suburban vans.

"What the hell?" I said.

"Calm down, Mapstone."

He wheeled in and parked.

"Stay here."

He left the engine and air conditioning running and approached the black Suburbans. Out of one stepped a slender man in khakis and an open-collar shirt. Eric Pham, special agent in charge of the Phoenix FBI. Even the head fed wasn't wearing a suit. The New Conformity. They shook hands and talked, and then they walked a ways talking more. Pham was gesticulating, as if laying out a map. Peralta nodded and pointed. Pham nodded.

I asked Lindsey for her iPad and switched the map to a satellite image. The dots had converged at a house at the end of Dunlap, about a mile away. From the photo, it looked like a mid-century modern house. Maybe it was on a little butte; it was hard to tell, but Dunlap rose as it went east before dead-ending at the mountain preserve. That could provide some easy escape routes if they didn't do this right.

Now a couple of Phoenix PD units arrived, along with the huge mobile command post. My stomach was wishing it didn't have breakfast getting in the way of contracting into itself. How long before the news vans and choppers arrived, too?

"Why aren't we doing this ourselves?"

Lindsey put a hand on my shoulder.

"We have to trust him, Dave."

I leaned my face against her hand, hoping she was right. I knew Peralta still had chits to call in and back channels. But I had a local lawman's mistrust of the feds. I had seen how these quasi-military operations could go very wrong.

The door opened and his bulk filled the seat.

"Phoenix PD is closing off streets," he said. "The FBI is preparing to deploy a SWAT team."

"And you explained to Eric Pham that we developed a break in this case...how?"

He took off his sunglasses and rubbed his eyes. "I have my ways, Mapstone."

"I bet."

He slipped the shift into drive and rolled back to Seventh Street.

"Wait!" It was an inane blurt, but it came out anyway. Anything to stop this circus. I knew it was too late, even though I had a bad feeling about going in with so many cops, so much firepower.

"Exactly, Mapstone. Wait. There's a baby in that house. The SWAT boys can't send an undercover to the front door with pizza, toss in a flash-bang grenade, and go in blazing. This is going to take time. They'll have to negotiate these guys to come out. We've got other stuff to do in the meantime."

I looked back with mixed emotions at the gathering army, hoping he was making the right call.

Chapter Thirty-two

The afternoon sun was cooking toward one-hundred by the time I was waiting for Peralta at the Deer Valley Airport in far north Phoenix, on the other side of the mountains. Since the city had turned Sky Harbor exclusively into a commercial aviation hub, this had become the major general aviation airport. It lacked the cachet of the Scottsdale Airpark, but it was one of the largest general aviation airports in the country. It was also probably the place where UNKNOWN had taken off and landed on his mission to drop the bloody baby doll on me.

But he wasn't unknown now. I had met Artie Dominguez for lunch downtown at Sing Hi. I left the Prelude on Cypress and took light rail downtown. No reason for all my movements to be known. The train was packed as usual. The light-rail system was one of the few elements of progress to arrive in recent years and its popularity made its critics more hysterical in their opposition. I liked it.

It only hurt a little to get out at the stop by the old courthouse. The building was as handsome as ever, although I wouldn't let myself look up to my office. It was a crime that they had ripped out the old palm trees, grass, and shade trees years ago. Downtown needed more shade. And they had added more parking on the south side, more concrete to help make the summers hotter and last longer. For all this, it was the best-looking building downtown. Across Washington Street, a little band protested against the new sheriff.

Sing Hi was two blocks south. Dominguez wasn't worried about being seen with me because the venerable Chinese restaurant had lost a good part of its clientele of deputies and prosecutors to the new restaurants at CityScape, the boring mix-used development to the north. I still liked Sing Hi's chow mein.

He played at being aggrieved over my hurry-up request, but he was clearly interested.

Bob Hunter and Larry Zisman came up pretty clean. Each had accumulated a few speeding tickets. The same was not true of Zisman's son, Andrew. The son had two juvenile arrests for assault and weapons at ages sixteen and seventeen. His father had paid a top criminal lawyer to get him out of both. He joined the Army but was discharged for being part of a white supremacist cell at Fort Hood, Texas, that was blamed for the beating of a black non-com and the rape of a female soldier. Three of his buddies had gone to military prison. Andrew Zisman had been sent back into the civilian population. His last known address was his father's condominium in San Diego but over the past year, he had racked up two moving violations in metro Phoenix.

ViCap was no help on either anti-personnel mines or women being pushed from balconies.

But I had also emailed Artie the list of Grace Hunter's clients.

"It's like the *Forbes* 400," he commented.

The list contained chief executives, investment bankers, a venture capitalist, doctors, lawyers, and one Indian chief.

The one exception was named Edward Kevin Dowd, age thirty-six.

Yes, Edward.

"This one has an outstanding federal warrant." Dominguez showed me the intelligence report. "He's suspected of involvement in the theft of anti-personnel mines from Fort Huachuca."

A sheet of paper had never felt so heavy.

"Dowd left the Army six years ago after serving for a decade in Special Forces. He had seen multiple deployments to Iraq and Afghanistan. Then Obama became president and Dowd started recruiting what he called the White Citizens Brigade among other disaffected soldiers. He was no redneck, but a trust-fund baby from back east, attended Andover and Yale. He was a captain. It was two years before the military got a hint of what he was doing on the side and brought him up on charges. But the investigators didn't find any laws broken, yet. So the Army quietly pushed him out."

Dominguez slid a photo across the table. Dowd had a lean face, a full head of reddish-brown hair, a narrow soul patch that looked like a Hitler mustache that had fallen to his chin, and small, mean eyes.

"This guy is a killing machine," Dominguez said. "He's also a licensed pilot."

Killing machine. I thought about what Ed Cartwright had told me.

"I need those back."

I reluctantly slid the material back across the table.

"Did Dowd know Andrew Zisman?"

Dominguez shook his head. "Unknown."

What was known was that Dowd had been a client of Grace's, meeting her a dozen times.

"So Artie, where was Dowd last operating?"

He smiled crookedly. "Phoenix and San Diego. What the hell have you gotten yourself into?"

It was a lethally pertinent question, but when Peralta arrived at the airport terminal we had no time to talk. Two tough, big men in suits came inside and called our names. They led us outside where an imposing Gulfstream jet was waiting on the tarmac.

"I'm going to have to ask for your weapons," one said.

"No," I said. It was one of Peralta's cardinal rules: you never give up your sidearm.

"It's all right, Mapstone." Peralta handed over his Glock. I reluctantly did the same. On a pat-down, they found my last-option knife and confiscated that, too. Peralta glared at me. I glared right back. We stepped up inside the jet, visions of being tossed out in the desert dancing through my head.

"Mike, how the hell are you?"

Mister *Fortune* Magazine, whose name was Jim Russo, looked older than his photograph, even though he appeared very fit with a golf-course tan. He led us to a sumptuous seating area where a young woman brought us bourbon.

"It's been too long," Russo said. "How's Ed Cartwright doing?"

Now I was confused and paranoid.

"Crazy as ever," Peralta said. To me: "We were all in the same unit."

"That crazy Indian saved my ass more than once," Russo said.

"Mine, too." Peralta savored the bourbon. The small talk continued for an interminable time. He even got around to introducing me.

"I appreciate you flying over here," Peralta said.

Russo stared at the floor. "I'm sorry, Mike. I should have contacted you sooner. But if this had gotten into the financial press..." He shook his head. "After Felix was killed, I didn't know what to do."

He had my attention.

"Felix was the head of my security detail," Russo said. "He was a Navy SEAL who lost a leg in Afghanistan. Won a Silver Star saving his comrades after an IED attack. He was a good man."

"Why did he have multiple driver's licenses?" I asked.

Russo explained that sometimes he needed to check into hotel suites under assumed names. Apparently like many billionaires, he was a target of threats and would be a tempting catch for kidnappers. I tried to pay attention while wondering how the situation in Sunnyslope was progressing.

"Scarlett." Peralta let the name drop ever so lightly.

Russo made a face. "Foolish old rich man, huh? I know what you're thinking."

"I'm not thinking anything, Jim. She was a pretty girl."

"I have a wife and children," Russo said. "But my wife and I drew apart sexually a long time ago. Grace..." He hesitated. "Grace helped me."

"Grace?" I said.

He smiled sadly. "I knew her name. Felix provided a complete dossier on her background for me."

"We're not here to judge," Peralta said. "Hell, I envy you, you horny wop. It might have helped to know you were the one hiring us instead of Felix."

"He did it," Russo said. "I only gave him your name. He didn't trust the police, and he was mindful of my privacy. I thought if anyone could help, you could."

"Was he seeing Grace, too?" That was my fart in church.

"Oh, no," Russo said, "Felix was gay. But he was the one to give Grace a ride to my place in Rancho Santa Fe and back. They got to know one another. Felix did love her, but like a brother. You see, when he was deployed his real sister was abducted and killed. He never forgave himself. He became very protective of Grace, especially after he learned she was being pimped out. He got her out of that situation and back together with her old boyfriend. I hated to have to give her up but she deserved a real life."

We waited. Peralta and Russo received refills.

"In the months that followed, Felix would keep an eye on her. He'd check up from time to time. Of course, her husband didn't know. Grace was very good at keeping secrets and compartmentalizing. About two weeks before her death, she called Felix. She was afraid somebody was stalking her. She didn't know who, or she didn't say. She didn't want to worry Tim, so I'd be surprised if she even told him. Anyway, Felix took a leave of absence, got an apartment in Ocean Beach so he could be close…"

"A guardian angel," I said.

"Exactly." Russo looked me over for the first time. A mixed verdict. "I didn't think it was necessary. Grace was smart and away from that life. But Felix was adamant, and he was a very good employee. He had also served the country. I felt I owed this to him. He gave her a panic button to push if she got in trouble. He was usually about a block away."

Peralta asked what happened on April twenty-second.

"For the first time, Grace pushed the panic button. It had a tracker and Felix was able to get to her…"

"What do you mean?" I was too impatient.

"He ran the car she was in off the road, onto a side street. But it was three against one. They beat him up pretty bad, which would be no easy feat, and they left him there. I didn't realize how bad when he called. He held it together, told me some guys had taken Grace and gotten away from him."

"Why didn't he call the police?"

"I told him to do it. I also gave him your number. I told him Peralta could get results."

He didn't call the cops, but he did phone us, getting the answering machine.

I took a tentative sip. It was very expensive bourbon. "But he called us from Grace's phone."

Russo nodded. "In the fight, he was trying to get Grace. Part of her purse spilled on the street. He ended up with her cell, which looked exactly like his."

Peralta said, "Why wouldn't he know it wasn't his phone when he didn't find you on the favorite calls?"

"My number had to be memorized," Russo said. "Security. Felix didn't realize he had the wrong phone until he had called me and was in the middle of calling you."

But he never made a second call to us. I asked why not.

"He passed out. You've got to understand, he wasn't as physically capable as he once was. He wore a prosthetic leg and was in constant pain. The next thing he knew, he was in the hospital. And Grace was dead. It was two weeks before he could come to Phoenix and see you. He still had her phone." Russo paused and suddenly slammed his fist into his leg. "And now he's dead, too."

I went through the names: Larry and Andrew Zisman, Bob Hunter, and Edward Dowd. They drew no reaction from Russo.

Peralta said, "And Felix?"

Russo set his glass down carefully into the brass cup holder on the teak table. "I helped arrange for his mother to bring his body home for a funeral in Indiana. I promise you, she'll never want for anything. She's lost both her children. It's a hell of a thing."

He seemed like as decent a master of the universe as there probably was, and he was at loose ends. Still, I couldn't finish his premium booze. I kept thinking how far ahead we would have been if Peralta's old war buddy had called us sooner. Tim might still be alive. The baby would be safe. It was all I could do to keep from exploding.

He ran a hand down his face and stared at Peralta. "Shit, Mike. How could this happen? I've lost them both. Who would do this? Why?"

I had a pretty good idea who had done it. I didn't know why.

Chapter Thirty-three

As we drove back and I reported on my lunch meeting, Lindsey texted me that she and Sharon were going shopping—she needed to load up on moisturizers now that she was back in the desert—and she would be home by six. I wanted to go back to Sunnyslope but Peralta vetoed that. So I let him drop me off at home.

With the house to myself, I lay down on the bed and actually started reading the biography of George Frost Kennan that had languished on the table for months. But it did not transport me away from this age of "business casual," tattoos on pretty women, and dunces saying, "No worries!" The perspective it gave me on geopolitics then and now was quickly forgotten. It was not the author's fault.

Too many anxieties hammered on my brain. Edward Kevin Dowd, killing machine, was foremost among them. In these insidious little moments, I noticed Lindsey's suitcases remained in the guest room, only partly unpacked. Was that because of the investigation she had been thrust into, or was her stay here only temporary?

I couldn't stop myself from inconspicuously rifling her bags. I fancied myself a good burglar. I persuaded myself that I was guarding my heart by trying to figure if she was going again. But my breathing was also the fast pant of the voyeur. What did I think I would find? Photos and videos of my wife being impaled by another man? *Billets-doux?*

I found it inside one zippered compartment: an envelope, addressed to me. It had a stamp, too, but had never been mailed. In fact, it had never been sealed and inside were pages of Crane stationery. Now every electron of good judgment in my body was telling me: *Stop, put this away, go no further!*

Of course I ignored them. Out came the personalized stationery I had bought for her two Christmases ago. I carefully unfolded it. Hers was not a generation that had been forced to learn and stick with cursive handwriting. "Keyboard proficiency" on a computer mattered more. Instead, Lindsey's block printing was instantly recognizable.

The letter addressed to me was dated May first.

Dear History Shamus,

This is not a "Dear John" letter but it's going to hurt. But please read all the way through. I'm trying to express things I don't know how to say when we're together. You're so good with words and thinking on your feet. I freeze up. So I'm going to try this way.

I said terrible things to you. I don't blame you for what happened to Emma. You know this, right?

As Robin probably told you, I had a baby when I was seventeen. It was probably a cry for help, as they say, from the one who always had to be grown up, always had to be the good girl. Linda called me a slut and put the baby up for adoption and I only got to hold him once. I didn't tell you this when we started dating because I still felt ashamed. And as the years went by, I always wanted to find the way to tell you, but couldn't. Like I said, I don't have your gift of words.

After that, I thought I didn't want to try again. I wouldn't make a good mother. There's madness in my bloodline. But when we conceived Emma, I realized I had been lying to myself. I wanted a child so much, a child with you. A child we could raise with the love and sanity I never had growing up, and the mother and father you never had. And everything inside both of us, good and bad, could go into the future. And maybe that child would remember us kindly and carry that memory with her, too, and pass it on to her children.

When the miscarriage happened, I went crazy. They say people have a "fight or flight" instinct. Mine was flight. So when the governor offered me the job at Homeland Security, I grabbed it and flew. There's no excuse for leaving you. My hope was that Robin would be there as a friend for you and more. I knew she couldn't help herself and neither could you. Did I make you polyamorous, my professor? I didn't realize she would fall in love with you. I didn't know if you would fall in love with her, too. But I figured I deserved it if it happened.

The first time I cheated on you, Emma had been dead exactly one month. I was sitting in a coffee shop near DuPont Circle and saw a man watching me. I smiled at him. He wasn't especially good looking. But he invited me to walk with him and I did. We went two blocks and he pushed me back against a streetlight and kissed me really hard. Then he asked me a question: he wanted to know if I was a slut. The question insulted and stunned me and I didn't answer. "I didn't think so," he said, and pushed me away. He walked off into the evening crowd. I felt so many things. Angry. Guilty. Hurt. Aroused. I liked that kiss. I had missed a man's touch, a man inside me. I wanted to kill this numbness in me. And I thought: yes, I was a slut.

I know this makes no sense to you. We had not had sex in a long time and after the miscarriage, even though you were so gentle and patient, I couldn't be with you. I can't tell you why. I couldn't explain anything, couldn't feel anything but the intensity of my grief. I didn't want five stages or closure or your love. I wanted my baby. And I knew that I could never have another one. That was it. Somehow that anonymous kiss on the street took me away from the pain.

Of course, I never confessed this to you. You wanted me to come back to Phoenix. I couldn't. The thought of it made me ill. So I stayed in Washington and I was a slut. Not with my husband or people I even really knew. Most of the ones I fucked and sucked were men. One was a woman. None of them knew I was mourning my baby. To them, I was a woman who was desirable and impetuous. They loved it that I was marvelously good in bed. The bizarre thing was, I could not come the way I did with you. I won't say it didn't feel good, but my body wouldn't give me a real orgasm. That was all right. Being a slut suspended the ache, the longing for Emma. These lovers didn't know much about me, certainly not the job I did. That only added to the sexual tension and the intensity when we fucked. I was a mystery woman.

Then I met a man at work and settled down. Crazy, huh? Settled down into monogamous infidelity. I figured you were fucking Robin and I kept translating my hurt and guilt over Emma into anger at you. So I became the mistress of a man who was the boss of my boss. He was married, of course, with a pretty wife and children in northern Virginia. He understood that I really needed to fuck and suck. Our encounters were incredibly intense. It took me awhile to realize he knew I needed this passion and riskiness like a drug, to help me forget. Did I write "me"? It wasn't me. None of them knew me. They knew the "not-me" that I became.

It didn't last. Robin's death happened. I sat in the cemetery with you. Remember how the rain started? "Not-me" became me for a while and I was so ashamed and I knew you would never understand or forgive me. How could I ask that? Things were different when I got back to Washington, too. I realized he was tunneling into me, getting past my defenses. But I didn't feel comforted. I felt manipulated. I felt like I was drowning.

Two weeks ago, I broke up with him. I left his apartment in the District and walked back to my place at three a.m. It was raining and I felt as if a very bad cold had suddenly passed. I don't intend to see him again, even though there will probably be consequences. I'm tired of the slut racket.

Dave, I am writing this letter to give you one big honesty dump, and I can only imagine how much it hurts, how mad you are. I want to come home and be with you, try to find us again. I miss us. I know that's a tough request after all that has happened. I don't expect you to agree to it once you read this letter. You will be pissed and jealous. I wouldn't blame you (don't think I didn't feel that way thinking of you with Robin). But I wish you would let me come home and let us find the way to forgive each other and forgive ourselves. You are the love of my life and always will be. When we first got together, you said that I saved your life. But you saved mine, too. I wish we could find a way to save each other one more time. I've written this letter ten times. I don't know if I'll have the guts to send it.

Lindsey

I carefully returned the letter to its envelope and that to the zippered pocket of the rolling suitcase. I rezipped it to exactly the position it had been before my fool's adventure. My hands were shaking, my mind seared. Burglary is a crime and I would pay the penalty alone. She would never know that I had read it.

As if on cue, Lindsey called. She and Sharon were at the Nordstrom at Scottsdale Fashion Square and was I doing okay? I gamely said yes. No, I hadn't heard anything about the situation in Sunnyslope. Did I mind if the two of them had dinner? Of course not. I told her to have fun, hoping my voice didn't betray my knowledge of the fun she had in Washington. After she hung up, I walked to the study, my mind in a soup of queasiness and arousal, barely feeling the old hardwood floor under my feet.

At loose ends, I turned on the television for the first time in probably more than a year. A handsome man holding a micro-phone was standing in the parking lot where Peralta had talked to the G-man this morning. The reporter had positioned himself so the "S" made out of whitewashed rocks on the slope of a hill above Sunnyslope showed over his right shoulder. I turned up the volume.

"...still no details about the police situation here in Sunnys-lope," the reporter said. "Officers have sealed off several blocks around a house on Dunlap, as these aerial images show..."

The screen flipped to an overhead shot of the house, with a long roof and several cars parked in its driveway. The nearest police or FBI vehicles appeared to be at least two hundred yards away. I shut it off. This was turning into the goatfuck that I had feared. I had to get out of the house.

Chapter Thirty-four

It didn't really matter if the bad guys were tracking me now. They had bigger problems. So I didn't even bother to remove the spy device from the Prelude before I rolled off to catch the freeway system that would take me to Tempe. Fortunately, I saw the disaster of the Papago Freeway before I turned onto the Third Street on-ramp. Rush hour, or hours rather, was not allowing anybody to move at more than a slow crawl, if that. So I settled for the street grid.

By the time I got to Larry Zisman's house at The Lakes, the sun was down and it looked as if most everybody who lived on the cul-de-sac had made it home, closed their garage doors, and were watching television back in their Arizona rooms. Not a single other car was parked at the curb. The lights were still off at Zisman's place, but you never knew. Unlike houses in the historic districts, most of these homes focused activity away from the front and the street. Zisman could well be in his Arizona room watching the "police situation in Sunnyslope" unfold. If so, I could finally ask some questions.

At the moment I didn't give a damn if he was a reserve police officer. I wanted to sit across from him and watch his face and body language as he told me about the night Grace Hunter was pushed off the balcony of his condominium. He wasn't on her client list, so why did he claim she was his girlfriend? Former football star or no, Larry Zisman seemed an unlikely man to attract Grace. I had seen recent photos of Zisman: he had lost his athletic body to a gut and his face was puffy. It wasn't as if Grace needed more chances to, as my once semi-prudish wife puts it, fuck and suck.

I wanted to know who he was covering for: his son, Andrew? Edward Dowd? And where was he when Grace died? Was he really already at his boat? If so, why did he leave her with her murderer at the condo? This was only the beginning of the questions I intended to ask.

But when I set the tip of my toe on the step of the arched entranceway, I knew that he would not be giving me any answers.

The big answer popped me in the nose: that unique, fiendish sulfurous smell I had first encountered as a young deputy, the scent of a body that had been dead for a while. In an un-air-conditioned building in the Arizona heat, it would become noticeable within a day. Air conditioning gave you a little longer. Often mail carriers or neighbors would be knocked down by the odor halfway across the yard.

We called them "stinkers."

A quick scan of the front door showed a mail slot. So no mail was piling up obtrusively outside. Maybe the mailman had a bad sense of smell. No newspapers were accumulating on the doorstep, either, but fewer people subscribed now, a sad thing for democracy.

It was tempting to walk around the house and look through a window. But that would definitely attract a neighborhood watch hotdog. So I walked back down the wide driveway toward the street, looking as if I belonged there in the warm suburban air, stealthily scanning to see if anyone was watching from the neighboring houses. Nobody seemed to be.

Out of the cul-se-sac, I drove north to Baseline Road and found a rare pay phone. There, I called 911 and reported a strange odor coming from the Zisman address. Larry Zip had thrown his last pass. Now I wondered if he had killed himself or become one more loose end for Dowd to tie up.

My phone rang. Peralta.

He was brief. "Get up here as fast as you can."

Chapter Thirty-five

He didn't have to say where "here" was. I drove as fast as I could to the parking lot on Seventh Street and Dunlap. Peralta's truck was moored beside a dozen marked and unmarked law-enforcement units, plus two giant command vans. All of the television stations had positioned satellite trucks there as well. Bright TV lights were focused ahead of me. I parked the Prelude and pushed my way through a crowd of civilians and cops.

Eric Pham, wearing a vest with "FBI" emblazoned on it, was reading a statement for the cameras. Peralta was standing beside him. He couldn't resist the cameras. He never could.

"….at five p.m., a SWAT team made entry into the home. A brief exchange of fire resulted in one man dead. Our preliminary information indicates he was armed with a semi-automatic rifle and fired on the officers. Five other men were taken into custody. A large cache of weapons was seized, including Claymore anti-personnel mines. We believe these mines were stolen from Fort Huachuca. We also took possession of computers and maps that indicate these individuals were planning to use the mines in attacks on shopping malls and federal facilities in the Phoenix area. We also believe they intended to use shoulder-fired missiles to shoot down an airliner landing or taking off from Sky Harbor Airport…"

His statement contained all the caveats about the early nature of the investigation and how he couldn't disclose further information that might compromise an ongoing probe.

"We believe," he said, "that we have disrupted what could have been a catastrophic domestic terrorism attack."

"Agent Pham!" A female reporter with perfect red hair shouted the question. "We have information that these men were members of the White Citizens Brigade, a domestic terror group. Is that true?"

"This was an organized, anti-government group. Beyond that, I'm not prepared to comment, Megan." He was cool and unruffled as a cascade of further questions followed. What were the names of the suspects? Who was the man who was shot by SWAT? What were the specific targets the terrorists intended to strike? He gave up nothing.

My stomach was an acid bin. No mention of the baby. Why had I expected anything different?

"Is this connected to the explosion in San Diego last week?"

"It's too early for us to draw conclusions, Brahm."

"What is former Sheriff Peralta doing here?" a reporter wanted to know.

Pham nodded knowingly. "Retired Sheriff Peralta is acting as a consultant for the bureau."

When the press conference wrapped up, Peralta worked his way toward me like a slow-moving bulldozer, ignoring the journalists' questions as only he could do. As I had watched countless times over the years, he didn't answer but he worked the crowd. It was showtime all over again. It made me wonder if he intended to run for sheriff again someday, maybe when sanity returned to Arizona.

"Where were you?" He wrapped me in his big arm and steered me toward his truck. I thought: *I was rifling my wife's luggage, learning about her fuckathon in the nation's capital while I was sleeping with her younger sister in our marriage bed. A normal family. Any other questions?* I said, "I wanted to talk to Larry Zisman."

"How'd it go?"

"He's been dead inside his house for some time. I called Tempe PD anonymously."

"Balls. Get in."

We closed out the noise with a swoosh of the doors and drove slowly out of the lot, turning east on Dunlap. The lights of the cars, streetlights, and houses rocketed by in streams of white and yellow, and ahead was the police roadblock of red and blue. As the road rose, the city lights spread out to my right in an endless jewel.

We are the night detectives. We would never be private investigators peeping on unfaithful husbands. That was not the trouble that we would chase, the trouble that would run us down. I would not write grand history in thrillingly reviewed best-sellers. I am with Gibbon, history being "little more than the register of the crimes, follies, and misfortunes of mankind." I am with Peralta, where we track it down armed. This is the job.

I gingerly fed my curiosity, afraid of what I might learn. "Are you a consultant for the FBI?"

"I guess we are now."

"Are you holding out on me? Have you been playing a side game all along with Pham?"

"Jeez, Mapstone. No."

I asked him what Pham was holding back from the press.

Peralta ticked off points with fingers on the hand that wasn't guiding the steering wheel. "The house was rented three months ago by Edward Dowd, using his own name. He wrote a check for a year's rent on a New York bank and it cleared without any problem. In this economy, the owner was glad to have a tenant who paid ahead. The suspects arrested are all confirmed members of the White Citizens Brigade, all former military. The Brigade is suspected of committing seven bank robberies in Arizona and Southern California over the past two years. It appears they used the money to fund their ordnance purchases, among other things…"

A Phoenix uni who looked about fifteen years old waved us through and we climbed up Dunlap as it narrowed and technically ended, turning into a dirt trail petering out against a metal barrier. Beyond it was the darkness of the Phoenix Mountain Preserve.

One sharp left turn put us at the house I had seen from television. It was built of gray cinder blocks with a wide over-hanging roof. The trail made another turn to reach a two-car garage. Black-clad cops from various agencies were milling about, many with nothing to do but try to look busy and officious. The SWAT guys wore helmets, boots, body armor, and, beneath that, T-shirts that were two sizes too small. Dazzling floodlights, running on loud generators, illuminated the scene. A police chopper was hovering overhead, vainly playing its spotlight over the mountain preserve.

I slid to the dirt and walked with him as he laid it out.

The electricity and air conditioning had been shut off early. FBI and ATF negotiators had tried for hours over the landline to persuade the people inside to come out. They had refused. Meanwhile, a SWAT member had been able to snake a tiny night-vision-capable camera into the ventilation system so they could see inside some of the rooms. A robot had scouted the perimeter of the house to make sure it wasn't mined.

They had pumped tear gas into the vents at four-forty-five and then had broken down the front door, tossing in a flash-bang grenade. Only one suspect had returned fire and a tactical officer had put him down instantly with one shot. He had been airlifted to Mister Joe's but was dead when he hit the floor. The others had put down their weapons without a fight.

"It could have been really hairy," Peralta said. It was interest-ing that he had walked onto so many crime scenes over the years that nobody thought to challenge him now.

Outside the front door, a tarp was spread. Most of it was covered with weapons: AR-15s, pump-action shotguns, assorted varieties of pistols, two shoulder-fired missiles, and enough crates of ammunition to make Ed Cartwright happy. The Clay-mores were probably safely in the custody of ATF. I barely paid attention.

"Where's the baby?"

"They didn't find him, Mapstone."

"What about Dowd?"

"Him, neither."

I used my hand to stop him at the door, no easy task given his bulk and momentum.

"What are you saying?"

His eyes shone black. "Dowd got away."

"I knew it…" All the cops, all the jurisdictions and expensive toys and command vans and they couldn't make a simple collar. I started a cursing jag notable for its creativity.

He pinched my shoulder until I thought it would fall off and leaned in to whisper. "Play well with others."

I did my best.

Evidence technicians were photographing the living room. The floor had traces of blood and was covered with yellow numbered markers. One marker was on the Halliburton briefcase. A laptop sat on a sofa, drawing another yellow tag. They had probably had plenty of time to realize the flash drive was phony, otherwise Dowd would have taken it with him.

My answer was next to evidence marker forty-two: the flash drive we planted in the expensive briefcase was shattered, as if by an angry boot. My feet felt as if they were sinking into the floor. The remains of the tear gas stung my lungs.

Another tech was taking inventory in the kitchen. The cabinets were fully stocked with canned goods, meals ready to eat, and bottles of water. A bedroom closet held body armor, helmets, and night-vision goggles.

"Dowd told them to make a stand here," Peralta said. "Kill as many police as possible."

"How did he get away?"

"Let me show you."

He led me down a hallway and opened a door that revealed a staircase down. I led the way as he talked.

"The house was built in nineteen sixty-two by a doctor. He put a fallout shelter in the basement. It was the height of the Cold War."

It was the year of the Cuban Missile Crisis, but I kept my mouth shut.

We came into a finished basement with wood paneling and an ancient pool table. He pointed to another, heavier door at the far end of the room. I stepped through that portal into a concrete-encased hallway that slanted down. Bare light bulbs protected by steel frames burned overhead. I started to sweat.

It reminded me of one of my maze dreams as I stepped more slowly, made a turn and went another twenty feet on a slanting concrete floor. Two doors were open. One led through thick walls into a shelter, maybe ten feet by ten feet, looking as if it hadn't been touched since Kennedy was president. A dusty yellow Geiger counter sat on a table. Ed Cartwright would look down his apocalyptic nose at such a primitive set-up.

The other door led outside, where a Phoenix cop stood guard. He greeted Peralta by name, as if the election had never happened.

We were at the bottom of the stubby hill. The house loomed above us.

"This is where Dowd probably got out while we were still staging," Peralta said. "We didn't realize there was this escape route out."

"What's this 'we,' Lone Ranger?" I said sourly. "I said we should go in and do it ourselves instead of setting up the para-military show that everybody could see."

"Mapstone, we would have been shot dead."

He was right, of course. But I was still angry. The only benefit was the hot west wind, replacing the tear gas in my lungs with good old Phoenix smog and dust. The sheen of sweat across my chest and belly remained.

"We think Dowd came out here and went into that neighborhood." He pointed to lights two-hundred yards away. "He kidnapped a woman and made her drive him through a checkpoint. Let her go down at Forty-Fourth Street and Camelback. He's probably already ditched her car."

Dowd's black Dodge Ram truck sat ten feet to my right, with its tracker no doubt uselessly attached to the back.

He faced me. "Where are the girls?"

"Shopping in Scottsdale."

"Call. Get them here. Now."

I already had the cell out. I asked Lindsey to bring Sharon and meet us back at Seventh and Dunlap.

He walked out into the darkness, kicking the hard ground, thinking.

"Thoughts? Ideas?" It was as if he were talking to the mountains as much as to me.

I moved toward him, wondering if Dowd was watching with night vision. He could take us out right here with a sniper rifle.

"We can't stay on Cypress." I stated the obvious through a scratchy throat. "Your place in Dreamy Draw is more secure but not secure enough. It's also dangerously isolated."

I had only gotten Lindsey back. Sure, she had left me twice before, but for now it was sweet. The idea of putting her at risk was intolerable, a rocket into my brain. Dowd knew we had defrauded him with the flash drive. He would come to kill us all. And he was the kind of man who would seek out Lindsey first, so my agony would be under way well before he got to me. I would have been responsible for losing them both, Robin and Lindsey.

I said, "You know we've got to find him ourselves. Get him first. You know this, right?"

He nodded.

"But for now," he said, "we need to get out of the Valley. How about San Diego?"

It sounded smart. But one other thing bothered me.

"How many Claymores did they find here?"

"Ten."

"You're sure?"

He shook his head and cursed. He could do the arithmetic as easily as I: a dozen stolen, one used on me in Ocean Beach, ten seized tonight.

One Claymore was still missing and I wagered it was with Dowd.

Chapter Thirty-six

The call came a little after eight p.m. Only one person had called me on the cheap phone I had bought in El Centro.

"Time's up, Doctor Mapstone."

"For you," I said. "You escaped once, you won't again."

"Did you ever serve in the military? In combat?"

"No."

"Then you don't understand anything. I gave you a chance to serve your country by giving me the list of Scarlett's clients. I appealed to your patriotism. I appealed to your intellectual side. But, no. You refused to obey my orders. You refused to negotiate."

"I'm really sorry about that."

"If you had served in combat, you would know that a soldier can't let his rage get the better of him. It can overwhelm discipline and training. Effectiveness. So I have to push you with some clearer incentives. I've researched you, Doctor Mapstone. I'm going to kill everyone you love. Then I'm going to kill you. And then I'm going to bring the war where it belongs, right here to America."

"Keep talking, General," I said. "The trace is working."

There was no trace.

He laughed as if a private joke had been shared between friends.

"I'm going to start with your first wife, Patricia." He read out an address in La Jolla. It was Patty's address. "I know you're in San Diego. If you come alone and bring the client list, then I'll let her live. I might even be willing to let you live. But you have to come within the next hour. You won't find her there. If I'm satisfied you're alone, I'll call and give you instructions. No cops. No bullshit. This is your last chance to negotiate."

Then I was only holding a useless plastic object to my ear, hearing nothing.

Chapter Thirty-seven

But I was not in San Diego.

I was in Phoenix.

I was in the valley of decision.

Sharon and Lindsey had driven the Prelude to Ocean Beach. Find a parking place and leave it, I had told them. It would be two weeks before the police towed it away. Then they had checked into a hotel downtown.

Peralta and I went to the Hotel Clarendon in Midtown Phoenix to wait for the call I knew would come. The Clarendon was where *Arizona Republic* reporter Don Bolles had been assassinated by a mobster's bomb in 1976. After its restoration, the new owners put a memorial photo gallery in a hallway.

What I hadn't counted on was him leaving while I was in the shower. "Checking on something with Eric Pham. Back soon," he had scrawled on the hotel stationery. He had known I wouldn't let him go without me. "I'm not an old man," he had barked at me. He had to prove something to himself. At least he was with Pham.

Or so I had thought. In thirty minutes, I had called Pham. He had told me he was held up in a meeting and had canceled on Peralta.

So he had gone on his errand alone. My calls to him went straight to voice mail.

Now, I dressed quickly in black jeans, black running shoes, and black T-shirt. I thought about stopping by the office and unlocking the Danger Room. But, no. There was no time. I didn't even bring the Python. Instead, I carried the Airlite and two Speedloaders. That would be enough or it wouldn't matter. At last, I didn't need the toolbox, only the hammer.

Dowd had let the woman he kidnapped off at Forty-Fourth Street and Camelback. Her car had been recovered at Tatum and Lincoln, in the parking lot by the statue of Barry Goldwater. I made a guess that there was one place nearby where Edward Dowd could hole up: the house of Bob Hunter, Grace's father. Like Larry Zisman, Bob Hunter had become a loose end that needed to be snipped. It was only a few blocks away.

I called a cab. While I waited, I phoned Isabel Sanchez and asked her to check on Patty, if Patty even still lived at that address.

Then I made one more call.

It was nearly ten when the cab let me out on McDonald. I gave him a twenty-dollar tip and hiked into the desert, a ghost passing the million-dollar homes. The night was moonless, a few prominent stars claiming the indigo vault above, and I was profoundly aware of the possibility of snakes. But I didn't move with a heavy step. I walked slowly and carefully, aware of every sound, each scurrying noise of an animal that had been disturbed. The sounds of the city were far away.

I came up on the Hunter house from the south and followed the pale adobe wall toward the front. The air was still and hot. My skin was cool and all my senses were notched up high.

The form on the ground was ten feet ahead. I crouched and watched. It wasn't moving and nobody seemed near it.

Closer, I saw a man prone in the dirt and rocks a few feet off the driveway. He was on his belly and his back contained a messy exit wound the size of a dinner plate. I turned him over carefully. His breathing was shallow and rapid. It was a miracle he was still alive. A bullet had struck him just above the heart. His face looked privileged and tan, even near death: Bob Hunter. He had made his last hike up Camelback. He stared at me without seeing.

"Who's inside?" I demanded it in a whisper.

He opened his lips and mouthed something. *My wife?* Maybe that was what he said. His eyes might as well have been glass.

The elaborate porch sconces were turned off but the door was cracked open, as if Hunter had left it that way and gone for a stroll. Or tried to make an escape. Once again, I scanned the terrain. The desert landscaping was done so well, too well.

I pushed the door open and entered with the snubnosed revolver out and up.

High-and-tight stood a few feet away, facing toward me and holding a black semi-automatic pistol in his right hand pointed down. This was the same man who had searched the Prelude at the office, the same man who filched the briefcase from the cheap motel on Black Canyon. He looked younger close up. His eyes narrowed as I kept walking.

"Who am I negotiating with? You?"

His gun arm started up and I made the smooth trigger pull of the Airlite. The walls echoed with the gun's quick *boom* as a dime-sized red hole appeared between his eyes and his head snapped back hard. In nanoseconds, the wadcutter bullet fragmented inside his skull and sent a wide shower of red and gray onto the wall. His body lurched back against an expensive floor lamp and both crashed to the floor.

And I was alone in the large living room. Cowboy paintings hung on taupe walls. But there was little time for art criticism. I swept the dining room and the kitchen, finding each deserted.

"Back here, Doctor Mapstone."

I stepped up into a hallway and followed the voice. It sounded unconcerned.

Edward Dowd was standing in the master suite, unarmed. He appeared ordinary except for the soul patch: medium height, average build, shaved head. The mastermind wore a loose, white Tommy Bahama shirt, shorts, and sandals. The hauteur of his military pretentions didn't extend to his wardrobe tonight. His calves were well defined by muscles.

Close to him on the white comforter of the king bed was an AK-47. I couldn't let even my peripheral vision linger, but the rifle looked lovingly cared-for, its wood stock highly polished. The distinctive curved magazine reminded me of its purpose, which was not to be an objet d'art. Anyway, my view was drawn a little farther. On the other side of the mattress a woman was lying nude as if on a snow bank. She was young and pretty and her lips were dead blue. She was the woman smiling next to Bob Hunter in a photograph in a silver frame on the bedside table.

I moved sideways from the door so I had a clean field of fire in case another bad guy came into the room. Measuring the distance between us, I was careful to make sure Dowd couldn't reach for my gun.

He said, "I wouldn't be quick to shoot again, professor. I'm not quite unarmed."

He slowly raised a hand that clutched a stainless steel cylinder with two small lights, a green one that was dark, and a second burning bright red. It had a button on the top. His thumb was holding down the button.

"You're shrewder than I thought," he said. "I didn't expect you here for some time. I've been trying to extract some information while you're in San Diego protecting your first wife."

"She'll be fine." My tongue felt as if it were covered with sandpaper.

"Well, no plan survives first contact with the enemy." His eyes narrowed.

I kept my voice steady. Dowd was right about one thing: anger would only get in the way of the training and experience that would give me an edge.

I ordered, "Put your arms out and get on your knees, very slowly."

He made no move to comply. "Aren't you going to thank me for my service to our country like every other civilian parasite did?"

"On your knees."

He shifted his weight, nothing more. "I want to show you something."

"Don't move!"

"I'll do it slowly."

I kept the gun on him as he stepped back toward a closet door, continuing to face me. Then he reached behind him and opened it slowly.

Inside, Peralta sat handcuffed to a chair. He'd been beaten badly. Blood was caked around his left eye. The last Claymore was strapped around his middle, with the front of the mine pointed inward.

"Kill him, Mapstone." He sounded groggy.

Dowd held out his other hand, the one with the cylinder. "He'll be dead in one second. This is a panic room, built for the family to hide in if there was a break-in. The walls are thick." He closed the door.

"And this," he indicated the device, "is a detonator for the Claymore. The walls aren't thick enough to block the signal. Right now, the only thing keeping your friend alive is the pressure my thumb is exerting on this detonator. So if you shoot me, the green light goes on and your friend dies. I told you I'd kill every one you love."

I kept the gun on him.

He cocked his head. "All I wanted was the list of Scarlett's clients. You thought you were cute, the expensive case in the motel room, the fake flash drive inside. I should have realized two can play the tracker game. Tonight, when your friend the sheriff showed up to check on her old man, I could have hidden, made daddy pretend everything is fine. But I thought maybe Peralta might have the list. So far, no list. This is really pissing me off. All I want is the list of johns. Why was that so hard for you?"

"I don't care." I didn't recognize my own voice.

His cheek twitched.

"Don't you get it? We'd been robbing banks, but that was too risky. Eventually the illegal government in Washington would have gotten us before we were ready."

He seemed eager to be understood.

I said, "You were going to blackmail Grace's clients."

"Exactly. I could have raised millions to fund the Brigade. Then the fun would have started. By the time we're done, this country will be under martial law, and every target we strike will have evidence that it was done by the hajis and the niggers and the spics who shouldn't be in this country. The Chicano Liberation Army. Al-Qaeda in America. The African Struggle."

"But the groups don't exist, right?"

"People will think they do. I've already got the Web sites reserved, so we can let these groups take credit when a shopping mall blows up. You don't know how savage the American can be. We'll make this a white man's country again."

"I think we're better than that." I nodded to the dead woman on the bed. "Anyway, she looks white to me."

"Collateral damage." He smiled. "Hunter said his slut-nugget daughter didn't have a computer here. If she had, it might have had the client list. Too bad for him she didn't. He had to watch while I humped his young wife a few times. She didn't like it at first, but I won her over. It was awhile since she'd had a real man. Must hurt like a son of a bitch to see another man screw your wife. It'd make me want to kill the motherfucker doing it, but ol' Bob just cried. 'Course, I had him handcuffed. Then I strangled her slowly while he watched. At least he didn't change his story."

He liked the sound of his own voice. I said, "So you knew who Scarlett was."

"I checked her out. She didn't check me out well enough, I guess."

"You had to kill her."

"It didn't start out that way. Look, she was a sweet little lay and I was happy to pay for it. It took me awhile to realize this magnificent piece of ass must have a very affluent group of men she was screwing, and this was going to be our funding source. By that time, she was gone. It took me a long time to find her again."

"But you did find her."

"We had a hero who tried to save her," he said. "It didn't take long to put him down. After that, we drove her around for a long time. I didn't want to hurt her, tried to reason with her just like I did with you. I wanted the list."

"You raped and tortured her," I said. "You waterboarded her in the toilet, right? That's why there was water on the bathroom floor."

"Very good. My thumb is getting tired."

I needed more time. I said, "Then you pushed her off the balcony."

"Young Zisman fucked up," he said. "That's who you shot in the living room. Andrew was supposed to hang her over the edge until she gave it up, but he lost his grip. Every unit has its FUBARs."

I almost pulled the trigger right then.

"Why that condo?"

"It belongs to Andrew's dad. Andrew had the fob to the front entry and the keys to the door. We didn't know his dad would be there, but it didn't take much persuading to get us some privacy. Old man Zisman knew what would happen if he didn't play along." He laughed as if we had shared an arch joke.

"But you eventually killed him, too."

"Not me. Andrew killed his father. Call it a test of loyalty. The unit always comes first. I couldn't take the chance his father would keep silent. Enough of your curiosity, professor. Give me your gun."

"No."

"Just so you know," he said, "whatever happens next, you won't make it out alive. I've got a sniper with a night scope positioned outside. He saw you come onto the property and told me. I let you get this far. Otherwise, you'd be dead. My man was trained as a Marine scout-sniper." He smiled. "I didn't realize you'd shoot Andrew straight off, but he was careless. So you can kill me, and I frag your friend, but you'll be dead, too. Just like Grace's daddy, who thought he could get away. If you do succeed in killing me, another commander will take my place. You can't stop us."

"We can make a start. After I kill you, I'll just call the cops."

His face flushed with anger. "Then you're gonna have a bunch of dead cops from my sniper. He's willing to die to take back his country and he'll take as many enemy with him as he can…"

"So far, all you've killed are white people."

He forced himself to speak in a reasonable tone. "You can give me your gun, I'll put the detonator on safe. We can do it at the exact same time. Then we'll take a ride to get that flash drive. The real goddamned flash drive. If it has the information I want, then I'll let you live…"

Dowd's cheek ticked in surprise. Ed Cartwright spoke behind me and then he was standing beside me.

"Your sniper is incapacitated," he said, cradling a pump shotgun on one arm.

"You killed him?" Dowd's voice shook.

"I just used the Apache Persuasion Hold and handcuffed him. He'll live. Probably."

Cartwright held up a black object that looked like a video-game joystick. He said, "I just made your detonator go limp, asshole. So why don't you slowly get on your knees."

Dowd stared at each of us, mouthed a profanity, lifted his thumb from the detonator in his hand.

Nothing happened.

He threw it at me and in those quick ticks of confusion, I allowed the distance between us to close. Rookie mistake—I had worried he would make a move for the AK on the bed—but it was too late. He dove at me and ferociously grabbed for my revolver. It quickly cost me my balance. We fell together onto the hard tile of the floor and I struggled to keep my panic from overwhelming my training. There was also the danger that Cartwright would use his shotgun on both of us.

Dowd's face was that of a feral dog and he was strong. So strong that he was close to gaining control. We sweated, grunted, and cursed. His face turned dark red. My attempt to knee him in the groin failed. So did his try at head-butting me, but he succeeded in rolling me onto my back and getting astride me. Every muscle in my arms and hands screamed as I watched the gun twist toward me.

That's when I released my left hand and grabbed the last-option knife.

"Ooof." He expelled bad breath in my face as I drove the sure little blade into his abdomen. Blood trickled onto my fingers. He still fought but his strength left him. The revolver came loose in my hands and I fired one shot point blank into his chest.

After an eternity that was probably five seconds, I pushed him off with difficulty. Cartwright just watched.

Grabbing Dowd's shoulders, I shook him hard.

"Where's the baby, you son of a bitch?"

A trickle of blood rolled out the side of his mouth.

"I tried to warn you…"

His eyes flickered and closed. He didn't deserve to die with his eyes shut. I shook and cursed him, but I was just yelling at a cadaver.

Cartwright waited a long time to speak. I realized that I must have had a wild look on my face. I patted down Dowd's body out of habit and forced my breathing down.

"Where'd you get that Airlite, kid?"

I told him: at a gun show.

He held out his hand. I gave it to him.

"You got Speedloaders?"

Digging them from my pocket, I put them in his other hand. "And the knife."

I rose unsteadily and gave him the knife and sheath.

"Now pay attention," he said. "I did the shooting here, not you. Right?"

I slowly nodded, feeling my senses return to human. The room smelled of discharged ammunition and vaporized blood.

"The Indian's here," he said, "and the cavalry are on the way. So you best be gone."

"Peralta's in there." I indicated the panic room.

"I'll take care of him. It won't be the first time. You go."

His voice stopped me at the door.

"You did okay, kid."

I nodded, then walked back through the house and slipped out into the darkness.

Chapter Thirty-eight

In the ensuing days, the FBI made a dozen more arrests and confiscated more weapons and explosives. It was being called the biggest domestic terror conspiracy in modern American history. Peralta gained major cred with the bureau, which promised it would lead to business for us.

The house on Cypress was back to something resembling normal. Did I dare trust it? Lindsey was reclaiming the gardens, fighting against the rising heat. I was cooking and reading. At the moment, we were both naked in the bedroom and sipping martinis. Coleman Hawkins was on the stereo with perfect synchronicity, *Cocktails for Two*. Among the things Lindsey had purchased on her shopping trip were two sets of garter belts and sheer stockings: bad-girl black and virginal white. She was wearing the black and draping one leg over me.

"Are you going to stay?" I asked the question that had been metastasizing inside me, fearful of the answer.

She held out her glass. "If you'll take me back, History Shamus."

I clinked my glass against hers. "Gladly."

Oscar Peterson came on. The Maharajah of the Keyboard, as Duke Ellington called him, sealed the deal.

"You're crying." She held my face close and wiped my wet cheeks. "Are they good tears?"

I nodded. But they were, in fact, a mixed bag.

"Happy that you're back," I said. "I want to do everything I can to put us back together…"

"Me, too."

"And I'm sad for all the ones we lost. At least some could have been saved if we'd been faster or smarter. I can't say we covered ourselves in glory on our first case. Grace, Felix, Tim, Larry Zip, Bob Hunter, his wife, all dead. We might have stopped some of it."

"Dave, you can't take all that on yourself."

"The only one who got away was Addison."

Lindsey cocked her head.

"Grace's friend," I explained. "Aside from Tim's parent's, she was the only one Grace and Tim had contact with while they were hiding out in O.B. She left school and went home to Oklahoma they tell me. A good thing. But I can't forget holding that baby after I changed him. Now he's in some hole out in the desert. What a shitty thing."

And I cried.

Lindsey held me close for a long time.

Finally, she said, "Addison is a really bad name."

"That's what I think."

"Mind if I try a hunch?"

Chapter Thirty-nine

We drove east from San Diego through Poway and Ramona on the old Julian Road. Suburbia slipped away and the hills and mountains surrounded us. Ahead were the Anza-Borrego Desert and the little town of Borrego Springs. We climbed around Grapevine Mountain, huge rocks leaning in on us, and then the desert valley emptied beneath.

Patty and I had been here many times. We made a ritual of staying one weekend a year at a little inn at Borrego Springs. It was a single-story speck in the desert surrounded by rocky, bare mountains. I remembered that it had a traffic circle. And I remembered a photo that Patty had taken of me on a hot day, surrounded by barrel cactuses in bloom.

But our trip to the badlands today was not for pleasure. The temperature was over one-fifteen and the town was emptied out of all but the hardiest year-round residents. A room would be cheap this time of year.

The traffic circle was still there: Christmas Circle, and a little beyond was a simple little motel with statues of desert bighorn sheep out front. Patty and I had stayed at the tonier Borrego Valley Inn, with its Southwest architecture and private patios. But I had seen this motel many times, never giving it a second look.

"There," Lindsey said.

She pointed to an older Toyota sedan parked in front of the ranch-style block of rooms. It was the only car in the lot. Peralta parked fifty feet away and we all piled out of the pickup truck.

"Let us go first." By this, Lindsey meant Sharon and her.

Peralta and I were well-armed, but I didn't think we would need firepower today. He nodded, and we watched the two women walk to the door directly in front of the Toyota and knock. They talked to the person who opened it, and after a couple minutes they went inside.

Peralta and I found some shade and waited, saying nothing.

Lindsey had followed her hunch and it pointed true.

Addison Conway's car was not in Oklahoma. It was sitting a few paces from us under the mid-day California sun. Thanks to Lindsey's black magic, the Chinese had hacked the phone company again and tracked Addison's cell phone. Last Friday, it had been in Ocean Beach, at Tim's apartment, an hour after I had left. Then it had taken the same route we had just driven and stayed here.

Sharon stepped out and smiled at us: come on in.

Lindsey sat on one of two double beds cradling little David Lewis in her lap. A young woman sat on the other bed. She turned her face to greet us. She was attractive in a girl-next-door way, no Southern California glamour, none of Grace Hunter's looks hot enough to warm your hands by. She was crying. Lindsey was crying.

"This is Sheriff Peralta," Sharon said, her voice so soothing. "And his partner David Mapstone. You're going to be safe now, Addison." She put an arm on the girl, who leaned into her as if she were a surrogate mother.

Sharon looked at us. "She's been out here with nothing but her fears."

I thought my insides were going to drop out on the floor. I tightened my diaphragm just to make sure it was still there. Lindsey's hunch had been more than rewarded.

Addison Conway spoke with a slight twang and no one would mistake her for a Rhodes Scholar. She had been operating on primal fear these past days, not logic or reason.

"I went to see Tim and Grace," she said. "I hadn't heard a word from Grace and I was worried. I knew about her... You know. I was always afraid it would get her killed. When I got to the apartment, Tim was packing up to leave. He was very scared. He told me what had happened to Grace and I just…"

Sobs took her over and Sharon lightly stroked her hair until she could speak again.

"Tim was getting out, going to hide with his parents." Her voice rose. "It wasn't my fault!"

The baby started crying, and Lindsey expertly rocked him into happy little murmurs.

Sharon told her nobody was blaming her. We just wanted to understand what had happened.

"It happened so fast. Tim told me to take the baby and go down to the car, you know, it was in the covered spaces in back? So I did. He said he was going to pack up a suitcase and come right behind me. Only…"

We waited beneath the sound of the air conditioning and the baby gurgling contentedly.

I spoke for the first time. "What happened next, Addison?"

"They came for him!" She looked at me with a red face, puffy eyes. "Two men. They called out at the door that they were cops, and then they barged in. I heard Tim yell. Something broke inside."

She shivered. Sharon coaxed her to continue.

"Tim yelled, 'Go!' I knew he meant me. I didn't want to leave him. And then David started crying and one of the cops looked out the window."

It was still jarring to hear the baby's name.

She said, "I ducked behind a wall and I got lucky. Right then, a garbage truck turned into the alley and stopped right there. It was making a racket and I went behind it and ran for my car. I was parked a block away and I've never run so fast. I was afraid to look back, but they weren't chasing me. Thank god for that trash truck. I left the city and I drove to the desert. I thought we'd be safe here. Then I saw the television, the explosion at the apartment and Tim dead. They called it terrorism. I didn't know who to call or how I could explain what happened, why

I just ran…" Her voice trailed into a pitiful whisper: "How did you find me?"

Nobody answered.

"The next day, I was going to call the FBI, but I got a call. He said he was a San Diego detective but he didn't sound right. He wanted to know where I was. I freaked. I told him I was in Oklahoma…"

I thought: *Good old Detective Jones.*

Peralta showed her photos of Edward Dowd and Andrew Zisman. "Are these the men you saw going into Tim's apartment?"

"Yes!"

"They're not police. And they'll never bother you again."

I realized that Dowd never had the baby. He thought we did. The baby was gone when he got to Tim's apartment. Dowd's elaborate air show, dropping the baby doll and the blood, had indeed been a threat. But he had never been in a position to carry it out.

She sniffled loudly. "The baby was my priority. I had to keep him safe. I didn't have the phone number for Tim's parents. You've got to believe me."

"We do," Sharon said. "It's going to be all right."

And it would, I supposed. Peralta pulled out his cell phone and slipped outside. I watched my wife cradle the baby with such natural love and wondered what might have been, wondered how she could ever doubt she would make a good mother.

Chapter Forty

The next morning, Mike and Sharon drove us to the ornate Santa Fe railroad station in downtown San Diego. He was healing quickly from the beating he had received in Paradise Valley. He made sure that I knew he had been ambushed and fought through two Taser shocks before he passed out and they got his gun. Beyond that, I was certain that we would never discuss it. I already knew that no bad guys would ever get his firearms without a hell of a fight.

Lindsey and I had tickets to Los Angeles, where we would catch the Coast Starlight to Seattle. We had a sleeping compartment reserved. I carried a bag full of books.

"You two have fun in the cool weather," Sharon said. After she hugged us, Peralta shook my hand and I saw the gratitude in his eyes. Nothing more needed to be said. Then he slipped his hand into Sharon's and, if even for a moment, everything seemed right with the world.

"When you get back," he said, "we've got work to do."

I had no doubt. I offered my arm, and Lindsey stepped up into the train car. I followed her and we found seats. From inside, we watched our friends wave one more time as the locomotive whistle sounded and we started to move.

I turned to Lindsey.

"Have you ever had sex on a train?"

"Not yet, Dave."

That night, as the train rolled through northern California, I made love with my wife and slept without dreams.

Paying My Debts

My editor Barbara Peters saw the possibilities in this series from the start. I owe her for encouraging me to keep it going, and especially for the skills, intellect, and inspiration that make her America's top editor of mysteries. She styles herself the Evil Editor, but I have only received the good. The Poisoned Pen Press is a treasure, and I am particularly grateful to Rob Rosenwald, Jessica Tribble, Nan Beams, Annette Rogers and Suzan Baroni.

Cal Lash, retired Phoenix Police detective and a private investigator, once again was exceptionally helpful and patient with my questions. Maricopa County Deputy County Attorney David R. Foster likewise provided valuable assistance.

Even before I finished my previous book, *Powers of Arrest, A Cincinnati Casebook*, readers wanted to know when the next David Mapstone Mystery would be coming. So I owe you all my biggest debt, whether you started the series at its outset in 2001 or recently got hooked. It's humbling to see how many people are moved by the lives of these characters, including the biggest of all, Phoenix. Thank you.

To receive a free catalog of Poisoned Pen Press titles, please contact us in one of the following ways:

Phone: 1-800-421-3976
Facsimile: 1-480-949-1707
Email: info@poisonedpenpress.com
Website: www.poisonedpenpress.com

Poisoned Pen Press
6962 E. First Ave. Ste 103
Scottsdale, AZ 85251